GUNMAN'

BEN THOMPSON

SPAWN

A GRAPHIC WESTERN

GUNMAN'S
SPAWN

PART ONE

Bullet Seed

1

YOUNG DUNCAN STEWART was to remember his trouble that day as marking his first sight of a real, live gunhawk—maybe the best in Texas, at that.

So Dunc always counted the day lucky, although it started ill. His brutish foster father, Dave Bridges, having returned from one of his secret trips half drunk and eager to go the whole hog, sent the boy to Big Bend's one saloon for a fifth of whiskey. Now he was headed home, the precious bottle clutched in his hands, his eyes on the lookout for Sam Peters and others of similar ilk whose pet recreation was baiting young Dunc.

At about that time, though Dunc could not know it, a comical little man was riding slowly toward Big Bend. Several miles short of the dusty cow town, he left the trail and began to keep clumps of mesquite and stunted oaks between himself and Big Bend's sparse false-fronted buildings.

The rider's modest height rendered him conspicuous in that land of tall, rangy men. His skin, the color of well-worn saddle leather, was excessively wrinkled about the eyes, long habituated to squinting against the pitiless glare of western sun. A tremendous sweeping mustache, of gray laced with sandy red and crooking upward toward the ears, was the most notable feature of his face, which also boasted carefully trimmed mutton-chop side whiskers.

The rider's worn, dusty and sweat-streaked clothing consisted chiefly of faded blue denims many times washed. Excellently fitted hand-tooled boots encased his feet.

A Winchester carbine in a saddle scabbard snuggled beneath his left leg. About his slim waist were buckled two heavy black-handled guns in peculiar holsters. They did not hang from the pull of gravity or with the help of whang-leather tie strings to keep them close to the thigh, in the fashion affected by some gunhands. These were more like harnesses than holsters; two large hip-fitting oblongs of leather with holster-case low on each, all strapped snugly to thigh. It was obvious that they were secure and would not drag at the gun in case of a quick draw.

Looping the reins over his saddle horn, the rider drew his side-guns one at a time, broke them, examined the loads, replaced them carefully in the holsters. Next he uncased the Winchester and went through a similar ritual. Satisfied, he squinted speculatively in the direction of Big Bend and encouraged his tired horse with a couple of clucks of his tongue.

Behind Big Bend where Rapid Creek loops so tightly it nearly forms an island, stood a grove of towering cottonwoods. Toward these the little man made his way. The buckskin he rode was streaked with salt, dust, the grime of travel.

"'Twon't be long, Leather," the rider said in a soft voice, patting the horse on the neck. "Smell that water?"

Leather tossed his head eagerly and increased his pace . . .

At sixteen, Dunc Stewart was a slim stripling giving promise of something rare in the man to come if he could but overcome the two fears that ruled him. Fear of his foster parent, Dave Bridges. And fear of Sam Peters who, three years older than Dunc, was the son of a prosperous merchant powerful in Big Bend's affairs. Sam and his friends took pleasure in ceaselessly tormenting Dunc, feeling themselves safe from reprisal. For Dunc never struck back. He was under the strictest orders from Dave Bridges never to lay a finger on Sam, because even a hardcase like Dave quaked at the vengeance Sam's father might take.

Now, as Dunc tripped happily along homeward with his father's whiskey, he congratulated himself on having missed, this one time at least, any trouble with Sam Peters.

But Sam, at that same moment, was also congratulating himself. He had found a victim for a trap his agile mind had contrived. He had drawn the nails from a board on the sidewalk and substituted a plank much longer that extended into an alley between the barber shop and the livery stable. Dunc came on, bare feet

11

slapping the boards. Suddenly he saw the plank spring up into his path but he was too late to avoid it and plunged headlong.

The bottle of whiskey cracked neatly around the bottom, dumping its amber contents into the muddy street.

Sam whooped with laughter, spanked his pants legs in glee, as did three other boys he had gathered to watch the trick work. Sam was thick and heavy, somewhat fat about the middle; but he was strong and mean. Dunc, who in a valiant effort to save the whiskey had cracked his head painfully against a porch post, for a moment saw stars. A moment later what he saw was red. For the first time in his life his blood heated up furiously enough to force him to battle.

Without a thought to the consequences he leaped up in a pantherish spring and swung the cracked whiskey bottle. Had it been full a lot of trouble might have been avoided in the future because it would certainly have smashed Sam's skull. As it was, it shattered into a thousand pieces and apparently each piece sought Sam's skin and delivered a separate laceration. His face was suddenly a dripping welter of blood. One boy went green and vomited, the other two ran as hard as they could go. Sam, no little stunned by the blow, stood stupidly for a moment, then fingered his stinging face. His hand came away red and dripping. He looked at the hand in horror for a moment then sprang to the sidewalk and ran off as hard as he could, screaming "Paw!" at every jump.

Dunc felt sick. Not because of the blood on Sam's face. Of that he was justly proud, after all the humiliation he had suffered from Sam. But he knew what awaited him when he got back to the cabin nestled among the trees by the creek. He'd get a beating and a bad one. He sighed, fought the knot of tension and sickness in the pit of his stomach, and dragged his feet toward home.

Dunc paused at the rickety gate. Dave Bridges was sitting in a shabby rocker in the front yard, his head happily fumed with the whiskey he had already consumed. He licked his lips and sighed in pleasant anticipation . . . then stiffened as Dunc came on. Dave's piggy black eyes narrowed and anger suffused his face with blood. "Where'n hell's my whiskey?"

Pale, his throat contracted with fear, Dunc faced the angry man. "Sam Peters tripped me on the walk. I fell. Broke the bottle."

Dave got to his feet slowly. "Why you clumsy. . . ." It was a hard open-handed blow and Dunc ducked it from sheer reflex but he couldn't duck the one that followed. It smashed against his cheek, knocking him flat. He came up and backed away from Dave. The same red haze that had dropped before his eyes when Sam Peters had tripped him now returned; he growled deep in his throat. "Don't you hit me again."

Dave looked at him, astounded. The boy's face was tight and pinched and the blue eyes were hard as stones. Dave snorted, "You damn sassy puppy . . . I'm gonna near kill you."

He waded into the boy and though Dunc fought back with fury he was soon dropped to the earth, beaten down by superior brawn, his nose and a cut above one eye leaking torrents of blood. Dave stood over him, sides

13

heaving as he panted, "Guess that'll learn you, you bastard. Learn you to git sassy with me."

A woman ran from the house and bent over the boy, a hank of colorless hair falling across her face. "Don't hit 'im no more, Dave," she pleaded. "You done nearly killed him."

"Git up from there," he roared at her. "Go get me another bottle of whiskey!"

"I got to help him to, Dave. I can't leave him . . ."

He lifted a foot and pushed her sprawling into the dirt. "Whiskey," he said savagely. "Or I'll beat your hide black and—"

"*Turn around!*"

It came with the sharp, cracking snap of a rifle bullet, so patently a command that in spite of himself Dave Bridges whirled swiftly.

A little man sat on a buckskin horse right at the edge of the yard. And though Dave had seen violence all his life, had been involved in no little amount of it himself, he felt a cold flit of terror along his spine. There was something chilling, something quietly dangerous about this little man, who now threw a foot over the horn of his saddle and slid blithely to the ground.

Still, he had a pair of silly mutton-chop whiskers coming to the angles of his jaws and a moustache to match. Why, he was hardly over five feet, and though compact and tightly assembled, he couldn't weigh over a hundred and forty pounds. Dave took hope, and with hope came anger and threat. "Git back on that hoss, Pappy, and beat it 'fo' I kicks your ribs in."

The little man walked closer with a curious gliding

14

stride. When he came within reach he unholstered his right-hand gun with a motion more blur than visible action and the gun crashed flatly alongside Dave's head. It rose again and before Dave could fall the barrel of it had opened a three-inch gash in his cheek with the efficacy of a cavalry saber. Dave rooted into the ground with such dead weight that his flaccid body sent up a cloud of dust. The sandy-moustached little fellow nodded pleasantly to the woman, then politely helped her to her feet.

"I'm plumb sorry, ma'm. I don't hold with bullyin' women. And while kids need whuppin', times is, they can do without the kinda hammerin' he gave bub there. Then kickin' you like you was a dawg . . . Nup. Can't see it."

He walked to the boy who had been dazedly watching the procedure. "Awright, son. Git up and let's go wash you off some in the creek."

He helped Dunc down the steep bank and watched silently while the boy washed away at the blood and let loose hard, tearing sobs.

"Might make yuh feel better if yuh tells me about it, bub."

The voice held a gentle undercurrent, a sound Dunc had never heard from another human save his foster mother. It opened the gates of his aching heart and he sat on a smooth waterwashed stone and talked fast and bitterly.

It came out in jerks and disconnected phrases, bits and parts rather than a whole. But the old man was a patient listener and, as it turned out, a skillful ques-

15

tioner. Gradually he drew from Dunc the complete picture.

He told the little man, as he had been told himself, of his rescue from a burning wagon train that had been ambushed by the Chiracuhuas—rescue by Dave Bridges and others. Of his mother naming him with her last breath while her throat bubbled with blood. Of his foster mother, a maid at the hotel whom Dave, to everyone's surprise, had married. Of his foster father whose background and employment were a mystery to everyone at Big Bend. He told of the fear that had ridden him since he could remember. Fear of Dave Bridges, fear of the night, fear of the older boys who had made his life miserable. He told of the cheap little rifle he had acquired by dint of sharp trading beginning with marbles, turtles and a garter snake and working up to animal skins. Of diligent practice and the rabbits he brought home when his father was gone, caring little whether those behind had enough to eat. He revealed that his foster mother had had a little education and had taught him as much as she could, that he was an avid searcher for knowledge and that he intended to learn a thing or two some day. He told of his dreams. The things he wanted for his mother, the finery he'd buy her and the servants he'd hire to relieve her of drudgery. Not once did he intimate that he wanted anything for himself.

When he had finished the little man smiled crookedly, lifting the tips of his moustaches until they pointed at his ears. "Sump'n tells me us two's gonna be pards. Le's go see whut your paw got to say."

Dave Bridges had nothing to say. He was still flat

on his back with the distracted woman trying to wash his horribly cut cheek.

"You're doin' right well, ma'm, but too gentle. Le's do it this here way." He took a full pail of water and let it pour unceremoniously on the face and chest of the fallen Dave, who sputtered, gasped, choked and sat up groggily.

"Pistol whip a man what ain't got guns," he said bitterly when a little sense returned. "That's the way they fights where you come from?"

"Nup, 'tain't," said the little man tartly. "Where I come from we don't fight kids and wimmen, neither. We ain't even 'lowed to watch it and stay still. You got guns?"

Dunc answered with short bitterness. "He got two of 'em."

"Go git 'em, bad fella. Go git 'em and put 'em on."

Dave remained where he was. Belated intelligence was telling him that this was no ordinary man and that if he put on his guns it might be the last thing he ever did. He didn't think the stranger would shoot an unarmed man so he remained sitting in the puddle of mud, his cheek bleeding nastily.

"I'll git 'em," said Dunc cuttingly. He went into the cabin and returned with twin gun belts and flung them with unnecessary force into his father's lap. Dave grunted but made no other move.

"Ain't you gonna put on your guns, Paw?" he asked sharply.

"The boy ast you a question," prompted the menacing figure before him.

17

"Who is you?" mumbled Dave stupidly.

"Knowed back east as Hampton Wallace."

Dave stiffened like he had sat on a scorpion. "You mean? . . . *Hamp Wallace?*"

"Gen'rally speakin' that's the substance of whut I said."

Dave touched the egg over his left ear gingerly. "Jesus," he muttered. "Jesus Christ and Godamighty."

"Your papa don't look like he feels good," said Hamp Wallace gently. "Son, le's me'n you amble up in town a while and see the sights." He turned to Dave. "What's your name, fat and stupid?"

"Dave Bridges."

"Um . . . Un hunh. Dave Bridges. Remember the Abilene stage robbery, Dave? You spent a lot of money 'round Fote Worth fer a while after that but couldn't nobody prove nuthin'. They did prove you got mighty free with a runnin' iron onct and seems like you done a soft stretch in the pen fer that."

Dave's face was as pale as dirty dough. Hamp Wallace gripped his gun harness with both hands and wriggled his hips like a cooch dancer. "Me'n the boy is gonna see the sights," he said softly. "When I git back I'd appreciate it mighty much if I find you'd unsaddled my hoss, washed him down good in the creek, t' git that there salt and dust offen 'im. Might feed him good too while you're at it."

Dave Bridges got up swiftly. "Yes *suh,* Cap'n Wallace. Anything else, suh?"

"Yeah. Take yourself a bath. It might kill you but

18

then it mightn't. Come along, bub . . . Uh, oh! Looks like we got cump'ny."

"Ed Peters," muttered Dave. "I wuz expecting him. Wonder he didn't show up sooner."

Peters was furious as he strode down the pathway flanked by two men, slickly dressed, obviously prosperous.

"Where's that boy . . . Ah, there he is. Dave, I want you to beat this brat half to death. He cut Sam's face to bits with a whiskey bottle . . . Come here, you . . ."

Dunc did not move.

Peters started for him, hands held menacingly.

"Just stay right where you is," said Hamp in a soft drawl.

Ed Peters stopped in his tracks.

"Yeah," growled Dave ferociously. "That young'un o' yourn tripped my boy and made him break a full bottle o' whiskey. If Dunc lambasted the fat bastard then he oughta git a medal." Dave's tune had changed radically and for a reason.

Ed Peters was fat and sported a forty-five inch waistline. His face was constructed of wave after wave of fat creases that disappeared into his nineteen-inch shirt collar. At the moment each separate crease seemed to be vying with every other in redness.

"I'll have the law on you, Dave, that's what I'll do."

"Tell it to Sandy Claws," snarled Dave, showing no fear. With Cap'n Wallace behind him he could afford to be hard.

Peters sucked in his breath, looked, balked, then

19

turned to Hamp. "I didn't stop because you said so, you dried up little weasel."

"What stopped you then, you over-bloated windbag, you tripe-eatin' sow dog. You overfed Poland China hawg. I bet you'd render out four hunderd pound of pure white leaf lard. On the other hand it might be all fertilizer." Hamp, knowing nothing of euphemism, did not say fertilizer.

Peters looked apoplectic and Dave Bridges, unmindful of the beating he had taken, grinned delightedly. The well-dressed gentlemen parted and stood to one side of their boss. "We don't like that kind of talk, Pappy," said one with long black sideburns. "In fact, we's plumb unhappy about it."

Hamp shrugged carelessly. "So fer, all I heared is wind. You his sons? You talk like 'im."

There was a momentary hesitation. They were hard men. They were handy with weapons. They hung about the Rock Bottom as trouble-shooters, the saloon being another of Peters' enterprises. They knew how to handle danger, a talent that must necessarily boast of some slight facility for sensing it. At the moment they sensed it like a fog of heavy stinking smoke. Like an overdose of cheap perfume, like the smell of a fat pine fire.

He was just a slightly built little fellow. His voice was gentle and soft and nothing about him seemed in the least threatening unless it was the peculiar harness that held his holsters or the heavily relaxed attitude of his long arms. He seemed completely relaxed . . . so much so that he seemed about to fall over from relaxation.

BULLET SEED

No one could be that relaxed so the men recognized it for what it was and conviction grew as hesitation clamored. One move would find them faced with thundering .45's. Of course, there were two of them, but they knew their contemporaries. They knew or knew of men like Clay Allison and Dallas Stoudenmire, of Jim Gillette and Rockwell Calandre, of Velice Devereaux and Braxton Bragg, of Wes Hardin and King Fisher. They knew that none of these men had ever let odds stop them if the occasion called for a drawn gun . . . and these men were still alive with the exception of Dallas Stoudenmire who had been shot in the back of the head.

Was this bristling bantam of the same breed as those renowned top guns, the two hardcases wondered. He certainly acted as if he was. He was small, of course, but he wouldn't be the first runt to maybe handle guns as good as anybody. You take that one who used to be with the Rangers, that Wallace everybody talked about. He was supposed to be high gun in all Texas—that's what everyone said.

The two made no move.

"Who . . . are you?" panted Ed Peters, now aware that something was definitely amiss. His men had been tried and found not wanting. Yet before this cold-faced, amber-eyed little man they hesitated.

"You got a handle, or not?" Peters pressed again, suddenly sounding almost hysterical.

Hamp Wallace smiled at Dunc. "You want to tell 'em, bub?"

Dunc stiffened importantly. "He's *Cap'n* Hampton Wallace," he said in a ringing voice.

No one spoke for a moment but Hamp did not relax the outpouring of a subtle threat, the overdone pose of relaxation. A thin smile spread over his lips, revealing teeth that were obviously false. "The wind sure is calm now, ain't it?"

Dave laughed gratingly. "Don't seem like there was ever no wind. Plumb peaceful."

"Your face looks like a little wind was taken out of you," snapped Peters, realizing that he and his men had taken water and shaking with fury because of it.

Dave laughed. "I know my match when I see it," he said derisively. "I don't hafta run inter a mountain to know how hard a rock is."

Peters faced Hamp. "Maybe we'll meet again, Mr. Wallace."

"More'n likely. I aim t' be around a spell."

"I wouldn't advise it."

"Yeah . . . I 'speck you wouldn't. Jest the same I'll be around a while."

Peters gave him a baffled look and with a savage gesture he whirled and pounded away, followed by his two henchmen.

Their necks were red but they didn't look back.

When they were out of sight Hamp cast a glance at Dave. "Better git along with that hoss. I might come back in a hurry."

"Yes, *suh*."

"Let your wife fix your face first."

"Yes, suh."

"Come along, bub."

His eyes wide with adoration, Dunc followed the quick-

22

stepping Hamp up the trail that led to Big Bend, three hundred yards away. As soon as they were out of sight of the house, Hamp stopped and motioned to a path leading away from the trail. "Le's me'n you go inter the bushes fer a minnit and have a pow-wow."

They found a log and sat upon it. "Now, bub . . . you been here most of your life."

"Sure. I told you."

"Unh hunh. 'Member back coupla years ago, a Ranger rid in here and got shot?"

"Yes, sir." Dunc nodded. "I seen it."

2

"Seen it?" Hamp leaned forward tensely.

"Yes, sir. I had went to the saloon for a bucket of beer for Papa. I was standin' right there."

"In front of the saloon?"

"Yes, sir."

"What happened?"

"Well, this feller . . . a tall man with yeller hair, he rid up t' two men who was standin' on the saloon gallery . . . Looked mighty like to me they was waitin' for him."

"Coulda been. They mighta got word he was comin'."

"Yes, sir. Well, he asked one of them the way to the sheriff's office and this man laughed and asked the Ranger if he thought he'd make it there."

"Unh hunh. Go on."

"This feller twisted 'round on his hoss and asked this man . . ."

"What man?" Hamp was pale now.

"Ash Zimmerman. He asked him who he thought would stop him. Ash just laughed and stood away from the wall of the saloon . . . askin' for it."

"Then what happened?"

"The Ranger went for his gun but somebody shot from the alley, a rifle from the sound of it, and hit him in the gun hand just before he got the gun out. Ash drawed and shot twice. Killed him."

"The sheriff didn't do nuthin'?"

"Well . . . ever'body said it was a fair break and the Ranger—if that was who he was—wasn't carryin' no orders or warrants. Looked like—if you wanted t' believe it that way—he just rode up and picked a gunfight with Ash and lost."

"I see. Didn't nobody mention the rifle shot?"

"Nope. Looked like I was the only one who heard it. Ash got credit for hittin' him in the gun hand first before he shot him in the head."

Hamp got up, his face glacial and his eyes molten pots of yellow fire. "Come along, bub. We wants to see the sheriff."

"Can I ask a question?"

"Sure you can."

"What's this all about?"

"The Ranger was a good friend of mine. I don't know how come he didn't have no warrant. He oughta had one. He was ridin' with a blank one to arrest a man who had shot another Ranger onct. We didn't know his name—but I know it now."

"Who?"

"Ash Zimmerman. What does he do?"

BULLET SEED

"He's a waddy for Felton Wade."

"Yeah. I heard of him. One of these days I'll have to have a talk with Mr. Wade. The time's comin' . . . Well, right now we got other things to do. Come on."

Sheriff Jim Walters was a bitter man. He was thin and looked sick. He was in his late fifties and time had dealt him ill. He had been a power in his day but now people openly flouted his person and office and the fact rankled deep within him like a slow cancer. He stayed at home or in his office and, unless forced by man or circumstance, kept his peace and allowed things to handle themselves. Age pressed down on every bone and muscle like a leaden weight; it was an effort for him to even walk. He was dozing when the door opened and Hamp and Dunc stepped in.

"Howdy, Jim," said Hamp, extending his hand.

The sheriff blinked and shook his head to clear the mud from his brain. "By *God*, if it ain't Hamp Wallace hisself." He got up, his stagnant veins tingling from his unexpected pleasure as he shook hands with the famous little man. "What brung you 'way down here, Hamp? Here, have a chair."

Hamp took the proffered seat and looked at the frail old man. "You oughta knowed I'd be here, Jim."

"Yeah . . . I knowed it, I reckon. Been a pretty long time, though."

"I been busy and my time wasn't my own. Done retired now. Got into that brush with Dayries up in Rockover right after I resigned. That held me up for a spell.

BULLET SEED

Been doin' a few other little chores."

Walters nodded. "I been hearin' 'bout you."

"From who?"

"Jim Gillette rid through on the way to El Paso not long ago. Said you told him you was catchin' up on some unfinished business."

Hamp's face was like stone. "Yeah . . . here'n there. Ain't got no rules t' foller now, Jim. I been doin' right well. I seen Dayries git hisn. I seen Kid Cantrell git hisn . . . Feller name of Bragg got 'im."

"So I heerd. You got anything on your mind?"

"Right now I got a man on my mind named Zimmerman."

"Story goes Willingham ast fer it. Rid up and made Zimmerman draw."

"Story I heard don't fit. Bub, here, 'members it as plain as yistiddy. Tell 'im, bub."

When Dunc finished there was a long silence. Walters rubbed the stubble on his chin. "Well . . . I reckon the boy could be right. He tells a straight story. I thought it looked funny but what could I do?"

"You done what you could. Somebody coulda got his warrant offen the body before you seen it."

"That's what musta happened. Whatcha gonna do, Hamp?"

Hamp smiled tightly. "Guess!"

Walters shook his head. "Don't know how you hold onter your young days like you do. Hamp, I'm dead already. Just ain't fell over yet."

"I keep goin'," said Hamp, ripping a generous chew from a thin plug and maneuvering it into his mouth.

"My two boys got a helluva big spread close t' Austin. They make the money and I have the fun. Killin' rats, Jim, is a powerful fine pastime."

"Better watch out, just the same. If they lined Willingham up like they did then you got to watch your step."

"I been watchin' my step a long time."

"That's *him*," hissed Dunc excitedly.

Hamp looked out of the window and saw a rangy man with colorless hair ride past on a big dark bay gelding.

"By hisself," said Walters suggestively. "I'll go 'round and cover the saloon door."

"Good! Bub, now you lissen hard t' me. It ain't gonna be safe fer you here after today. You know how t' git t' Yucca City?"

Dunc nodded excitedly. "I know the way. 'Bout twenty miles."

"Good." Hamp spoke rapidly for thirty seconds, leaving Dunc pale but excited.

"I'll do it. I been wantin' to get outa here a long time."

Ash Zimmerman tied his horse to the hitching post in front of the saloon leisurely, then looked up and down the drab dusty street. It was the same as always with its ugly stores and rickety boardwalks. The street was ankle deep in powdery dust and the sun beat down fiercely. He saw the sheriff come out with a double-barreled shotgun, take a wide flanking circle, then head for the saloon. Zimmerman paused, puzzled by the old man's actions. Coming straight for him was a slim figure with two guns in a harness that made them follow every move of his thighs. Ash's lips tightened. The little man was coming straight for him and even at the distance he could see the burning pits in the pale eyes.

Forty feet away he stopped, his arms hanging limply. "Git out in the street, Zimmerman. I wouldn't want t' hurt a hoss or a person. Dawgs is my specialty and that's where you come in. *Move.*" The word cracked out like a pistol shot, making Zimmerman flinch.

"Who the hell is you?" he growled, careful not to make any unwary move.

"I'm a friend of Walter Willingham. That tell you anything, Zimmerman?"

Zimmerman turned casually as though to finish the hitching of the horse but Hamp could see the animal was already hitched. Like a flash Zimmerman turned and his guns came out in a glitter of light, but Hamp's big weapons flashed and bellowed twice. Ash's bright silver-plated weapons described an arc in the air and fell with a plop in the dust. He stood erect for a moment, then fell backward against the steps of the saloon.

For a moment, Hamp didn't move, his eyes restlessly searching for any signs of further hostilities. Heads were poked out of practically every door but no one seemed disposed to take action. The sheriff, a grin on his face, started forward, stopped and without even raising his weapon to his shoulder triggered off both barrels with a stunning detonation. A man fell forward from an alley, a Winchester carbine clattering to the walk. The twin charges of buckshot had nearly torn him in two.

Walters looked like he had shaken off twenty years. "Just got a glimpse of him but, by God, I can still move."

Hamp nodded and holstered his weapons. "Where's that boy . . . bub . . . Git on this here hoss and fog it. He won't be needin' it no more. Remember what I told you."

"Yes, sir. Could I have his guns, too?"

"'Course you can. Take 'em."

While a gaping citizenry looked on, Dunc gathered up the guns, pulled the holsters off the body of Zimmerman and made a flying leap for the horse who shied momentarily but didn't bolt.

Dunc's face turned red when he realized he hadn't untied the animal. Hamp with a grin performed the office for him and stepped back. The big horse with its slim rider tore down the street.

With the sheriff Hamp crossed the street, went on through the sheriff's office and disappeared. Twenty minutes later he showed up at Dave Bridges' cabin. Dave was drying the buckskin, whose hide now glistened with cleanliness. The horse still nibbled at the remains of a good feed and nickered softly as he saw his master.

"Saddle up," said Hamp shortly. "When you cinch him, make sure he don't hold his wind. He's good at that and it makes a loose cinch job."

"Yes, suh . . . what happened?"

"Another good rat fer Boot Hill. Where's your wife?"

The faded woman came to the door. "Ma'm," said Hamp, "I taken the liberty of sendin' your son on a little sojourn fer his health. He was a power of help t' me

today and I give my word that he'll come t' no harm.
I hope to send 'im back t' you a growed up man and
a fine one. He's got the makin's."

"He's a good boy," she said tiredly, with a sidelong
glance at the puffed face of her husband. "I'll miss
him."

"I wouldn't want to leave him here after what he told
me today. It might get out and that would be dangerous.
When he comes back he'll be able to take care of hisself."

"Will you talk to him . . .? Tell him I'll be waitin' . . .
I'll pray fer him."

"I'll tell him, Ma'm. I'll tell him. And now I'll bid
you good evenin'."

Dave brought the horse. Hidden from the woman in
the doorway by the animal, Hamp looked into Dave's
eyes.

"I come onto a perty ugly sitchiation here when I rid
up," he said in a low cutting voice. "If I ever git back
in these parts, and it ain't onlikely, I better hear good
reports about you. Git me?"

"Yes, suh," said Dave profoundly.

"Awright. Just remember it."

Hamp mounted the buckskin and rode toward the
southeast at an easy trot.

Yucca City was considerably more of a town than Big
Bend, having three saloons, two of which boasted girls
of uncertain virtue. There was, however, no uncertainty
about the daring cut of their clothes and the paint

with which they were lavishly decorated. Their voices were shrill, their laughter brittle and their eyes bright with acquisitiveness and spurious joviality.

Hamp had found Dunc waiting for him just outside town and together they rode to the largest hotel.

"Now here's your first baptism in the evil ways of the world," said Hamp in an undertone. "First we'll go in and wash up if this place can afford a tin tub and some hot water. Then we'll go out and git you some clo'se. When you're proper dressed we'll come back and take in the sights."

Two hours later Dunc walked alongside his benefactor, striding proudly. He was clad in new denims, new boots, blue shirt and his arms were loaded with other purchases. On his slender hips the two silver guns with their pearl handles looked out of place.

When they got to their room Hamp said, "Take them things off 'fore some ranny makes you eat 'em."

Dunc's face fell but he did as he was ordered. "They sure are pretty."

"Yeah, they're dangerous in a kid's hands. You'll learn soon enough. Let's go down to supper."

They went into the tremendous lobby that was saloon on one side and dining room on the other. In the center was the desk.

A person having a meal could watch the dancing and other activity in the saloon and only Dunc's hunger kept his attention on his plate. The girls he thought were the most beautiful creatures he had ever seen but his stomach demanded attention first. He ate a big steak, hashed brown potatoes, seven slices of light-bread, the first he had ever tasted, and two big wedges of dried apple pie.

Hamp watched him with amusement enjoying, vicariously, the boy's youthful appetite.

"Think you're full enough t' lissen a while?"

Dunc started guiltily. "Yes, sir."

"I'm gonna put you on your own . . . in a stable sort of, so you can grow up. I think you got a lot of git up and spunk but you're undergrowed and underfed. I'm sendin' you t' Mexico to a hacienda owned by a friend of mine. He'll give you bed and board. He's a prince of a man and he'll take you on my sayso. I want you t' stay there till you're twenty at least. Then you can do what you want to. Maybe you won't want t' leave. If I was you I'd come on back and see your maw and look around fer me. When that time comes we'll see what's t' be done."

Dunc's face fell. "I can't go with you?"

"Not now. When you come back we'll see. I ride too fur and too hard to have a kid along. Too many people'd like to line me up in their sights. Tag onto me, and you might die without ever livin'. I'm gettin' you outa this part of the country and inter a spot where you can grow up safe. I'll write the man a letter and you'll give it to 'im." Hamp's bushy brows came together. "I don't want no report o' you actin' up down there, neither. Long's you stay with the Camara-Peon family you'll do just what they tells you, when they tells you. They'll be your boss and if I ever hear of them havin' trouble with you I'll find you and beat your head in, and don't think I won't be able t' do it."

33

Dunc, remembering his father's torn face, nodded but didn't speak. He was perfectly certain that Hamp would do just as he said.

"Now you got a good hoss, a Winchester and two side-guns. Take 'em with you. Turn the side-guns over t' Don Rolando Camara-Peon when you git there. That'll keep you outa trouble."

"But I want to practice."

"He'll let you have 'em fer practice and if he takes a notion he can teach you plenty. He's a greased streak hisself. You can keep the rifle and practice with that. We'll buy you some ammunition in the mawnin'."

3

RESPECTABILITY, as Felton Wade had discovered, not exactly to his surprise, was a condition guaranteeing a certain degree of immunity from malicious or careless tongues.

"Felton Wade's a big man," folks would say. "A man as big as him's got to shave the edge sometimes." Or, "Felton Wade's too big a man to stoop to something that small. Why, they only run four Bar W steers off . . . Sure, Stinger Blue got shot and Stinger's one of Wade's men. But he can't keep track of all them as works for him. Four steers. That's small pickings!"

So it was. But multiply four steers by a hundred widespread raids on various ranches—not all of which were limited to four head, either—and the total mounted. Still, there was nothing to tie the raids in with Felton Wade. His land was the poorest forage on the Border but he owned so much of it that it supplied more than enough grazing for thousands of head of cattle and a goodly remuda of top mounts. He had even dug a canal that led across his ranch property to the Rio Grande and on every rise of the river he'd flood a tremendous lake that he had built by throwing up an earth levee across a wash. Thus, he had not only land but water. A lot too much land to handle, really, but because it was not of the best he needed it. So said his neighbors, and with reason. Jared Walker, for instance, had better grazing and he hadn't had to dig a canal for water although his place was smaller. The same was true of other nearby spreads. Smaller but richer ranches, well managed, well stocked and quite self-sufficient. Walter Koenig, a German immigrant, had a hog ranch and had made a fortune killing and curing meat. His customers numbered just about every man, woman and child in that region because hams and bacon kept well in the dry climate and were a convenient staple.

Not even Koenig was free from raids. Once when he, his fat wife and his three fat daughters had gone for a week's vacation to San Antonio, his biggest smokehouse had been raided and a year's harvest of meat stolen. It was known that the pickings had been sold across the Border to one of Mexico's countless "generals" who had an idea that the people in power were bad for the people not in power and had set out to do something about it. Something, in this case, had so far only amounted to gathering a few lean and hungry peons and arming them with bad rifles . . . Still, the general had money and money was all the smokehouse raiders had wanted.

BULLET SEED

In vain the ranchers sought protection for their herds and property from Jim Walters, their sheriff. Jim had seen his best days and seemed in the grip of a dreadful malaise which always made him look upon the dark side of things. His attitude was wholly negative. Sure, Stinger had been killed on Jared Walker's Bar W, Jim said, but could he jail Felton Wade on evidence like that? Had the Mexican informer identified any of the men who had sent the wagon loads of meat across the Rio Grande to the general? What, then, could he, Jim Walters, do? Jared Walker, a great giant of a man, grizzled and square-faced, had cursed under his breath and stalked out of the sheriff's office. In the Rock Bottom he had taken a seat at the table around which were waiting Walter Koenig, Kenny Remington of the Circle X, Joe Favron, a dark silent man of French descent, and Jeff Keller who owned the 6-20 spread. They watched Jared as he morosely poured a small glass of whiskey from a nearly emptied bottle.

"Vell," asked Koenig, "vat did he said?"

Jared clamped his square jaw shut behind the drink and glared about him, hard gray eyes slitted and furious. "What do you think he said? No evidence! What could he do? And, dammit, he's right! Not that it excuses him from his shiftless lazy attitude. Not that he shouldn't go ahead and retire and die and be buried. He looks half dead now! Just like he said, Stinger Blue was Wade's man but it wouldn't be the first time a ranny took it on hisself to up his paycheck with some runnin' iron art. There wasn't but four steers in that bunch anyhow. . . That's the sort of pattern this thing's got. I guess

37

in two years I've lost maybe two hundred head. It won't put me out of business but it's a damn irritation."

"I've lost not quite that many," said Favron softly.

"I've lost seventy-five or eighty," said Jeff Keller, ruffling his coarse red hair.

"Vat about me?" exploded Koenig, his fat face purple with indignation. "Me, I lose a whole smokehouse full up mit goot meat."

"I know, Walter," said Walker placatingly. "It's just as easy, with you gone, to steal a houseful of meat as a ham. Where was your boys?"

"Here in town," fumed the fat man. "Vun of the boys iss finding two twenty-dollar bills stuck in der front gate and dey say to demselves, "Free money . . . joost vun night. Vat could happen in vun night? So dey come to town and get drunk."

Keller sniffed suspiciously. "Who goes around leaving twenty-dollar bills stuck in gates?"

Remington smiled tightly. "People who want a free hand for one night to steal meat."

Jared Walker poured another drink and downed it. "Nobody, you see, has lost enough to really make him go on the prod. But let's look at it this way. It's a pattern. A little here and a little there. We're just a few of the people involved. It's more trouble to steal a little from many but it's a hell of a lot safer."

"A liddle vas nod stolen from me," moaned Koenig. "Four thousand pounds off goot meat . . . dot is nod a liddle."

"Your case was different, just like I said," Walker reminded him. "Well, what'll we do about it?"

BULLET SEED

There was silence for a moment. "It all started when Wade came to these parts," remarked Favron.

"We know that," said Remington. "He bought up the mortgage on that big spread and got it for a song."

Walker glared at them ominously. "Yeah, when old man Pickering fell off his hoss and was killed."

"Pickering was as good a rider as any man in Texas, for his age," murmured Favron.

"Yeah," bristled Walker, "and I'm older'n he was. Any of you think I'll fall off my hoss and get killed?"

No one answered but Koenig moaned something else about four thousand pounds of cured meat.

"When does Jim's term run out?" asked Favron.

"In three years," snapped Walker. "He was just elected last year. How do you suppose he beat Matt Crosby?"

"Money," said Remington, shortly.

"Money from where?" asked Walker with a growl. "He sure as hell ain't got any.".

"Money," persisted Remington. "Maybe not Jim's. But somebody's."

The meeting ended on that sour note.

Dave Bridges, his face swathed in bandages, sat before a heavy expensive table and poured drink after drink, throwing them down with thirsty concentration. It was a richly furnished office, plastered white and hung with Indian rugs. On the floor lay a well-tanned buffalo hide. The furniture was massive plain oak that had cost a lot of money.

BULLET SEED

A thick door opened on silent hinges and a tall slender man came in. His hair was bleached almost white but his skin was saddle brown. The eyebrows that bushed over eyes of incredibly intense blue were also the same light shade as his hair, and so was the neat military moustache that decorated his upper lip.

"Put that whiskey down," he barked. "You drink too much."

Dave leered. "Free whiskey. Always did like free whiskey. Good brand, too. Bet it cost a lot of money, hey, Wade?"

"It did. What's that got to do with it?"

"I've made some little of that money fer you. You oughtn't t' mind if I drink."

"What in hell's the matter with your face?"

"Better set down. This is gonna jar you."

The tall man took a seat and put his elbows on the table. "Well . . .?"

"Well, is right. Know who put that bump and gash on my head?"

"I asked you, didn't I?"

"Cap'n Hamp Wallace!"

The other stiffened, his long slim fingers knotting into fists, his face looking like muddied milk.

"Hamp Wallace?" he whispered.

"The same, and still pizen as ever, as maybe you'll be seeing fer yourself. Where's Ash Zimmerman?"

"Don't know. He rode into Big Bend . . . hasn't come back, and that isn't like Ash. He never gets that drunk."

Dave looked steadily at the man. "Ash ain't comin' back. Ted Coulter ain't neither. The sheriff got Coulter

40

right after Hamp Wallace got Zimmerman. They tried to work the same thing on Wallace that they worked on that Ranger."

"How did they know Wallace was there?"

"Way I git it, Coulter come in first and he musta seen Hamp go inter the sheriff's office. When Zimmerman come in Hamp flagged him 'fore he even left the street. Zimmerman musta been a pretty big fool t' think he could take Wallace. Wallace got him 'zactly like him and Coulter got the Ranger . . . in the hand and in the head, 'cept it warn't but one man who done it."

The light-haired man took the bottle, got a glass from the table drawer and poured a drink with trembling hands. "Zimmerman was good, too."

Dave snorted derisively. "I done seen a boatload o' mens like him. They just think they's good. They kin knock over some hidebound ranny with his hands all stiff from ropin' or some sodbuster what thinks like 'lasses runnin' on a cold day, but let 'em go up against a man like . . ."

The blue eyes shot sparks as he slapped the table. "Is Wallace bullet-proof? . . . He can be taken."

"By who—? Name 'im."

The other leaned forward. "Where did he go? He isn't going to stick around in these parts, is he?"

"He didn't say. I think he was headed for Yucca City."

"All right. Go get him . . . Don't give me that look. It won't be the first time."

Dave looked outraged. "You must be crazy. I done took orders and I done well by you but you ain't sendin'

41

BULLET SEED

Dave Bridges up against no sich a rattlesnake as Wallace. Why that there man don't even shet his eyes when he sneezes. He rid right up on me at my place . . . I was takin' the hide offen my boy fer sump'n he done. He rid right up on me and there ain't no cover fer a hundred yards 'cept towards town. Not me. You got plenty o' high-powered gunslingers . . ." Dave grinned evilly. "Like Ash Zimmerman and Coulter. Send them. I flat ain't goin'."

The man opposite him flushed. "You'll go if I say so."

"You said it. I still ain't goin' and don't crowd me."

"I'll crowd whom I please, Dave. Don't get too big for your britches."

"I fill 'em," said Dave toughly. "I take orders and git my pay—and sometimes what you call bonuses. But that's a order I don't take."

"And I say you will."

Dave grinned infuriatingly. "Don't crowd me, man. I know too much Hamp Wallace'd like t' know."

"Dave, when you make threats your usefulness is done. You know that, don't you?"

"My usefulness to you, you mean."

The other ran his left hand over his pale hair and his blue eyes seemed to deepen in color. "Dave, I really should kill you." And he did. But only because Dave, taking the words as a threat, tried to draw. The gun in Wade's right hand exploded below the level of the table and Dave's big body jerked, banging into the table hard. With a magnificent dying effort Dave managed to bring up one of his guns but the slender killer's weapon exploded again and Dave's fell to the floor with a thump.

BULLET SEED

There was the sound of running feet and the tall man got up with a gesture of annoyance. He cracked the door and filled the crack with his body. "Jugg, you come in here. Rest of you go on back. A man tried to draw on me and he wasn't fast enough. That's all."

Jugg Allison, hardy, tall, with muscles like whipcord and broad sinewy shoulders, came through the door and looked at Dave's body on the floor. Jugg's hard lean face didn't change expression. "Thought that'd happen some day."

"So did I. He was smart enough to do simple chores and he was valuable for that reason. But he got too big for himself. Just now he was threatening to tell what he knew—I had no more use for him, then. Get rid of him."

Allison shrugged. "Let him lay till dark. Ain't no use to advertise who he is."

"Maybe you're right. He brought news. He saw Hamp Wallace in Big Bend."

"What of it?"

The slender man eyed his big foreman narrowly. "He got Zimmerman. Coulter tried his sideline and the sheriff cut him in two with a shotgun."

Allison drew taut. "He got Zimmerman? How?"

"He cracked his skull with a cream puff," said Wade sarcastically. "How do you think? Shot him exactly the way Zimmerman and Coulter shot the Ranger . . . in the hand first, then in the head."

"Where?"

"Right in the middle of Main Street. Dave seemed to know Wallace. I know him. Don't you?"

Allison shrugged. "Might of heard of 'im some place. What is he, some sorta ghost . . .? You look like you seen one."

"I know him. I don't want him in these parts."

"Then let's get him."

"You're too valuable to risk. Send three good men. He's in Yucca City—or that's where Dave thought he was going. It'll be a good test for any men you aren't sure of."

"Give me a description of him."

The hand pawed nervously at the pale hair again but Felton Wade gave the description, with a feeling of misgiving. Allison was smart, he was fast with a gun and could handle men. But he didn't know Wallace and thus was unimpressed with one of the most dangerous men ever to ride the trails of Texas. To send such as Allison on such an errand would be dangerous. The other three would do just as well— maybe better. Allison was conceited and arrogant, and had never been taken in a gunfight. Yet no one knew better than his employer that this could mean something less than superior gun-handling on the part of his foreman. It could mean, rather, that he had never gone up against a man of truly high caliber. On the other hand, the rancher had working for him a number of men carefully chosen for their abilities as fighters, men with a ruthlessness that would allow them to do his bidding without a single twinge of conscience. He nodded to himself. Yes, it would be better to use three of these men and keep Allison from meeting the fate of Zimmerman.

44

BULLET SEED

His mind went back to Hamp Wallace and he made a wry face. Did he really want Hamp killed?

Captain Hampton Wallace, formerly of the Texas Rangers—and a man known so far and so wide that ignorance of his reputation was equal to an admission of hopeless dullness—was definitely luxuriating. Dunc Stewart had been sent southward loaded with newly acquired weapons, ammunition, a letter and considerable advice, also with promises of the direst sort of retaliation if said advice was not followed to the letter. Now Hamp was spending the rest of the morning soaking in a huge wooden tub filled to the brim with several boxes of Arm & Hammer soda and hard Yucca City water.

After scraping and soaping and honing himself until he was red and sweating, Hamp, dressed in new clothes and with a sharpened match in his mouth, sauntered down the street to a barbershop. There he got a haircut and shave, calling for several extra hot towels in addition to those normally used in the procedure. "Now," he said, muffled in towels and breathing steam, "strop up that there butcher knife till it'll split a hair. Don't use no gapped-up piece o' cutlery on me, son. And mind them there side-whiskers. They's my pride'n joy. Got any moustache wax?"

"Yes, sir."

"Well, dip some up and ladle it on the las' three inches . . . both sides. I want t' make 'em set up and take notice."

BULLET SEED

When Hamp came out of the barbershop he was a changed man. His mutton-chop whiskers were so perfectly trimmed they looked stenciled on. His moustache was combed and trimmed, the points twisted upward at a debonair angle. His hair was carefully combed, sandy and as straight as a shingle. At the moment it reposed beneath a "Sunday" hat, a wide-brimmed flat-crowned sodbuster, new and clean. His blues were new and pressed and his shirt revealed by its fit that his body was not that of an old man at all but a man in his prime, compact and hard.

Hamp paused in the door, held down his gun harness tightly with his hands and wriggled his hips. Then he strolled briskly northward until he reached the courthouse and walked boldly into the sheriff's office. That worthy, a paunchy, heavy-jowled individual dressed in faded khaki with a gun strapped to his hip, almost turned his swivel-chair over scrambling up. "Well, bus' mah galluses if it ain't He Himself. Howdy, Hamp. When'd y' git in?"

"Las' night," said Hamp shaking hands. "Simp, you ain't changed a bit in twenty years."

Simpson Madison grinned and motioned to a chair. "Put on a little weight. You . . . dammit you look plumb young with all that there goo in your hair and a fresh shave. Las' time I seen you you had to hunt fer yer face in a patch o' brush."

Hamp grimaced as he sat down. "Never could git used t' shavin' on the trail. Damn nuisance. I just let the weeds grow."

The sheriff brought out a half-full bottle of red liquor

and two shot glasses. "Fill up, Hamp, and tell me the news."

While Hamp and his old friend were lazily emptying the bottle and chewing the rag, a hardbitten trio rode into town and turned their horses over to a livery bucko for a night's feed and stable. Doug Ellis, small and rat-faced, shook the dust from his sombrero as they gained the boardwalk and headed toward the hotel. Sam Trask, tall and skinny as a crane, his auburn hair bushing behind his hat, led the group. Doug, a little behind, walked with John Morgan, thick of shoulder and belly, solid and expressionless of face.

Doug was distressed about something. "That there name keeps stickin' in my craw," he complained. "Looks like I ought to know him. Nair one o' you boys don't 'member seein' him or hearin' the name?"

"We done tole you we don't. Ain't never heard of him." Sam looked at his companion disgustedly. "We's frum up in Montana and we don't recollect ever' cross-roads hero. He ain't nuthin' a bullet can't stop nohow!"

"I musta been drunk or sump'n when I heered about him," persisted Doug. That might have easily been true. At the moment his struggle to remember fought with his desire to get this job done and return to a cool bar, where his insatiable thirst could be treated. It had never been slaked.

They strolled before the hotel-bar and huddled for a moment. "Now," said Trask, "we gonna separate and visit all the hotels and the bars. We'll ask t' look at the registers . . . We'll be lookin' fer a friend. If you see 'im or git a line on 'im, don't try a thing. Just keep sight till you kin git t' one of us. If he's so all-fired rough mebbe we'd better play close to the titty. Fust we gotta locate 'im then we'll decide what t' do."

They separated and went their several ways but it fell to Doug to sight Hamp first. Doug ducked into an alley so quickly that he fell headlong. He picked himself up, cursing softly. Doug had sighted his quarry walking down the steps of the courthouse, and this alley was the only place of concealment handy.

Hamp, his old eyes sharper than those of many a youngster, and habitually on the alert, saw from an angle the hurtling figure of Doug as the latter made his headlong dive into the alley. Hamp promptly dived into another alley—a narrow board street running between courthouse and livery.

Doug waited and sweated, but nothing happened— no slight little man with ridiculous moustaches crossed in front of the stalker's hiding-place. Doug began to fidget and was about to take a quick peep out when a gentle voice sounded behind him. "Lookin' fer me, bub?"

4

Doug SPUN around so quickly that he almost dislocated a vertebra, his hand going to his gun instinctively; but he arrested its motion with bone-snapping suddenness. A heavy black gun stared him solemnly in the left eye, its enormous bore seeming to grow as he watched it.

"Tch, tch," clucked the little man chidingly. "Now, that ain't a friendly move . . ." He peered at the rat face and chuckled. "Up t' your old tricks, hunh, Mousy? Good old Mousy Larkin who broke outa the pen killin' two guards. Now don't you know Cap'n Hays'll love to find out I located you. He been lookin' fer you all over creation."

"I ain't Mousy Larkin," whined alias Doug Ellis, "and I been goin' straight ever since. . ." He stopped, realizing he had trapped himself.

Hamp laughed. "You been usin' that tale so much it pops out automatic, like. Now, just around the corner is a man who'll be tickled t' death to see you, Mousy. Name of Simp Madison."

Mousy jerked stiff, but then his shoulders slumped. Bitterly he cursed his taste for drink. His memory now sufficiently joggled, he recalled well the night in Austin when he had been drunk and bragging—the night this very man had come in. Before Mousy had known what was happening, a length of chain had been secured about one wrist and his gun tweaked deftly from its holster.

Almost as bitter as this memory was the utter contempt the little man now proceeded to show for Mousy's prowess as a badman. They were on the street and headed for the courthouse but Mousy's guns still remained in their holsters. Anger raged within him at this palpable insult, then it occurred to him that there could be reason behind it. Maybe Hamp actually wished Mousy would go for his gun. He stole a glance at his captor but Hamp seemed interested in the northern landscape where low mountains were growing purple in the afternoon haze. They were close to the courthouse but Mousy, knowing that a rope awaited his transfer back to Austin, went for his gun with all the speed at his command, backed by a frantic desperation. Then the world seemed to come apart at the joints. A hard wrist smacked into Mousy's adam's apple, a harder leg smacked him just below the knees, this combination attack landing Mousy on his back on the boardwalk with stunning force. The gun had been drawn and lay in Mousy's flaccid hand. Hamp, lips tight and thin, deliberately lifted his left boot and brought it down hard on the hand. Mousy, though dazed, had not been out and he screamed like a burning horse.

"That'll learn you," gritted Hamp. "Git up and le's march."

So it came about that Mousy sat in a chair in the sheriff's office and answered questions, holding his hand and whimpering. True, he showed a certain understandable reticence. But after he had been tapped with authoritative solidity by the barrel of a gun he talked long and earnestly on subjects in which Hamp professed interest.

Night had fallen but Yucca City's stores, bars and hotels were bright with the light of kerosene lamps. At the hotel bar, after regretfully evading the blandishments of several painted girls, Sam Trask and John Morgan stood shoulder to shoulder and carried on a stiff-lipped conversation over two drinks.

"Where'n hell could that jasper of got to?" John wanted to know.

"You axed that befo'," complained Sam Trask. "I ain't seen hair ner hide of 'im. You didn't git a eye on Wallace?"

John shrugged.

"Ain't seen but five mens with moustaches and they was yaller or black. Nairy one sandy gray. Looks like we gonna hafta wait till he comes in. He's registered right here."

"This ain't a likely place, neither. Fo', five gents standin' around not doin' nuthin'. The take at them

51

gamblin' tables is heavy, and they ain't takin' no chances."

"That lobby is got a back door. We could hang around back there."

"That might be the best thing. He'll be back in sometime, we knows. Tell you what. You hang around out front and maybe you can spot 'im comin' up the walk, then slide back and we'll both open up when he comes in. It ain't far t' the livery stable. I'll drift down there right now and tell that jig t' saddle up."

"Good idea. I'll git out front now." The hotel veranda was long and wide, covering the entire front of the building. Six feet from one end was a general store giving out with plenty of light so John Morgan took a seat on a bench at that side of the veranda and relaxed, rolling a smoke. Across the street, hidden in the shadows of an unlighted store, Hamp Wallace grinned wickedly. Then he slithered off, disappearing into still deeper shadows.

Ten minutes later John heard a whisper at his elbow. "John?"

"Yeah," he whispered back. "Who's that . . . Doug?"

"Yeah, come down heah a minnit."

John leaped from the veranda into the dark alley cutting back beside the store, and simultaneously felt a violent tug at his waist. His hand slapped downward and struck an empty holster. "What the hell . . ."

"*Walk.*" A hard cylindrical object dug deep into his stomach, wringing a pained grunt from him. He started for the street but the gun barrel tapped him painfully across the knuckles. "Not that way—the back way."

BULLET SEED

Sam Trask, after arranging to have the horses saddled immediately, had been making a cautious way back to the rear of the hotel lobby. The night was warm and the twin doors stood open, giving Sam an unobstructed view of most of the lobby. He found a stout packing box just out of the light and sat on it. He wanted to smoke but was afraid the light might draw some curious person. For twenty minutes he sat, waited and fidgeted. He stood up and stretched and as he did he heard a rustle behind him. Before he could turn, he felt twin tugs at his hips, and he knew that he had been disarmed. In a moment his eyes, turned away from the lights, became sufficiently accustomed to the gloom for him to make out the slight figure before him.

"Lookin' fer Hamp Wallace, Sam?"

"Yeah . . . uh . . . *no!*"

"Well you found 'im. Come along and don't spook on me. I got a hair-trigger pair o' blunderbusses here."

Sam Trask went along, wondering who, after all, this character was and what, if anything, he had to do with the law. He had been in the jail break along with John Morgan and Mousy Larkin and he had hired out to his present employer because the pay was good and the locality isolated; but had justice, in the shape of Hamp Wallace, caught up with him?

Half an hour later Sam had the answer. Sheriff Madison ran his thumbs under his galluses and snapped the elastic absently. "How'll I handle these here hombres, Hamp?"

"How many deputies you got?"

"Two."

"Swear you in another good man and handcuff one each t' these birds. Mail the keys t' Austin—don't let 'em carry no keys, 'cause things have been knowed t' happen. When's the nex' train through?"

"In the mawnin' about three o'clock."

"Git 'em on it. Don't let nobody know what's up. Git that, Simp . . .? *Nobody!*"

Madison frowned but nodded. "Sure, Hamp, if that's the way you want it. But how come the big secret?"

"Two reasons. We don't want somebody boardin' the train and tryin' a rescue. Also we can let Mr. . . . What'd you say their boss is called?"

Madison told him and Hamp nodded, grinning. "Let 'im wonder what the hell happened to his men." He rubbed his chin reflectively. "Too bad I'm in a mite of a hurry. I'd like to pay that in'restin' gennleman a visit. Fact is, I might just . . . later."

"I been hearin' 'bout him from Jim Walters and Jim says they ain't got a blessed thing on him yet."

Hamp's eyes slitted. "I got a notion I'll soon have a slant on that hombre. It's a plumb habit fer mens t' turn up like right outa a gopher hole with money and set theyselves up in the cattle business. Then their neighbors starts losin' stock. A plumb habit. I think when I find me the time I'll amble back down here and track around a little."

Sheriff Madison looked dubious. "Hamp, you're ridin' a dangerous trail. All sorts o' men is layin' fer you."

Hamp grinned. "I done lived a long time, Simp. I'll git it some day but it'll take some doin'. Like t'night. Three come a-gunnin' and look where they is."

BULLET SEED

"Well, pard," said Madison regretfully as he held out his hand, "play it careful and come see me again."

"I'll do that thing, Simp, and much obliged fer your help."

Madison grinned. "Hell, all I done was open and close the door."

A month later the boss of the Flying Y spoke angrily to Allison, his foreman. "Dammit, Jugg, I just got a letter from Austin explaining the disappearance of those three men. You knew they had broken jail and killed a guard?"

"I'd heard it," said Allison shortly.

"Well, I got a lawyer friend I told to be on the lookout if anything like news reached his ears. He got to talk to Doug. What do you think happened?"

"You're tellin' it."

"Hamp Wallace caught all three of them, turned them over to Sheriff Madison who put them on a train handcuffed to a deputy. . . one apiece. They'll stretch rope sure."

Allison felt a strange emptiness in his stomach. "Y' know, since you seemed so all-fired scared of Wallace, I been askin' questions. Three outa four men here know him and generally they look like you shoved a snake in their face when they hear the name. Why didn't you let me go with Doug and them?"

The long fingers brushed the silvery hair. They could have been seen to tremble slightly. "Jugg, you'd be no good to me, dead in Austin." He walked away leaving the stiff-necked Allison pallid with an insult that sat in queasy company with the fear the news had produced in his stomach. Such is the effect of deserved and sustained reputation. . .

Jugg Allison turned uneasily and marched himself to the bunkhouse. There he poked around under his shuck mattress, coming up finally with an unlabeled bottle of Missouri moonshine. Sitting on the hewn-pine edge of his crude bunk, he drank until he could feel himself on the edge of intoxication. Then, being a man of forethought, he cached the bottle, shook himself, left the bunkhouse for an open spot behind the hay shed. There, for the best part of an hour, he carefully practiced his draw.

Meanwhile Sheriff Jim Walters was having an unwelcome visitor. At the moment he was concerned with the deadly lassitude that suffused his own body and mind and here was a woman telling him of the trials of another. Unwelcome or not, the woman had no intention of leaving until she had had her say and this fact Walters knew from long experience. She was his wife.

"And would you believe it, when I went in that cabin Jenny Bridges didn't have a single smidgen of anything to eat. Looked like she was starved. She said she was sick but she was plain hungry. Well, I turned right around and went back home and brought her some grub. She ate like an animal. Now, we're going to have to do something about that woman. It ain't Christian to sit here and let her starve. Nobody seems to know what happened to that no-good dawg of a husband she tied herself to and the boy can't come back till these criminals around here forget he pointed out Ash Zimmerman to Hamp Wallace. Now there's a man."

"Yes, Hamp is a man. I mind the time I was one just like 'im."

"I declare to goodness if I know what's come over you these last few years, Jim. You look and act so peaked all the time."

"Just a old man, I guess," he said sadly.

"That ain't so. I know a lot of men older'n you what don't set around and mope like this. I don't see why you don't go see this here new doctor. He knows a lot of things them old butchers didn't know. Why when Lovey Denton had her last young'un she didn't feel a thing. He gave her chloryform! Did you ever hear anything like that? Go see him, Jim."

"Well, now, I might do that," he said. A faint glow of hope warmed his veins. After all, he had felt good a whole week after that Ash Zimmerman episode.

"Anyways, we'll have to do something about Jenny Bridges," said Marthy, returning to her first subject. "Any ideas?"

He shrugged. "Looks like we could feed her fer a week, then some of the others could help. . . a week at a time. She could set with sick folks or old man Turner who can't hold his water no more. . . or tend children fer wimmen like that Dora that cleans up at the hotel . . ." He spread uplifted palms. "Hell, I don't know."

A gleam came to her eyes. "Fine! Each of us in the sewin' circle can take a week and bring her grub till she gets on her feet again, then she could tend children and sick folks and such. I think that's a plumb good idea."

"Heah," he said dryly, "I just mentioned it. I mean—I dunno if—"

"Never mind. Once I gets my teeths in a ear of corn I eats it. Well, I'll be gettin' along and don't you be late for supper again."

5

TIME PASSED.

Walter Koenig lost no more cured meat.

Every six months, Jared Walker came up short on his tally sheet, as did Kenny Remington, Joe Favron and others. Not many cattle lost . . . just a few here and there. Sheriff Jim Walters sat and nodded in his office, putting off the visit to the new doctor.

The sewing circle took care of Jenny Bridges and Jenny sat with babies, or with the sick when needs be and with old man Turner who was still tottering this side of his grave.

The white-haired boss of the Flying Y frowned over his acres and nursed memories of a little man with a ridiculous moustache and gimlet amber eyes.

Jugg Allison did his work with the swift cold efficiency for which he was noted, his pride still remembering that he had been afraid when he had heard what had happened to his three men in Yucca City.

59

BULLET SEED

In Yucca City, Sheriff Madison idly gnawed on dead cigars and wondered what Hamp Wallace was up to now and if he'd keep his promise to come back and look into some things.

And far to the south Dunc Stewart grew and filled out his frame, stretching and maturing with hard work and good food . . .

On a rocky cactus-studded knoll Dunc sat his deep-bay gelding and looked toward the west, seeking and finding the green spot that marked *La Hacienda de los Palos Verdes.*

He was well over the six-foot mark now and his long bones were plated with hard muscle. For six months now he had been wearing a pair of beautiful pearl-handled Colts, and he had burned a great deal of ammunition. Safe from observation, out on the rimrock, far from the hacienda, he had practiced by the hour, day after day, whenever his work permitted it. He labored at the business of drawing and firing until his back would ache and his hands burn like fire. The skin of his thumbs began to take on a smooth horniness from the scrape of the mule-eared hammers. As Hamp had predicted, Don Rolando had taught the boy much, and to his education Dunc had added quirks of his own. He could now juggle his guns like a sleight-of-hand artist; to him the border shift was a split second affair. He could single- or double-roll so swiftly that the guns would resemble a speeding wheel, a circle of light. He could draw, spin and return his guns to their holsters with such speed that the guns striking leather simultaneously were a flashing, thwacking blur.

BULLET SEED

Still, he worked and worked. His rifle was a source of joy to the hacienda because the *vaqueros* were notoriously poor shots, but Dunc could always bring home venison. He had learned in his youth, when ammunition was precious, never to throw lead carelessly; he was always sparing of shots and rarely took more than a single round to bring down a buck.

So his education progressed. Nor was it all concerned with arms. The priest who presided over the hacienda chapel lent him books to read and taught him Spanish. Often when they talked, the gentle old man had a sense of foreboding about the eager Dunc. Father Ortiz had seen killers, and this one somehow reminded him of them though he knew Dunc had never shot a man.

Some three years after Dunc had first come to work at the Camara-Peon hacienda he ran into his first trouble there. That it arrived with his first love was perhaps inevitable.

Carmelita Molina was fourteen years of age. She was just completing the transition from adolescence to maturity, early, as befits a true daughter of Mexico, when Dunc first saw her. She happened to be washing clothes in the middle of a small stream that wound lazily through the groves of tamarinds and willows. In the process, of course, she had become thoroughly drenched. Her wet dress, clinging to her figure, revealed it with outrageous frankness, and her young breasts were as sprightly as hyacinth shoots. Her face had a sultry beauty—her skin was olive, sunkissed to a deep tan. Her lips were full and sensuous, their healthy red making them look like a rose held stem-in-teeth. Her masses of dark wavy hair tumbled in disarray to her lithe shoulders. She was a thing of the outdoors, the woods and streams; a wild flower. Dunc sat his gelding, watching her while the animal drank. She was unaware of his presence, his approach having been quiet, and she was singing at the top of her lusty voice.

Dunc listened and looked, his eyes wide and his heart kicking him painfully in the ribs. There was a sweet sickness in the pit of his stomach and he seemed to be having trouble breathing. Carefully he got off the horse, in the thrall of the wholly new and delightful emotion. Screening himself in low bushes he stalked quietly closer, finally walking out in full view not ten feet from her. She let loose a frightened little cry, but in a moment was smiling. *"Por Dios, señor,* but you frightened me!"

Dunc grinned foolishly and answered in Spanish almost as liquid as her own. "I . . . I was watering my horse."

"He is a very nice horse," she said, to make conversation. "I have seen you riding him many times."

"You mean you've seen me before?"

"But of course. I have watched you. You ride so strongly. . . so well." A slight flush curtained the satin of her cheeks but her eyes were bold and sparkling.

Dunc flushed scarlet and looked down at his feet. Then attraction and desire, which have routed shyness before, took over and led Dunc through a series of speeches and actions that were sheer torture yet a compulsion upon him.

"This is the first time I have seen you, which I regret." He sat down, for his knees were shaking.

Her smile was loaded with coquettishness and deviltry and her perfect teeth gleamed. "You like the way I look, señor?"

His face reddened again. "Just call me Dunc. Sure I like seeing you. You're . . ." He choked but continued. "You're—pretty!"

The smile widened and softened. The high conical breasts lifted and fell as she breathed excitedly. "Oh . . . Dunc . . . That was a nice thing to say."

"*Es nada,*" he scoffed with a touch of hysteria. "Why, you—you're more than pretty . . . beautiful . . . *magnifico!*" He remembered something he had read. "*Adorable,*" he finished, sweat breaking through his plain gray shirt.

At the beginning it had been she who was the steadier and more composed of the two, but now with his words ringing in her ears, words she had never before heard but of which she had dreamed, the tables were turned. She, being a creature perhaps closer to nature than he, and certainly with fewer years, left the rock on which she had been standing and as though she were being pulled on a string came straight for him, stepping boldly through the shallow water, her wet dress clinging to her swelling thighs and hips. Dunc got to his feet, wishing that he had the strength to flee. The sight of her crossing the water, her hips swaying with the natural grace of her blood, was so thoroughly shattering that he was leeched of whatever equilibrium he had so far maintained.

For an instant or two they stood staring at each other, as if this were a moment of revelation. Neither spoke.

That is to say, neither spoke aloud. Their eyes were doing all the talking. Dunc's mouth hung open and he was panting like a stallion after a race. Carmelita too was breathing hard, her youthful bosom rising and falling in a manner that to Dunc was utterly enchanting.

No one can explain quite how such things happen but, with neither the strength nor the will to resist, they suddenly found their arms about each other. Dunc nearly fainted from the touch of her rosy lips. She too was reeling from the impact of this miracle encompassing them. Without a word, they walked a few steps away from the water and fell rather than sat on the grass. Her body was wet but the heat of her skin struck through his clothes, fanning the flame already ignited the moment she had touched him. His arms were tight about her, crushing her to him, squeezing a delirious little note of eagerness from her throat. . .

Some time later, they clung together, now seeking in their embrace not passion, but reassurance and respite. Each seemed trying to find refuge from some nameless fear.

Carmelita sobbed briefly into the rough fabric of his shirt, arousing in him a fierce sense of protectiveness.

Finally she raised her head and looked into his intense blue eyes. "Do you love me, Dunc?"

"So much," he said brokenly, ". . . so much."

This had a reviving effect on her. She sat up and smiled slowly like a well-fed cat. Her face was satin smooth now and her eyelids were almost sleepy with

BULLET SEED

peace. "I love you, too," she said, leaning over and kissing him again . . . nuzzling his lips and eyes with her cool soft nose.

That her dress was in an appalling state of disarray and that a great deal of her was exposed did not seem to trouble her now. "I love you so much that I hurt in the heart," she cooed. "When may we meet again?"

"Every day! Why not?"

And nearly every day they did meet thereafter. The spring roundup had been completed and the market drive finished without incident, so his duties were not arduous. For weeks they sought each other on every possible occasion, intelligent enough to make it seem all very casual and accidental. No one appeared to notice except one Carlos Vaca, a lithe *vaquero* who had acquired himself a crush on Carmelita long before Dunc had but whose Latin training had prevented him from speaking his case. He could court a girl only through channels—with proper arrangements involving hacienda protocol, parents, chaperons and such. Carlos was thus at a severe disadvantage and after the first meeting between Carmelita and Dunc the *vaquero*'s chances were slim. Even at church, where he had been accustomed to making sly eyes at her or stealing a few words of conversation, he now reaped only her contemptuous glance and a haughty tossing of soft round shoulders. Being no fool, he placed his own interpretation upon this change in her. Although he could never catch her in an intimate moment with Dunc, by assiduous spying he did discover they were holding secret trysts and his quick temper almost blew him apart. He had never

liked the *gringo* from the start and now his hatred became a fearsome thing. He nursed it for a week until he
could stand it no longer and then he took his troubles
to Rolando—who turned out to be quite cold about
them.

"Have you ever known me to interfere with the lives
and loves of our people?"

"No, Don Rolando, but this man is a *gringo* and it is
not right."

Rolando, his mind on other things, shrugged. "Then
take your difficulties to the *gringo*. However, I must
warn you, if he beats you half to death do not come
running to me."

Carlos bowed to hide his rage and departed. Still in
a steaming fury two days later, he met Dunc just as
the latter was entering the bunkhouse after supper.

"*Señor*, I would have a word with you." He was pale
and trembling. Dunc stood dumfounded.

"Sure. What's the trouble? You're shaking all over!"

"I wish to warn you. Stay away from Carmelita."

Dunc, staggered for a moment, recovered enough to
laugh. Carlos took this as insult added to injury. He
clenched his fists.

"Carlos," said Dunc, "whatever put that idea in your
head?"

"What idea?"

"The idea that I'd stop seeing her. She and I are in
love."

The *vaquero*'s voice carried a deadly edge. "That is a
lie."

Dunc's blue eyes flamed dangerously. Where he came

66

from there was no deadlier insult. He slapped Carlos, if an openhanded blow with enough power behind it to fell a calf could be called a slap; and Carlos, who was seven inches shorter and thirty pounds lighter, rolled in the dust. By this time they had quite an audience but no one interfered.

Carlos' face was pallid, except for the livid imprint of Dunc's hand.

He got up slowly. "*Señor* Stewart," he said, holding onto his temper by a powerful effort of will, "I cannot fight you this way. I am small and you are large . . . But you are wearing your guns, I see!" His right hand was raised and slightly forward, the fingers slightly crooked.

Dunc felt no fear. He was certain that in a draw he could easily beat the Mexican. But a dead man in the dust would not be a gift with which to reward his benefactor, Don Rolando, who had helped Dunc, the outlander, in every possible way, who had treated the boy as a member of his family. On the other hand, Dunc's courage was being challenged and the pregnant silence that hung over the assembly did not allow him any illusions on the matter.

"You are a fool, Carlos," he said evenly. "I will see Carmelita whenever I wish and whenever she wishes. I will not fight you with a gun, or a knife either. Because if I did I would kill you. You are one of Don Rolando's best *vaqueros,* and I will not repay his kindnesses by killing you."

He turned on his heel and entered the bunkhouse.

Sleep did not come easily that night. Dunc tossed

67

and turned, thinking. If his promised four years had been up he would be free to leave; but there remained at least eight months to go. It did not occur to him that he was a fine figure of a man now, and not a slim fearful stripling. Hamp Wallace had ordered him here and Dunc believed himself bound to obey. Still, it would be difficult to remain now that the hornets had been stirred up. He had not missed the looks of contempt on the faces of the *vaqueros* with whom he had ridden over many a rough trail.

Then there was Carmelita . . .

It was from her that the greatest shock came. That Sunday, with a flock of young girls dressed in their finest, she was walking through the brilliant sun on the way to church. Catching sight of Dunc standing at the well, she boldly detached herself from the crowd and ran over to him. Her eyes flashed dangerously. "Dunc, I hate cowards. Especially cowards who allow Carlos Vaca to make them turn and run." She tossed a silken shoulder contemptuously and ran back to her giggling companions.

Stricken and miserable, Dunc tottered back to the bunkhouse and began to gather his scanty belongings. Hamp's injunctions upon him seemed as nothing now. The bottom had dropped out of his world and the hurt was his first as a man, therefore terrible. Tears of self-pity welled into his eyes but he dashed them away out of shame. His packing completed, he went to the big house to speak with Don Rolando.

An Indian girl-servant went to search for the head of the house while Dunc sat in a hide-bottomed chair in the cool flagged patio and waited numbly, his brain pickled in the sour brine of curdled love. Don Rolando walked in, his high-heeled boots making enough noise to arouse the dead, but he had to speak to Dunc twice before he was noticed. Dunc started and forced a stiff grin to his lips. "Don Rolando," he said, rising solemnly from the chair, "I have come to take my leave."

Don Rolando sat down in the chair Dave had vacated and crossed his long legs, his hawk-handsome face concerned and serious. "What is the meaning of this, Duncan?"

"Haven't you heard about Carlos and me?"

Don Rolando grunted. "The man is a fool. He came to me with his troubles and I sent him away. I told him to see you. I make it a practice never to intervene in matters of love."

"He tried to make me draw on him."

Don Rolando sat up stiffly. "The ass. You would have killed him with ease."

"I know that, but I wouldn't fight him. I couldn't . . ."

"What? Surely you're not afraid of him!"

"You know different, sir. But he's a good man, and you—you've been a friend to me. You've been kind, helpful. Your beautiful spread here has been my home for more than three years. I couldn't kill one of your men."

"That is a sentiment I would have expected from you, Duncan. I admire you for it." Don Rolando was suddenly pensive. After a few moments, he resumed: "Hamp was right. He saw the mettle in you. But then, I've rarely known Hamp to be wrong." He smiled.

"Nevertheless, I can handle Carlos. You need not leave on his account."

"It isn't that," said Dunc bitterly. "The men think I'm yellow. No one has spoken to me, since he tried to prod my draw. No one but Carmelita, I mean. And all she had to say was that I'm a coward."

"You have showed a great deal more courage than the occasion warranted, Duncan. I tell you that for your own peace of mind. As for the girl, she is allowing appearances to influence her . . . which makes me think she was not so much in love as either of you believed."

"Maybe you're right, sir." His voice was low and cords stood out on his lean neck.

"*Pues,* I can see how you feel. Wait here just a moment."

He came back after rather a long while and handed Dunc a letter. "This is for Hamp in the event that he does not understand your leaving me prematurely. It will explain what happened and that I gave you permission to leave." He handed Dunc a buckskin bag that clinked richly. "Hamp was very emphatic that you were to be paid nothing while you were here." Don Rolando smiled. "He said nothing, however, about paying you when you left. These are your wages for three years and four months. Exactly what I pay my own *vaqueros.* Except that I added a little because of the respect you showed my house by refusing to shoot a man who had challenged you. It is also a token of . . ." The smile came on again. "Of my own personal esteem. Please consider my doors always open to you."

Dunc did not trust his voice. He shook hands hard

and walked through the big house, a damp mist blurring his eyes.

Ten minutes later he was in the saddle, heading north for the Rio Grande. For miles he rode at a hard gait, choking with misery and hardly aware of his surroundings. The horse automatically followed an old cattle trail leading toward water.

Then Dunc, warned by his shying horse, saw a rattler coiled in the dust and heard its whirr. He drew his left-hand gun and with a single slug blasted the snake's head. After that, he began to sit up and take notice.

6

ROCK BRIDGE was so named because of a legend that there was once an Indian maiden who, fleeing from some ogre of the times, found Lost River blocking her flight. She prayed to the Great Spirit for deliverance and lo, there appeared a bridge of solid rock over the river, across which she sped. The demon followed, but the bridge collapsed, crushing him. To this day there remained two mighty outcroppings north of town which conceivably could have been joined together, bridge fashion, once.

Being surrounded by good range, and accessible by both water and trail, Rock Bridge was a natural spot for two saloons, two general stores, a gaunt boxlike hotel, a livery stable, a blacksmith shop, and a leather worker's shed where a one-eyed Mexican plied deft hands at saddle repair, also making chaps, belts and other handy articles.

Rock Bridge had never felt any need for an officer of

BULLET SEED

the law—a fair enough commentary on the kind of citizen occupying the cabins scattered on the slope above the one street of the town, as well as those without need for the atmosphere of home who lived and ate at the Traveler's Hotel. It was a hardy soul indeed who ventured into Rock Bridge unless he carried nothing that its unprincipled denizens might covet. If he did, he was in danger, to put it mildly.

Duncan Stewart arrived at this oasis after fifteen hard days of travel, sick of beans and camp food, tired, caked with dust, thirsty, his heart as sore as a boil and his face grim with the bitterness in his soul.

He rode straight up the single dusty street to the livery stable on the north end, ignoring the glances of curious people, ignoring various gibing remarks and the guffaws they induced.

He stabled his horse and walked back to the hotel still scarcely conscious of his surroundings. He registered and asked the clerk, a thin, consumptive-looking gentleman with a sharp red nose, "You got a place where a man can wash the dust off?"

The clerk jerked his head toward the rear of the lobby. "Through that door. Want hot water?"

"All you got."

"Cost you fifty cents extra."

Unnecessarily inflamed at the remark, Dunc looked straight at the other. "I'll stake you to a bath too. You need it."

The clerk, startled by the drilling intensity of the blue eyes, swallowed jerkily. "No offense, sir . . . It'll be ready in twenty minutes." Then he added nastily because it was within his province, "The room is two dollars a day—in advance."

Dunc hauled out his buckskin bag and spilled a double eagle from it. "Just hold onto that till I've eaten and slept it up. Now where can I buy some clothes? I want the lot from boots to hat."

"B. U. Price General Merchandise, or four doors down at the Main Street Merchant."

B. U. Price proved a giant of a man with a brutish jaw covered by inky beard. His shoulders bulked with heavy muscle and he wore a six-shooter at his right hip. About the store, Dunc noticed with some surprise, lay two double-Greeners and three Winchesters strategically placed. He looked at Price, who was studying him with impenetrable black eyes. "Sort of funny to display your hardware like that," said Dunc. "They don't look new."

Price said, "They ain't for sale. They're for use."

Dunc's sun-whitened eyebrows rose questioningly. "Bad actors here, hey?"

Price shrugged. "Bad enough. If I was a notcher I'd have them guns all carved up."

Dunc's jaw hardened with displeasure. It sounded like a boast. "Oh. You're the toughest."

"I'm the carefullest," said Price without taking offense. "You look like a younker."

"No. Nineteen."

Price laughed. "Better look out, bub. Some of these hardcases pull your pants off right on the street."

Dunc nodded but there was no expression in his eyes. "I want an outfit, so's they can start pullin'."

"Like what?"

"Like a hat, a pair of black high-boots, some denims and a couple of shirts. Six pairs of wool socks."

"Ain't many people around here what wears socks."

"Ain't many people around here what bathes either," retorted Dunc.

Price looked at him, then laughed deep in his cavernous chest. "You'll make it, bub, or you'll go down fast."

While the clothes were being laid out, Dunc pulled out a pair of clean socks from a hip pocket and put them on his feet with a grimace of distaste. He would have washed first but the thought of putting on his dirt-glazed garments over clean skin revolted him. He picked up the first pair of boots, lifted them to his nose and replaced them in the box. "If you don't have some that a dirty foot hasn't been in I'll keep on wearing my own."

Price frowned then grinned. "Wal, I'll look." He searched and found a pair of brown boots that had never been tried on. "How about these? They smell just like the steer."

"That's a good smell," replied Dunc laconically and took the boots, tried them on and kicked his own worn-out footwear aside. "I'll take 'em but they sure do glare. I wanted black."

"These are dress boots," said Price.

"Who dresses up around here?"

"Not many people. That's why they never been tried on." So saying Price made a bundle of the purchases. "Now, lemme see. Two pairs of denims—that's five dollars. Boots, eighteen dollars . . . that's 'cause they's dress boots. Shirts, three-eighty. Total . . . Nope, six pairs wool socks at fifty cents a pair . . . Two dollars. Total, twenty-eight fifty. Right?"

"No. You shorted yourself on the socks. Should have said three dollars 'stead of two."

Price looked positively startled. "Wal . . . damn if it ain't so." He accepted his money and got a look at Dunc's poke.

"Son, I think you're a plumb honest boy. Don't walk around with all that money on you. You'll lose it shore's shootin'."

"If I lose it," Dunc said easily, "you can bet on the shooting."

Price shook his head. "You don't know this place like I do. But you'll learn. If things git rough, turn your back this way. You won't git one in the spine."

"That's the kind you got here?"

"That's the kind. Some of the others too, but they's not so much picked on. Mainly the real old or the awful young are the prey. That last part takes you in."

Dunc flashed Price a look and the merchant caught a short quick breath. A killer, he thought. Young, but a killer. There'll be smoke in the air . . .

Dunc walked back to the hotel, took a long thorough bath, shaved clumsily the few blond hairs that had begun to fuzz out like threads of gold against his tanned hide. He dressed in his new clothes and sought the hotel dining room, such as it was. He ate a huge meal of steak and onions with boiled potatoes and butter, a soup plate full of canned tomatoes, three pieces of apple pie and two cups of hot strong coffee. He sat for a while and rolled a cigarette, a habit he had acquired among the *vaqueros.* He sat back and surrendered completely to the feeling of well-being. But it took only five minutes for his mind to work its way back to Carmelita, whereupon his supper seemed an intolerable load and he wished he hadn't eaten it.

Feeling miserable and truculent at the same time, he walked out of the hotel and down the street to the first saloon, a sawdust-floored barnlike establishment with the usual complement of thirsty cowboys, as well as cold-faced men whose sole interest seemed to be cards and others whose interests would be difficult to determine.

There were no women, for which Dunc was thankful. Even a painted dancehall girl would have reminded him of Carmelita and he needed no such reminders.

He went to the bar and motioned to the greasy-haired bartender. "Put out a bottle of Hogans and a glass."

It was his intention to get drunk. It would be his first time but he felt he should have the experience. The wine and other drinks he had tasted at fiestas had made his stomach burn prettily but he wanted experience with a man's drink.

"Got no Hogans," said the bartender, taking in the evident youth of his customer. "What about Rodden's Best?"

Dunc nodded shortly. "Make sure it's the best."

The bartender palmed a smile. Rodden's was the worst liquor that had ever been bottled. It wasn't long before the news was circulated about the wet-eared kid drinking Rodden's Best and snickers went the rounds, but they were lost on Dunc. He stood solidly on his two

77

feet and plied himself with drink. The resultant burn within him mounted until it was wildfire and he began to feel restless and eager to do great things.

A thick-shouldered man with a broken nose and black foul teeth, his face red with drink and obviously on the prod if he could find a victim who didn't offer too much resistance, spied Dunc and heard the story about Rodden's Best. He swaggered over while others stopped what they were doing to watch.

He shouldered into Dunc, making him spill half a drink. The boy's natural civility made him move and mutter an apology. For an ordinary jostle that should have sufficed but Blackie Hogan didn't feel like listening to apologies. He swelled and looked hard at Dunc. "Clumsy, ain't you?"

"How can a man be clumsy leaning against a bar standing still?"

Blackie's talents did not extend to verbal tilting and he felt taken aback and put upon. No man should take refuge behind words.

"Purty boots you got on there."

"Thank you."

"Thank yew," mocked Blackie, then, tiring of conversation which promised to be an effort, he lifted a big boot and crashed it down on Dunc's left foot. This hurt. The boy's temper, already as thin as a shed snakeskin, snapped violently. He spun around and slammed a left fist as hard as an oaken mallet into the very center of Blackie's unpleasant visage. Bone crunched, blood spurted and Blackie struck the floor so hard on his back that he almost went over in a somersault. Like a tiger Dunc was on him, snatching him up and propping him against the bar. With his opponent in this momentarily erect position, Dunc loosed three terrific blows, one to the pit of the stomach, then two to Blackie's jaw. A fourth and fifth slid Blackie almost across the bar, so Dunc caught him by the heels and with a titanic heave hurled him halfway to the door where he rolled on his back, beaten and unconscious.

Dunc gave his tense shoulders a heave, deliberately turned his back and resumed his drinking. He felt a tap and turned to face a scrawny ugly man dressed in tight black clothing. His eyes were slitted so nearly shut that Dunc could hardly see them. "That was a friend of mine," said the man, his lips moving stiffly as though they were too tightly drawn for the rest of his face. He wore two guns low on his hips.

Dunc was unaware that there was a collective catching of breath throughout the whole saloon. He was high on anger and alcohol.

"Is that a fact?" he said coolly.

"That's a fact."

Again the left whipped up like a streak of lightning and Bugger White stretched out beside his friend.

Dunc looked about, his eyes lances of cold light. "He got any more friends?"

No one said anything except the bartender. "You better be gone when he comes to, younker."

"I'll be nowhere but here."

He turned, poured one more drink, then put his back against the bar and watched the two men come gradually out of their respective comas.

79

BULLET SEED

An old man, too old to cause offense, hobbled over to Dunc. "Ye're a guid lad with ye're fusts," he said with a thick Scotch burr, "but when he cooms to ye're a dead mon. I council ye to be gone."

"Thank you, pappy," said Dunc, but made no move, his eyes watching the men on the floor. Blackie was sitting up now, staring vacantly about. Bugger White was struggling to get to a sitting position.

"What's ye're name, lad?" asked the ancient.

"Duncan Stewart."

The old man straightened, his rheumy eyes flashing. "Aye . . . a bonny name. A name a mon would be prood to wear. Stay ye here and show the scum how a mon o' Scots bluid conducts himsel'."

"Yes, sir." Scotch, Indian, Spanish, plain American—who knew? Dunc was thinking. Anyway it was his blood, mixed or pure and at the moment, boiling.

The two men were both erect now and White's wandering eyes had located Dunc. His face grew livid and he got slowly to his feet. He called Dunc a filthy name and took a step forward. Dunc stiffened, his feet spread and his face as taut as rawhide. "Pat yourself, friend."

White looked as if he had expected someone to tell this fool of his, White's reputation; he was surprised because either it hadn't been done or hadn't made an impression.

He made his move almost contemptuously and realized in one blood-freezing fraction of a second that he had made the mistake so many men had made. He had underestimated an opponent. Dunc's guns flamed and the big slugs smashed White from his feet like a pitchfork tosses hay and skidded him on the rough floor.

The old man cackled with glee. "A bonny name . . . a bonny name. Aye and still honor bright."

A lanky man with sandy hair and pale colorless eyes, dressed in range-town garb walked to the bar where he could speak without talking over or around anyone. "Good shooting, kid," he said tonelessly, "but we can't use you here. Don't let morning find you in my town. You savvy?"

"Your town?" Dunc faced him, still tense and drawn, his guns pointing at the floor.

"My town," came the flat reply.

Dunc looked steadily at the man for a moment, then reloaded his guns. He had killed a man and he felt nothing except a certain grim elation. Also there was a feeling of soaring self-sufficiency, which he was careful to keep curbed.

He spun his guns until they were circles of light and snapped them back in his holsters. He raised his eyes to the lanky man. "Since this is your town, I take it you personally run people out of it." He raised his hands to his new flat-crowned hat and set it firmly on his head. "Well, get to running."

A wispy smile touched the other's lips. "No, sonny, I order people run out of town. I don't dirty my hands."

Dunc laughed with such terrible derision that the fellow's face flamed. "I see. Yes, sir . . . I see. I'll think about your invitation. I'll let you know in the morning."

"That'll be too late," came the strangled reply.

Dunc shrugged. "The hell you say. I don't like to be

pushed in my thinking. Good night, you big bad man, you."

He left the saloon in a horrible silence, but no one shot him in the back. One reason was that the old man followed him out closely. When they were in the dark the old fellow stopped him. "Ye're a credit to yer clan but ye're outnumbered. A Scotsman besides being a mon o' courage is a'so canny. Ha'n't ye heerd?"

"You think he'll try to run me out?"

"Sure, laddie, and what chance ha' ye when he's got twenty men to do his dirrrty worrk?"

Rage was still plucking at Dunc's reason. "What's your name, pappy?"

"Rory MacNabb."

"MacNabb, if anybody starts on me tonight, this town is going to be hell in a bundle. I don't want decent folks hurt, if there are any here, so tell any you know to keep out of my way—" Like a cougar's, the eyes shone now with a foxfire glint and the old man sucked in a slow breath.

"Ye've convinced me. The Bruce dinna lay doon his claymore when short o' men. I'll do my best and I'll do more. My eyes are na' too auld to look over the sichts o' a rifle."

"Shucks, I don't know about this Bruce, but just stay out of the way, pappy. Won't need more'n just me to take care of things."

Dunc went straight to the livery stable, told the attendant to saddle his horse. He took his rifle from the saddle boot, returned to the hotel. There he found the news of his fracas had preceded him and the clerk looked at him with a respect that was almost fawning. He leaned over as he handed Dunc the key. "There's some hardcases just come in. Upstairs. Watch your poke."

Dunc nodded and walked up the dimly lighted stairs, his arms folded, and in the crook of one nestled a cocked .45. One smoky kerosene lantern burned midway of the hall and toward this he made his way, so tense that his back ached. Nothing happened. He let himself into his room and closed the flimsy door but he did not lock it. He turned and walked quickly to the connecting door of the adjoining room, tried his key and found that it fitted. This adjoining room was empty so he unlocked its outside door also. Then he closed the connecting door but didn't lock it, went to his bed and arranged a not too lifelike dummy of his bedclothes under the blanket. The hour's wait seemed interminable but at last from the vantage of the other room, the connecting door barely cracked, he heard the dry rasp of an opening portal.

Two men entered softly and a third stood in the doorway.

"There he is," muttered one.

"Best tap him on the head and wake him," whispered another, " 'cause he mighta dumped that poke summers. We got to make 'im tell us where it is."

"It's under the bed," shouted Dunc, and suddenly the room seemed filled with flames and ear-splitting concussion. The commotion shut off with startling suddenness as the third man, the one who could still run, got a cute idea, turning and dashing for the adjoining

83

room. The door flew open in his face . . . the door from the hall. Again came the ear-shattering detonation of a heavy-caliber gun fired in a confined space and the man slid forward on his face.

With a leap that carried him back through the room to a window, Dunc snatched up his rifle and stepped out on a low flat roof. He followed it toward the back of the building until it dropped to one still lower. From this one the jump to the ground was nothing and he was free of the hotel. His face shone whitely in the gloom and his berserk rage seemed to be having the effect of clearing his senses rather than dulling them. "They'll remember this night," he said grimly to himself.

When he entered the back of the Price store, the owner spun like a cat but he faced the black eye of a Winchester held at hip level, steady as a rock.

"Mr. Price, I'd like to have you either neutral or on my side."

Price's lips tightened. "Heard what you did to White and what you said to Chance Naught . . ." He smiled. "How about that for a name? Chance Nothing."

"By morning there'll be that much left of Rock Bridge —nothing."

Price's big shoulders hunched. "By God . . . I felt it when you went out. Maybe you're what this town has been needin'. What do you want that I can give?"

"Five gallons of coal oil . . . and this Chance Naught, what does he own around here?"

Price went to his front doors, closed them and barred them against the rising roar the hotel fight had set into being. Dunc could hear loud shouts but he knew he had moved unseen. Also he had stayed out of the light while talking to Price.

Price arrested himself in the act of filling a can. "Good Godamighty. You gonna burn the place out?"

"His places."

"The hull town'll go."

Dunc shook his head. "No wind, and a storm brewing up north. Didn't you see the lightning? Wet your place down. I'll give you time. What does Chance own?"

"Hotel, both saloons. A warehouse next to the saloon you was in, the Top Chance. The other'n is the Last Chance. He owns the Main Street Merchant, the other general merchandise store and ... Well, that's all. Mostly his stuff is on the other side of the street." His face grew black. "By God, younker, I'm in this with you. He's begun t' threaten people who trade with me and not him. Couple of his men tried t' burn me out, too. A couple of weeks ago I fixed their plows with buckshot, but he's out to get me first and last."

"I'm cleaning out him and his rats. Want to take one of those shotguns and drift around in the dark with me? There'll be plenty of light after a while. Then you can pick you a place and stay there."

The square face looked like a piece of roughly carved granite. "Tie a white rag around your hatband ... never mind. I'll know that hat."

By this time every tough gun in Rock Bridge, aroused by the slaughter in the hotel, was hunting for Dunc high and low. But not a sign of him did they find and after an hour they gave it up, going back to the Top Chance for a drink on the house.

Dunc thereupon set up his incendiary bombs and all he needed was rain to discourage the flames from spreading too far and fast. This came soon. With the first drops, Dunc was well beneath the Top Chance establishment laying a thin trail of kerosene away from the mass of soaked rags to give him time to cross the street before the fire was noticed and take cover behind a boulder of sandstone carved with hundreds of names and obscene verses.

It was a night that Rock Bridge would long remember. Men with wives and children had long since gone home and taken their families higher on the slope and put them in places of protection. Old Rory had done his job well. Trouble began when the tinder-dry Top Chance seemed to explode into lurid flame and men poured from the saloon in a stream. Dunc with an extra loaded Winchester he had borrowed from Price, called out, deliberately showed himself around the edge of the boulder. Immediately, shots from twenty or more guns came his way. He answered with a deadly fire into the packed mass of men fleeing the Top Chance, sending them scattering in all directions, those who could move at all. He snatched up the second rifle and began to squeeze off careful shots, cursing audibly at an occasional miss. Dunc was not accustomed to missing but the light, though bright enough, was not good to shoot by because of the flicker.

Frenzy entered their ranks and some even fired at one another in their hysteria, which mounted with the flames. Thunder and lightning crashed about their ears. Occasionally Dunc could hear the dull-throated boom of a Greener shotgun. Dunc withdrew into the shadows, following the fleeing figures carefully, his head cool and deadly. Reloading his rifles, he made it to a spot opposite the hotel. Feeling safe here from Price's shotgun he joined a group fleeing from they knew not what and went with them unnoticed across the street. Ten minutes later the hotel burst into flame, and a few minutes after that the Last Chance.

Further down the street the warehouse and store followed in like manner and now the town was lit up like a forest fire. Dunc coolly awaited his chance and crossed the street, taking advantage of a sudden roll of smoke that billowed low, and climbed to the cabin level on the slope. There he exposed himself, deliberately drawing a hail of bullets. This gave him an excuse to shoot back. The Greener boomed oftener, Price becoming more than a help. He was now a force. Dunc could see the Mexican saddlesmith frantically pouring water on the roof of his place and in Price's store there were four men likewise occupied. He was careful not to fire in their direction. So far only the houses on the river side of the street were burning.

The street was spotted with men sprawled out in the stillness of death or crawling painfully for cover. The rain was still coming down lightly, but the lightning had stopped. There was much less to fire at now because hysteria had spent itself and caution had grown. The Greener was silent for lack of targets but Dunc, his eyes searching, managed to spot a knot of men hitting

87

up the slope on the other end of town. They had been in darkness, protected by a still unfired building, but it caught with a puff like ignited gunpowder and this exposed them. He opened fire, scattering them like leaves, but they kept on up the slope. The night was turned into a horror of flames, of desultory gunfire and the cries of wounded men. Dunc almost shot Price who, panting like a steam engine had crawled up the slope to bring him sorely needed ammunition.

"I been talkin' to them fellers on the hill," he said, sobbing for breath. "You done turned the tide, boy. They been skeerd of Chance Naught fer years but to-night changed that. They got a man fightin' fer 'em and they're ready to pitch in."

"Good," said Dunc. "I'm going to have to leave this spot. Just spotted a bunch angling up the slope, trying to flank me. I'm going to make tracks and get lost up in the hills there. Draw your folks back over the rim and tell 'em I'll be around just short of daylight. The women and kids'll be able to go back before that." He stood up and distributed ammunition through his pockets, his eyes flaming greenish in the reflected light. "Not many left, Price."

"Younker, you ain't tellin' me a thing. Where did you learn to shoot?"

Dunc grinned tightly. "Shooting an old worn-out single-shot rifle. I'll speak to your people about resistance in the morning. There won't be too much and when Naught's men realize they've got a force against them there'll be less."

"I'll take care of that end. See you just before dawn.

BULLET SEED

It's wet out there. You got a *poncho?*"

"My blanket is enough. Your store all right?"

"Fine. I got six men watchin' with plenty of water. So far they only got a couple of bad sparks. I see Pedro is doin' all right, too. Guts he got, gettin' up there in plain view."

"This rain is helping. It's coming down heavier, now."

Dawn broke cold and gray on a smouldering, wrecked Rock Bridge. As soon as it was light enough to see, a solid volley of rifle fire broke out directed at Chance's hardcases and badmen gathered about in groups across the river. Though the range was extreme several were killed and the rest were scattered.

Buck Price, at dawn, had been elected marshall by public voice, Price being a man they all knew as a bull in courage as well as in strength.

Chance Naught was wiped out in Rock Bridge but, in his rage, refused yet to recognize it. He could not believe that things had gone so badly against him, not even in the face of that early morning shooting which could mean only one thing—a rising of angered citizens.

He had ruled and intimidated them for a long time and when finally the rain stopped he came back at the head of five men on horses. They crossed the swollen river, rode down the street that was now a sea of mud, their faces black with the sight of the utter destruction of the Naught enterprises.

"Yonder they come," hissed Price, looking out of his store door.

"This should be fun," said Dunc, his voice like the edge of a saw. "Price, send a few men around back so they can step out and support me. I'm giving him his showdown as soon as he comes opposite your store."

"Go ahead," growled Price. "You'll be covered."

Slowly Chance and his riders came on, looking from side to side and gathering confidence as they proceeded.

As they drew opposite Price's store, Dunc's feet struck the boardwalk.

"Looking for anybody, Naught?"

They reined in and stared at him, Naught's face as red as a sunset.

"You," he said. "I'm lookin' for you."

Dunc's laugh was harsh and brittle. "Still got ideas like running me out of town?"

Quietly, armed men had drifted from their places of concealment and gathered on the walk, rifles held ready.

The battle of eyes lasted only a few seconds, then with a gesture of defeat, Naught slowly turned his horse toward the south.

"Hold it right there," said Dunc, the gun on his right hip flashing in the sun as he drew. "Get down, all of you."

There was nothing they could do except comply. Dunc lined them up before Price's store and took their guns. Walking over to their horses he took their rifles as well and made a stack of them on the store steps. Dunc then jerked his head toward the horses. "Get on and ride. Any of you who puts foot back in Rock Bridge will feed on lead . . . Right, Price?"

"You said it," growled Price, standing solid as a

granite boulder on the sidewalk. "Get movin'."

There was a momentary pause while Naught looked hate at Dunc, then he and his crew turned, got on their horses and rode south out of town.

Price looked at Dunc. "Me and the folks been talkin'. How'd you like for to be marshal around these parts?"

Dunc gulped, embarrassed. "Won't need no lawman around here for a while. Come on, Price. I'll set you up to a shot of Rodden's Best."

"Hoot mon," chuckled old Rory MacNabb admiringly, in the fringes of the crowd.

7

Two weeks later a small but wiry man rode a big buckskin horse into Rock Bridge. He was stained and streaked with travel and was looking forward to a bath, shave and haircut in the town. He hitched the horse in front of Price's store and walked stiffly inside.

"What'n hell happened to this here town? Lightnin' strike it?"

"You might say it did. What kin I do fer you?"

"Some chewin' terbacco. Some bacon and a sack of beans. Might add some canned stuff, tomatoes, corn and such. 'Bout ten pounds o' flour. What happened?"

"Shoulda been here," chortled Price. "Younker come in here, killed the local gunslinger, beat the hell outa his pard and made the town boss back water. He was tole to leave town the next mornin' by sunup. Wal . . . he didn't leave till sundown and this is the way he left it. The boss man got run off, and a whole slice o' his men was killed or so momucked up they won't never

92

fight no more. Boss rode back in 'bout dinner time with a few men and we run them off. It's a man's town now. All the riffraff gone. The ranchers won't mind lettin' their hands come to town Saddy nights no more."

"Damn," muttered the little man, twisting his extravagant moustache. "This here younker must be a ringtailed cycloon."

"Three of 'em," said Price proudly. "When I seen 'im I said, 'Son, you better take it slow or they'll have yo' poke sure as shootin'.' Know what he said? He said, 'If they try there sure will be shootin'.' Never a man spoke truer words. See that there old Winchester over there? Barrel's plumb burnt up. It was pretty wore before he used it but it's a frazzle now. Bet the boy didn't miss a dozen shots all night long."

"Well, I vow," breathed the other, pounding the dust out of his clothes. "What's this here Billy the Kid's name? I knows a lotta people."

"Younker name of Dunc Stewart. Ever hear of 'im?"

The little man reeled slightly, caught himself on the counter, his eyes widening in astonishment. "Well, I'll be a suck-egg mule. Yeah, I know 'im. He's a relate, sorta. I took 'im under my wing once and give him some good advice."

"Now ain't that sump'n? Wal, you done a good job, I'll say that."

"Tole that boy if he come back in lessen fo' years I'd skin the tail offen 'im."

Price looked critically at the little man. "Mister, I don't know who you is. Mebbe you's John Wesley Hardin and mebbe you kin do it. All I got t' say is, that

93

there feller is a flyin' rattler with tushes all over 'im."

"Say where he was headed?"

"Seems as if he did. Said sump'n about he thought he'd amble over Texas way and see his maw. Seems he hadn't seen her in some time."

Price accepted the money for his purchases and helped stow them in saddle bags on the rangy buckskin.

"Wal . . . so long. If you see your relate tell 'im he's always welcome in these parts . . . an' you better go easy on that skinnin'. The boy looks like he's seven foot tall."

The moustached little man smiled and nodded, placed his hands on his hips atop the strangest gun harness Price had ever seen and wriggled it into a more comfortable position. "I'll tell 'im and thanks. By the way, you know Hamp Wallace?"

"Cant' say as I do. But everybody's heerd of that gunhawk, includin' me. How come you ask?"

"Oh . . . nuthin' much. That there younker you spoke of. He out-gunned Hamp Wallace. They buried poor Hamp with his boots on."

Price, jaws agape, watched the man and his moustaches ride off.

Along the devious frontier grapevines spread the advice that a smooth-cheeked youngster named Stewart had killed Hamp Wallace. Soon this news caught up with Dunc and passed him. Trouble rode his heels because hot-tempered youngsters or green gunfighters, in spite of the reputation of some of those Dunc had tangled with, could not look on the tall, mild-appearing boy as being dangerous. Mature men, on the other hand, men themselves widely known for their fearlessness and speed with a gun took one look at him and nodded to themselves. Here was a lad who would not backtrack. That he was good they were willing to accept. Meanwhile the tales of his exploits, as is natural, were becoming adorned and magnified out of all proportion. It was to this type of exaggeration that Dunc attributed the news that Hamp Wallace was dead by the guns of a youngster not yet twenty, the youngster being himself.

When Dunc first heard the rumor he was shocked to the quick. Had he, after all, shot Hamp at long range in the frenzied horror at Rock Bridge, without even knowing the man was in the town? On consideration, he decided this highly improbable. If a man of the caliber of Wallace had been there, he would have been fighting on the right side, and in any case more than able to protect himself from gunfire.

Hamp's abilities were always veneered in Dunc's young mind and had been attested to by many a story he had heard since that day when the one-time Ranger had killed Ash Zimmerman at Big Bend. Hamp was such an omnipotent creature in Dunc's imagination, that the boy was soon laughing to himself about the rumor and speculating on how it ever had got started in the first place.

Among gunmen, Dunc learned, there were two attitudes. Some were jealous of another's reputation, with a psychopathic jealousy that fired them with an irresistible itch to see which was the better man. Others, realizing a fight could always mean a slug in some dis-commoding spot, were out to make friends with another gunman if they could not stay out of his way.

Before he reached Big Bend, Dunc had met both types more than once—as in that incident at Crazy Water.

Dunc had developed a taste and a capacity for liquor. He also had developed a magnificent store of animal caution and never allowed his drinking to proceed to the point where it endangered his reactions. Which was fortunate, considering the fact that the gun-toter he ran into in the local bar was a big man with a broad back and the bleak unblinking eyes of someone who killed because it pleased him to do so. He hated all humanity the way humanity hates snakes. His presence grew increasingly unwelcome as he rode aimlessly through the country, working only when his grubsack grew slack. Jap Brody, he was called, because of the abnormal narrowness and slant of his hard gray eyes. He hated the nickname.

He had worked two months for the Buzzard-on-a-Stump brand and when he quit he went straight to Crazy Water for a binge. To Jap Brody a binge was the process of building up a nice belligerent glow at a saloon, then buying a bottle and taking it to his room or to his bedroll where he would proceed to get blind drunk. No man who had as many enemies as Jap Brody could risk getting actually drunk in a saloon. Crazy Water was just another dusty cowtown where punchers drank and gambled their wages away but it did have a flop house that bore the imposing title of Banker's Hotel, and one fairly large saloon. Jap and Dunc

BULLET SEED

Stewart rode into town thirty minutes apart and soon found themselves standing at the bar, not too far away from each other. Jap was openly contemptuous of the youngster sipping whiskey. "Serve wet-eared saddle tramps in here?" he asked, loud enough for everyone to hear.

Dunc ignored him and the bartender said, "We'll even serve you, Jap, if you got money."

Hearing the nickname spoken, red rage boiled up in Jap. But bartenders, he had found, often had hideouts behind bars. They were habitually barricaded and, moreover, they nearly always had friends. It didn't pay to pick trouble in that direction.

After several more asides that gained him nothing except a single stony glance, Jap bent to his drinking and let Dunc alone.

Later another stranger came in and went to the bar on the other side of Dunc. Here was your other type of gunman. The make-friends variety. This man was of moderate height, his clothes clean and well-fitting. He wore two guns high in a Wes Hardin vest and few men at that time wore such a rig. It was enough to get him considerable attention.

He glanced at Dunc, looked away and looked back again. "Didn't I see you at El Paso a month ago?"

Dunc looked up, saw nothing threatening in the man's attitude, liked the steadiness of his pale green eyes, took in the peculiar gun rig and nodded. "I've been there."

"Stewart's the name, isn't it?"

"That's right."

BULLET SEED

"My handle is Cash Crowson. Glad to know you." He held out his hand and Dunc took it, wondering. Cash Crowson was a man whose reputation as a sort of floating peace marshal preceded him in all directions. He was ranked in some quarters the superior of Wild Bill Hickock in the taming of wild towns.

"That true what I hear about you downing Hamp Wallace?"

Dunc looked steadily at his drink. "Can't help what a man hears."

Crowson laughed good-naturedly. "Sorry to pry."

There it was. A peace officer many times, and maybe right now; and a gunhawk of wide renown. Yet Crowson did not try a play, either for the sake of his ego or out of sympathy for a fellow lawman.

Dunc said mildly, "Have one on me."

"Thanks. I will and I'll return it."

Dunc felt a tap on his shoulder and turned to meet the cold eyes of Jap Brody. "That right what the man said about Hamp Wallace?"

Dunc looked at him stolidly for a moment, then said, "Why don't you go plow a field with that nose you like to stick into things?"

"I asked y' a question," grated Jap, his nostrils pinching at the sides.

"You got the only answer you'll get."

Jap snarled and spat directly in Dunc's face. A hush fell on the assembled men and the bartender glanced around, making certain his armament was in place.

When Dunc moved it was so sudden that the sharp crack of his hard fist on Jap's chin startled the on-lookers. Jap rocketed backward and slid noisily into an empty table, knocking over chairs and a spitoon. Dunc stood clear of the bar and looked down at the crumpled man, his face still expressionless. Finally he took out a handkerchief and wiped his face carefully, then threw it away with a gesture of repulsion.

Crowson put a hand on his shoulder. "That man's looking for trouble."

"He's got it."

"You're young," continued the older man. "Never let anybody who's out for trouble get all covered with chairs and a handy table." He walked over to the prostrate man and started kicking furniture until Jap was clear of all impeding objects. "A good oak-bottom chair'll stop a slug, son. Remember that."

"I'll remember," said Dunc, without lifting his head.

Jap Brody emerged from the downy nothingness of oblivion by slow degrees. A man coughed over to Dunc's left and was soundly cursed. This was drama of the highest and no one wanted interference, not even vocal.

Jap got slowly to his feet, his mind now clear, but he felt it would help his cause somewhat if he appeared to be still groggy. His eyes focused on Dunc and he said slowly, "I'm gonna kill you fer that."

"You do a lot of talking," said Cash Crowson, who only now moved out of the line of fire.

"I'll tend to you later," snapped Jap malevolently.

"I'll be here."

Dunc spoke for the first time. "You going to stand there and yap all night, or you going to pat yourself?"

Goaded, but still not ready, Jap Brody grabbed for

his last gun. It had hardly cleared the holster when Dunc's .45 thundered, drawn and fired left-handed. It knocked the big man backward, then exploded again and, as Jap folded, a third time.

Out of the hubbub that rose now came the excited voice of the bartender. "What was them last two for?"

"Insurance," said Dunc shortly and turned back to his drinking.

Trouble once more had reared its head in the Big Bend country. An attempt had been made to steal more meat from Walter Koenig's smokehouse and had come to a bad end for the marauders. The Koenig family had widely announced they were going to visit a distant rancher and in sight of anyone who cared to look Walter had driven off behind a span of bays hitched to the buckboard.

Just how he managed to get back to his place so fast no one ever knew, but he did, he and his hands killing two men, wounding a third, before the thieves managed to get away leaving two huge wagons and four spans of fine mules.

Walter's Teutonic shrewdness had paid off and the county was astir again. One of the dead raiders had been identified as a rider of Jared Walker's. Yet no one seeing Walker's purple rage at the fellow could have seen in the rancher an accessory. In fact, Walter Koenig assured him and reassured him that no blame was attached to him. Hadn't one of Felton Wade's men been killed running Walker's cattle off into a maze of coulees?

BULLET SEED

That part of the trouble was settled amicably but soon the flame stirred again. The second dead man was a newly hired man of Wade's.

Then came the stage robbery. Ed Peters was sending ten thousand dollars to a bank in Claytown and that day the stage was held up at Cutthroat, a pass that knifed through a low range of wooded hills to the northeast. The driver, Will Packer, was killed and one of Ed Peter's slick gun gentlemen, Lief Andstrom, riding shotgun, was shot between the eyes.

Ed Peters was fit to be tied and together with a number of indignant citizens descended on Sheriff Jim Walters, meaning to make things uncomfortable for him.

Later the same day Felton Wade, riding a magnificent cream-maned sorrel stallion, also paid the sheriff a visit and had a few things to say.

"Looks like I'm gonna hafta git up from here and do sump'n," said Walters complainingly. In truth, since his visit to the new doctor he had been feeling a lot better and had gained weight and appetite.

"What can you do?" said Felton, his bushy white brows contracting over his beak of a nose.

"I can go look."

"A lot of men have looked and what did they find?"

"True, they didn't find nuthin'. But I guess I oughta get out there and ack like I was bein' sheriff."

"I think you're doing all a man could do," said Felton heartily, offering an expensive cheroot which Walters took with thanks.

"Well . . . I reckon I is at that . . . but this sounds a

101

mite funny comin' frum you. Ain't you been complainin' too?"

"Certainly. I've lost a hundred head in two months. That's heavier than anyone else's losses in that time, but I know a man can't fight ghosts."

"Ghosts," argued Walters reasonably, "ain't what's stealin' them cattle."

"Well," said Felton getting up, "I'm not one to lay it on you. Either you gather evidence and pin it on someone or you don't get evidence . . . and naturally can't pin it on anyone. I just rode in to report the loss. Not to complain."

"That's plumb white of you, Mr. Wade. I appreciates it."

"Not at all. How about a drink, Sheriff?"

"Reckon I will. The new doc says a drink is just the thing for a man my age. Keeps the arteries loosened up or sump'n."

That night a tall slender man rode to the cabin among the trees on the outskirts of Big Bend and got down from his horse. The door of the cabin opened and a woman looked out. "Who is it?"

"It's me, Maw . . . Dunc."

She sprang from the door and ran to meet him, crying his name. "Dunc . . . *Dunc* . . . My *boy!*"

For a long time he held her close, blinking the tears from his eyes and squeezing down by pure physical force the sobs that rose in his own throat.

"Come on in," she said brokenly.

"Where's Paw?"

"We don't know, son . . . we don't know. He ain't been

back in . . . well, right after you left he went out and never come back. I had a . . ." she snuffled and wiped her nose on her apron, "quite a time of it."

"How did you make it?" he asked in an agony of contrition.

"I was plumb low. I was sick and hungry and Miz Walters she come around and took care of me. Then she made the Sewin' Circle pitch in and they all helped. I been doin' right well lately settin' up with sick folks and babies when their maws is sick or wore out. Don't worry. Been doin' right well."

She looked it. A sparkle had come into her once muddy eyes and now they shone an attractive brown. Her figure had fleshened comfortably and she was nearer to the beauty that he had in his dreams envisioned.

"Well, you won't have to work any more," he said gently. "I got some money and I'm going to get more."

"How?" she asked, suddenly afraid.

"Why . . . work, of course."

"Oh . . . I was hopin' you meant that. You see, we done heard some pretty bad things about you."

"What's that, Maw?"

"Oh, that you burned a town down and fit a lot of men and killed a bunch . . . includin' Hamp Wallace."

"I heard that too," he said, a distant look in his eyes. "Don't know how it got out. I haven't seen Hamp since the morning I left him at Yucca City."

"Then you didn't kill 'im?"

"No'm."

"I'm glad, son. First time I ever seen Sheriff Walters

real mad was when he heard that."

"I'll have to talk to him. I'll ask him about Paw, too."

"Why?"

"Just curious."

"Dunc . . . I know he wasn't very good to you but I . . ." She dropped her head. "I been wantin' to know what happened to him."

"You loved him in spite of all his bad, didn't you?"

She nodded but wouldn't look up.

"Well, I'll see what I can do. Is the sheriff still ailin'?"

"He's been lookin' pretty pert here lately. The new doc fixed him up and he's been lookin' right good."

"Think I'll walk on up there and see him. I don't suppose he's gone home yet."

"Ain't you hungry?"

"Not much. I'll get something at the hotel . . . Maw, can you make tortillas?"

"No, son, but old José's wife makes them all the time. You remember Carmelita . . .?"

His face went pale. "Never mind. I just asked."

He went out, leaving her baffled at the shocked change that had come over his face at mention of the girl's name. She shook her head but in a moment was singing happily and went about making up his bed.

Sheriff Jim Walters, when Dunc came through the door, stared hard until recognition seeped through, then did something he hadn't done in years. He leaped to his feet and swept a big gun from his desk, covering the dusty visitor. "Git outa here," he snarled. "The onliest reason I don't cut you down right in that there doorway is because I'm a officer of the law and I ain't s'pposed t' have no personal feelin's about things."

The hard blue eyes didn't waver. "What's got into you, all of a sudden?"

"You look just like when you was sixteen . . . Bigger and harder, that's all. I heerd about you. The man what killed Hamp Wallace I wouldn't give breathin' room. Now git 'fore I loses my temper."

Dunc looked unimpressed. Deliberately he turned and, skidding a straight chair around, sat on it and hung his long arms over the back. "If I was good enough to beat Hamp Wallace to the draw, sheriff, I could draw and button you up before you could back that hammer."

Walters felt discommoded and embarrassed. The boy talked straight and didn't scare at all.

"You denyin' you killed Hamp?"

"The last time I saw him was nearly four years ago at Yucca City. Now put that thing away before it goes off."

Walters flushed and thumped the gun back to the desk. "All right, tell me."

"There isn't anything to tell. How that rumor got started it'll take somebody else to tell. I haven't seen him and after what he's done for me . . ." Dunc straightened up. "If someone has killed him then that man's my meat. Hamp couldn't make me draw on him . . . and if I did it'd be me they'd bury, not him."

Walters nodded slowly. "Come to think of it, you make sense. Lessen Hamp had a broke arm I wouldn't pick you t' take 'im."

"Now you're talking right. I'd like to ask some questions."

105

"Fire away, son. I'm right sorry I blowed up like that."

"Can't blame you! I'd do the same under the circumstances. What do you know of Paw's disappearance?"

Walter's eyes narrowed speculatively. "You interested?"

"Not too much. Maw is, though."

"Unh, hunh. Well, all I know is he worked for Felton Wade, although it'd take Jesus hisself to tell just what he done for 'im. Your pappy went out one day ridin' and ain't nobody ever seen 'im since."

"What'd he ride, the pinto or Jeff?"

"Happens I seen him go out. He rid Jeff. Now that's sump'n I hadn't thoughta. That there hoss was the joy of your pappy's eye and with that blaze face and them four white-stockin' feet he oughta be easy to spot. Figgerin' on lookin' around?"

"Maybe."

"Better stay clear of the Flyin' Y. They don't take kindly t' strangers."

Dunc shrugged. "I'll remember what you said."

"But you ain't takin' my advice?"

"No, sir."

The old man sighed, remembering the turbulent days of his youth. He wouldn't have taken the advice either. "Anythin' else I can tell you?"

Dunc grinned. "I want a job that pays money and'll still let me nose around. Know anybody that big a fool?"

Sheriff Walters studied the man and liked what he saw. Close cropped golden hair, hard angular face, sun-seared with tiny squint wrinkles about the eyes, rawhide lean body, relaxed with a lithe catlike readiness. Then, too, there was the reputation he had gathered in a very few months. The Rock Bridge rampage, Jap Brody in Crazy Water. The local badman at a cow camp out on Lonesome. And others. A boy shoved too fast into manhood, but still level-headed and deadly.

"Matter of fact, I do know where you can git a job like that."

"Where?"

With slow deliberation, Walters opened a desk drawer and took out a star. He burnished it on his shirtsleeve and, getting up, went over to Dunc and pinned it over his left pocket. "Raise your right hand and repeat after me . . ."

PART TWO

The Gunfighter

8

"THE BOYS," said Jugg Allison, "is gettin' restless."

Felton Wade dragged a nervous hand through his bleached hair. "What now?"

"They're tired doing all this riding after small bunches of stuff. They want to start some real operations."

Wade spread his slim fingers out on the top of his desk and looked at them carefully, then raised his almost colorless eyes to Allison.

"We're doing well. Everyone's making money. No one's getting rich, it's true. But practically every man on this spread is a fugitive from justice, and here they're safe because the most wanted ones are always with the herds or on line camps where they're not likely to be seen. It's carelessness and the itch to pull something big that always spells the end of such men. I have no intention of pulling anything big. I'm going along just like I've been going. If something falls in my lap I take it. If it doesn't I let it alone. If the men aren't satisfied with a good hideout, good grub, more money than any cow waddy in the west makes, then they're stupid and stupid men I've no use for. By the way, what was my advice on that Koenig deal?"

Allison flushed. "You didn't want it pulled," he mumbled.

"Who did want it pulled?"

"Wal . . . er . . . It was like this . . ."

"You and that thundering ass of a Jim Beasley. Jim brought the news that Koenig was leaving with his family. He wasn't satisfied at slipping behind Walker's back and knotting up a few steers for us to pick up easily and getting his cut. Oh, no. He wanted to climb right into the eagle's nest. That first raid someone made on Koenig gave him ideas. You're a good man, Allison, as long as it involves no thinking. From now on I'll do it. If that Koenig affair doesn't convince you, then you're a lost cause. Remember what I told Zimmerman about him and Coulter shooting that Ranger?"

Allison's eyes wouldn't meet those of his boss. "Yeah."

"What?" The question came out like a shot.

"That if he killed a Ranger he'd better take it over the border."

"Precisely. He laughed, didn't he? Laughed as though I had told him a joke. He was just too good. Nobody could take him. I wonder what he's thinking now between drinks of boiling tar. Wallace shot him twice before he could clear a gun." Wade made a vulgar noise with his mouth. "Just as well. I never could abide these two-penny heroes who're so damn good that it shines. It does, until they meet a man."

THE GUNFIGHTER

"You includin' me in . . . I mean with him?" hissed Allison, his face purple with anger.

Wade smiled insolently. "I don't know. How good are you, Jugg?"

"I'm good enough to do your dirty work, ain't I?" Wade laughed.

"Quite right. I've said before that you're a good man. You're tough and unprincipled. I don't know whether you're a gunfighter or not."

Allison got up, backed away, his right hand held in front of him. Like a blur of light it swept down and Wade found himself staring into the bore of a .45. "That fast enough for you?" Allison asked.

Wade shrugged, unimpressed. "I wear no gun. I have no reputation as a fast man. You had no opposition. I'd have to see you under fire before I'd know. That kid they say killed Hamp Wallace must be something to see. He's Dave Bridges' adopted son."

Allison, feeling theatrical and foolish and well-snubbed, sat down again. "Reckon he'll come lookin'?"

Wade shook his head. "Not a chance. I've made inquiries. They say he hated Dave." Wade did not know that almost as the words were being said someone was tethering a familiar horse to a spike in the stone fence surrounding the sprawling ranchhouse. His Chinese cook came back and knocked on the office door.

"What is it . . .? Dammit, Wing, didn't I tell you never to disturb me when I'm in conference?"

The celestial bowed impassively. "So solly. Young man come on holse. Alla same sit on velanda light now. Think you want to know."

113

THE GUNFIGHTER

"Who is he?"

"Not knowing."

"What does he want?"

"Not knowing."

"Le's go out and come around the side of the house," said Allison with the innate caution of a man who had long lived outside the law.

"That might be a good idea."

As they rounded the corner of the house, they found that their visitor also was conversant with the rudiments of caution. He stood with his back against the log walls, out of line with the door. He had heard them and he was now standing tall, loose-jointed and calm, commanding all approaches. When they saw him, he advanced and stood at the top of the steps as though blocking their approach.

"Come in," he said, remembering the door at his back. "Welcome to your house."

"Who're you?" asked Allison truculently.

"Duncan Stewart." The voice was soft and cultured. "Who're you?"

"Me?" Allison was taken slightly aback. "I'm Jugg Allison."

Dunc leveled a quick finger at Wade, making the latter jump. "And you?"

"Felton Wade. What do you want?"

"I came to see if you could tell me something about my father."

For the first time Allison saw the star on Dunc's shirt and he felt a swift cold pain whip through his stomach. He wasn't afraid of the boy but a star always

114

gave him the jumps. "What's that tin badge fer?" he asked harshly.

"It isn't tin," said Dunc gently. "It's silver . . . says so on the back, anyhow. I'm Sheriff Walters' new deputy."

"The hell you say," blurted Wade, startled out of countenance.

"Why of course, Mr. Wade. What's wrong with that?"

"Nothing. Only I thought Walters was doin' a good job."

"You're the only man in the county who thinks so, including Walters himself. He hasn't made an arrest in years."

"Well, this is a very law-abiding section."

Dunc's smile widened and he emitted a single derisive, "Ha!"

"You don't agree?"

"Again I think you're alone in your opinion. However, every man is entitled to one. My father worked for you, didn't he?"

"Yes," Wade admitted.

"When was the last time you saw him?"

"It's been a long time ago. He just up and disappeared. Not a soul knows anything about it."

Dunc nodded pleasantly. "I'm intending on making friends all over." He smiled winsomely. "I don't like jumping at conclusions like some of them did when they found one of Mr. Walker's hands dead over at Koenig's place. I don't like that sort of law-officering. You had an experience like that, didn't you, Mr. Wade?"

"Yes," said Wade, so vastly relieved that he made a mistake. "Stinger Blue was shot one night, running

Walker's cattle. A man can't keep a twenty-four hour watch over every man on his payroll. Walker's discovered that."

"That's my point. Where did you bury Blue?"

"Over on Juniper Creek near Red B . . ." A dead poisonous silence fell and Dunc smiled thinly. "Thank you, Mr. Wade. Now, gentlemen, if you'll just come along with me—"

Allison was white with fury and fear. Before Dunc had gone ten feet he started off the veranda and said in a strained voice, "Where you think you goin'?"

Dunc whirled like a striking cobra and Allison's hand died on his gun butt. Two long revolver barrels were trained on his middle. To Wade the whole thing smacked of sleight-of-hand. It was incredible. He had only seen the man turn around. He had seen no movement of his hands.

"Turn your back."

Allison, as pale as watered milk, turned and held his hands stiffly shoulder high. Dunc whipped out both Allison's guns and, backing several feet away, flipped open the loading gates and rodded the cartridges out on the cultivated grass.

He replaced the guns and returned his own to their holsters. "Now, Mr. Wade, you and Mr. Allison will ride out and take a look at a grave . . . or some graves."

"I'm not going anywhere," said Wade, looking desperately about for help. The Chinaman was of no assistance in a battle. The hands, for the most part, were out on the range. Shorty Belker was sick in the bunkhouse with a tequila hangover and couldn't be depended on. Abel Quant, the blacksmith, was deaf as a post, couldn't hear himself talk. He couldn't be counted on.

"I ain't goin', neither," said Jugg Allison tightly.

Dunc smiled understandingly. "You make it hard for me, men. However, I'll say this one thing. A live man can ride. A dead one has to be carried. But one way or the other, you're both coming."

Wade, plucking foolishly at his lips, came down the steps and started toward the front gate.

Allison stood his ground. "I ain't goin'."

Dunc stepped up to him and before Allison knew what was coming had dug two fists wrist-deep in the man's midsection. Jugg's breath went out with a sound like a tremendous belch and he floundered around on the grass in the manner of a beheaded fowl. It was some minutes before he could crawl to his feet.

He finally made it, only to become violently and productively sick.

Some time later, two subdued men were riding silently toward Juniper Creek, Dunc bringing up the rear with a look of seraphic innocence on his young face.

Juniper Creek was a rivulet that ran toward the border from up in the hills around Lonesome, and closely hugged a rim of rock that stood sheer over the thread of water some three hundred feet. The three reached the rim and paralleled it for half a mile before they came to a slide they could safely put their horses to. They wound carefully downward until they reached

117

the creek, then followed it southwest for a mile.

"I'll have to depend on you keeping away any men you might see, or who might see you and want to chat," said Dunc mildly. "You may use any method that seems best to you, bearing in mind that I'll shoot you in the back if anyone comes within two hundred yards."

Wade broke out in a sweat and Allison, his stomach still leaping about like a lass rope trailing from a calf's hind leg, maintained a humid silence.

"Also," said Dunc almost apologetically, "we don't want to have to do a lot of searching. Riding is tiring and so is digging."

Jugg Allison looked around with a lethal scowl. "If you think I'm gonna do any damn diggin' . . ."

"I guess you will. I got the loaded guns."

Since there was no argument to offer against this, silence persisted until they reached a spot where the cliff base and the Juniper were separated by only thirty feet of dense undergrowth. There, in the heart of the thick brush were three graves. Two quite weathered and beaten down. The other one fresh. None of the three bore markers.

"Off your horses," Dunc ordered. "All right, Allison. Get to digging and if I have to get off my horse it won't be to dig. That I promise. I'd advise you to choose the right graves. By that I mean I have no interest in Stinger Blue. The other two graves we'll open."

"Two?" yelled the outraged Allison.

"One and one. That makes two. Wade, we didn't bring two shovels because we were afraid one would break. You take the other one."

THE GUNFIGHTER

An hour later the graves were open. The fresh one contained the body of a puncher with violent red hair, still in his clothes and boots; he had been rolled in a tarp before burial.

The second grave was old and the corpse only a bag of bones in a rotted tarp and again the man had been buried in his clothes. The clothes were rotted but his two big guns, clotted with corrosion, were still in evidence. Dunc frowned.

"The guns, Allison, and don't try to throw them. I can shoot straighter than you can chunk." He unholstered a gun and laid it across the swell of his saddle.

Allison was careful to hand the rusty hunks of metal, still in their brittle holsters, to Dunc with gentleness. Dunc reined his horse backward twenty feet and dug the rusty revolvers from their rotted leather. He smiled thinly and held up the butts for them to see.

"Eagles . . . gold pieces countersunk into both butts. I know these weapons. Thank you, folks, one and all. Wade, don't try for that gun in your saddle bags you've been itching to get at. Sudden moves make my trigger-hand itch. Neither of you, I suppose, would like to make a guess about these here corpses."

Allison was silent but Wade smiled, passed his left hand over his hair and wiped the sweatband of his sombrero. "No, Mr. Stewart. That's Stinger Blue's mound, yonder. But we know nothing whatever about these two corpses. Someone must have buried them here."

"Sure, but who?" Dunc sighed. "Well, that's the headache of the law, not honest ranchers."

Wade's smile grew broader. "Very well put, Mr. Stewart. Very well put."

Dunc nodded his thanks. "I thought you'd feel that way . . . You appear anxious to say something, Allison."

"I is. Where did you git that there hoss, that saddle and them pearl-handled guns?"

"Why, didn't you know? Hamp Wallace gave them to me. He said the man they belonged to would have no further use for them."

"Unh hunh. Think you can keep 'em?"

"I think so."

"Just be sure you do."

Dunc's eyes slitted and he got down slowly from his saddle. "There's always a sure test for a windjammer, a bushwhacker, or a man." He walked up to Allison, took one of Allison's guns, loaded it from his own belt and jammed it back in Allison's holster. He backed ten feet away and let his hands fall limply at his sides. "All right, Allison. Take the horse, saddle and guns."

Wade watched his foreman curiously as Allison's face drained white. The rancher couldn't restrain a swift thrill of admiration for this boy—Dunc was hardly more—bucking one of the most dangerous men Wade had been able to find. Not for nothing was Jugg Allison foreman of the Flying Y.

For a long minute the two faced each other. But Allison couldn't bring himself to draw. Finally he shrugged and threw a glance at Wade, who was watching with his face frozen and expressionless.

"There'll come a day," Allison muttered. Sweat poured from his face in streams and his shirt was stained dark blue at the armpits. Dunc nodded affably and flipped his right hand forward with a casual gesture, but there was nothing casual about the weapon the hand held. "Get your hands up, Allison. I'm taking my cartridges."

When he had stuffed them back in his belt, he got on his horse, a broad grin revealing the whiteness of his teeth against the tan of his lean face. "There you are, Mr. Wade. There's your foreman." He looked at the other man who was now trying to quell the shaking of his hands and knees, a man who was coming apart at the seams after showing a white feather. Dunc made each a mocking salute and said, "Allison, you sure had us fooled. We all thought you was real bad, didn't we, Mr. Wade?"

For ten minutes after Dunc had disappeared, Allison cursed. Passionate broadsides of blasphemy poured from his lips and his face grew apoplectic from the fury that rode him. Wade said nothing. After Allison had run out of breath and voice, they mounted and rode homeward wrapped in embarrassed silence.

"Let's have a drink," muttered Wade, as they turned their horses into the corral.

"A whole goddamned ocean of drinks," fumed Allison. "It'll take that much to get that wet-eared kid out of my hair and off my stomach."

They went into the office and Allison sprawled out on a hide couch, his face black with dammed-up anger and mortification. He swallowed the drink Wade gave him and returned to his silence, which lasted through several more drinks. At last he straightened up, his eyes burning dangerously.

"Well, for the brains, you pulled a snorter, didn't you?"

Wade's lips thinned. "What do you mean?"

"Him, a kid with guns, a saddle tramp with a tin badge, trapped you about as neat as I've seen in many a year. The great Wade with all his brains. You oughta seen your face when he really broke it off what he was after. Naturally, to keep the ranch from bein' cluttered up with graves all over the place we'd bury 'em together. That was what all that lead-up was for. Didn't believe in makin' no man suffer just 'cause one of his riders was caught stealin' . . . Huh! Wound you right around and brought you to the point. He was smart. He didn't ask you where his daddy was buried. Asked about Blue, a man you wouldn't mind tellin' where he was. Suckin' eggs at your age ain't pretty."

Wade's smile was not mirthful. "It has not been my lot to meet a man who never made a mistake. I have never claimed to be such a man. I have never claimed to be a gunfighter either," he concluded significantly.

"I wouldn't push that too hard," said Allison, that dangerous light in his eyes.

Wade shrugged. "Wouldn't that have been a nice set-up—say at the saloon in Big Bend? He not only beat your breadbasket into a mush and made you puke your breakfast, he stood you down . . . And all you could do was mumble something about there being another time!"

Wade chuckled and felt again a tingle of admiration for the youngster.

"There'll be a time, all right."

"When his back is turned, you mean? He drew you a picture. A test he called it. Whether you were a windbag, a bushwacker or a man. I wonder what he's got you sized up as right now?"

Allison's eyes glinted. "Don't you like your foreman, Wade?"

Wade grinned. "Of course . . . as a foreman."

"Look," said Allison in a deadly voice. "I was shook up. I had been workin' diggin' up them graves. You think I'm gonna set myself up like that for a man who's knowed to be pizen with a gun. Do I look like a fool?"

"Indeed not. Let's forget about it. Let's just say I made a mistake and you got crowded down. It happens, sometimes."

"It'll never happen again. I know you think I'm yeller . . . But I wanted to go after Hamp Wallace, didn't I?"

"Yes, you did. Well, maybe it would have been better if you had."

"How's that?"

"What happened today wouldn't have happened to you. It would have happened to someone else. Let that comfort you." Wade laughed.

Allison got up and slammed out of the room, his mind seething with a dozen hatreds, none of them very concrete, mostly because the greater hatred was toward himself. He, a distant cousin of the great Clay Allison, a man tall among tall men—backed down by a downy-

123

cheeked youngster! Death had been riding with that youngster, however, and Allison had seen it, standing in the chill blue eyes, a spectre and a promise. He shuddered. He'd hate to be wrapped in a tarp and put out there in the brush alongside Dave Bridges, Tom Connors and Stinger Blue. He went to the bunkhouse and, pulling a bottle from beneath his bunk drank until he passed out cold. Later that evening, after supper, he sought Wade, thoroughly sick and with a full compliment of the shudders and mutters.

"I just thought of sump'n when I was eatin'," he said with a jagged edge to his voice.

"Be careful about that," said Wade, grinning infuriatingly. "Might sprain something."

"The hell with you. Do you want to hear it?"

"Let's hear it."

"What about Bridges' woman?"

"What about her?"

"Well, as long as there ain't no witnesses t' where he went and no suspicion that he started out for here, then we's in the clear even with him found on your ranch. But let 'em get someone who'll swear he was on his way to us, and it won't take too much else to leave us danglin' at the end of a rope with the hosses runnin' off with empty saddles."

Wade chewed this startling thought over in his head for a moment. "You've got some brains, after all. I hadn't thought of that. Wouldn't she have told the boy already?"

"I wouldn't think they talked about it much. Not yet. I got the word that he just rid in las 'night."

THE GUNFIGHTER

Wade drew a hand lightly over his pale hair. There was an opaque flatness in his eyes as he stood in deep thought. Both Wade and Allison were too preoccupied to see the man with the froglike face standing motionless beneath the window.

9

WITH A RIGID enforcement of caution Dunc willed elation out of his mind. Elation was like a drug and
bred overconfidence. A bullet aimed right would kill
him just as it would any other man, and he knew it.
He took back trails and moved like a lobo toward town.

Still staying away from trails and chance meetings,
he worked his horse around to his mother's cabin and,
taking off his saddle, rubbed the animal down with
a tow sack before turning him loose in the little corral
to feed.

He ate the supper his mother fixed and listened to her
breathless chatter, understanding her need for talk and
gossip. Himself, he spoke in monosyllables, if at all.
Finally she smiled at him affectionately. "You never
was a talker, was you, Dunc? Why, even as a baby you
hardly ever cried."

"I guess there's plenty of people to talk. You don't
have any idea where Paw went when he left here that
last time?"

"I been thinkin' about that," she said. "Looks like ever'body in town knowed he worked fer Felton Wade but me. He wasn't goin' no great distance I know, 'cause he didn't take his rifle ner his saddle bags. I axed him if he wanted me t' fix grub and he said no. Said he wouldn't be gone long."

Dunc nodded and got up, rolling a brown-paper cigarette. "I guess I'll walk up and talk with the sheriff a while."

After Dunc had given his news, Jim Walters looked at the new deputy with respect, not unmixed with concern. "You're a mite young, Dunc, t' be makin' a target of yerself so soon."

Dunc shrugged, arranged his long legs comfortably and sat on his spine. "It had to come."

"Well, I'll give it to you. You found out plenty."

"Yes, but I'll have to have something to tie it all to. I got some evidence but it's not the pointing kind. Wade could make it stick that he knows nothing about Paw's death. What I want is some evidence that he went to the Flying Y that day."

"Yer maw don't know nuthin'?"

"She didn't even know he worked for Wade. She did say, though, that he couldn't have been going very far because he didn't take his riding bags or rifle. Wouldn't take any grub."

"Well, that's sump'n."

"Not enough."

Jim Walters stirred in his chair. This youngster with his cold blue eyes and hard willowy body seemed to im-

127

bue the older man with energy he hadn't felt in years.
Things 'were beginning to happen. Here was a man
undaunted by hours in the saddle, cold camps and the
rigors of the blistering south Texas sun—or by human
wolves. His courage and strength were contagious.

"With you runnin' around with your eyes peeled, it
won't be long 'fore somebody puts a foot in a pile. I
feel it in my bones."

Dunc said nothing for a while, then he asked suddenly
the question which had been on his mind a long time.
"Tell me something about Sam Peters."

Jim rolled a cigarette and moistened the paper with
the tip of his tongue. When it was burning evenly he
looked at the ceiling reminiscently. "Well, his face ain't
very purty, on one side. That's where you ruint it with
the whiskey bottle . . . He's a loud-mouth and a wuss
and wuss bully as time goes on. He picks his victims and
fights with his fists. He carries a gun but ain't never used
it to my knowin'. He's a overgrown pup what needs
a bastin' with a blacksnake. He's ramroddin' Ed's Broken Egg over to the southwest—joins the Flyin' Y on
the east boundary. Young all right but the men swear
by 'im. Pro'bly 'cause he's a good-timer and they good-
times right along with 'im."

"He's three years older than me," said Dunc quietly.

"Well . . . I wouldn't a thunk it, but I guess he is.
He always was bigger'n the rest of you younkers. How
come you thinkin' about him?"

"No reason. Except I got a idea that he'd do anything
he was a mind to if there was enough in it."

"Sure that ain't that old sore he left you with?"

"Might be. I won't push it. That all you know?"

"Weeel . . . Maybe another thing. Old José Mercader, a Mex what's got a little spread below town a ways, raises corn and beans for the *vaqueros* hereabouts and a few cattle. He come in all excited one day. Said Sam had given his daughter some trouble. Tried to drag her inter the bushes one time, then threatened to run the old man offen the place if he said anything. Was right nasty about it. Cute little trick, that gal, too. Named Carmelita after her mother . . . Great grabbs, boy, what's got holt o' you?"

Dunc had snapped taut, his face pale and his eyes pits of blue fire. "Nothing . . ." He got up and looked at the sheriff with peculiar intensity. "Nothing." He turned and walked out of the office. Walters shook his head and dropped a foot on his cigarette butt. "Got sump'n in his gizzard for sure."

The Forgey brothers were well known to law officers in numerous localities and said officers knew nothing at all good about them. In fact the brothers were becoming so well known that it seemed imperative, from their point of view, to move their base of operations for a time. So the night before the visit of Dunc Stewart to the Flying Y they had ridden in and had got themselves hired after some blunt words of wisdom delivered by Jugg Allison. He didn't like them but Jugg liked few people and he didn't let this fact interfere with his duty as he saw it. They were men on the run and from the looks of them they were hardcases of the kind the Flying Y could use. Big and Little Frog they were called although they were the same size, both heavy, both pot-bellied but giving the impression at the same time of tough endurance earned from hard living. Big Frog was the oldest and had the same close-set gimlet eyes as his brother, the same receding chin and distended nostrils, the same sloping forehead and colorless hair.

Allison questioned them with care and was satisfied to take them on, but he did not know a great deal he should have known about them. He didn't know, for example, that they had a burning curiosity, a sneaking furtive way of acquiring a great deal of information which they stored in their tight little brains. They were ignorant but they were neither stupid nor slothful. As Allison and Wade talked privately, Big Frog, coming in from the south section, "happened" to pass beneath the window, his abnormally keen ears taking in everything. Actually, this was no more than normal deport-ment for either of the Forgey brothers. That Big Frog managed not to be seen at his eavesdropping was merely testimony to his talent.

He went back to the bunkhouse and sought his broth-er, telling him what he had overheard. "Now me'n you wasn't never cut out t' be no cow waddies nohow," he said in an undertone. "And I got a idee how we can sorta ease up a notch here and mebbe show off a little. Gotta ketch the big guy's eye and that's where the idee comes in."

"What's 'at?" inquired Little Frog eagerly.

"Well, seems there's a old lady name of Bridges in Big Bend what might know sump'n on the boss. If she tells off on 'im hit might not be a good thing for him . . . and so, bad fer us too. This here is a good place to hole up fer a while and I ain't lettin' nothing I can help run us out. We got a million acres of brush and rocks t' hide in. Only thing is we's workin' too cheap. Now if this here old woman was t' take pizen and die off, sorta, then that'd put us in plumb solid with the boss. Might be able t' pick a plum er two."

Little Frog looked at his brother admiringly. "You always was a smart one, Frog."

Big Frog accepted the compliment gracefully. "Sure. Born thataway, I guess. Le's make a move . . . but not a word to nobody."

"Sure, Frog . . . notta word."

Duncan Stewart stumbled toward the little cabin sick at heart, old wounds torn open by hearing the name of Carmelita. He walked along, his feet prodding woodenly, the old bitter feeling inside him.

So absorbed was he in his own grief that the twin reports of hard guns surprised him with such suddenness that he almost fell. But his own gun instantly snaked out and he stood for a second, tensed. A first bubbling scream came from the cabin he knew as home, seconded by another that was not bubbly but high-pitched and freighted with terror.

"Got 'er," muttered Big Frog, and started trotting up the trail that led back to town and Little Frog, whom he had left at the saloon to cover him, if need be, in escape.

Duncan's left-hand gun seemed to blow up in the

131

batrachian face and Big Frog died without even seeing the man who killed him.

Dunc holstered the gun and ran into the cabin. On the floor lay his mother, the light in her eyes fading fast. Cradling her gray head was a girl whose beauty, at the moment, Dunc could not appreciate . . . He didn't even see her. He dropped to his knees beside the stricken woman. "Maw . . . Maw . . ."

"Did . . . you . . . ?"

He nodded, "I got him." A faint smile touched her lips only to be banished by a wave of pain. She struggled against it weakly for a moment, then went limp. Dunc, boiling with grief and fury, placed a gentle hand on his mother's breast. "Dead," he said, to no one.

"I'm afraid so, señor."

He turned suffering eyes to the girl, took in the alabastrine smoothness of her skin, the sapphire blue of her eyes and the richness of her thick brown hair, but reacted to none of it.

"Who are you?"

"Carmelita, señor. Carmelita Mercader. I came to bring you tortillas. Your mother asked my mother if she would make you some."

"What happened?"

"He stood by the window. He put the gun inside the house and shot her. I saw him when I walked through the town on my way here. Going into the saloon with another."

Dunc jerked taut and sprang to his feet. "Another?"

She nodded. "Two of them. They were very ugly. They looked alike . . . like twins."

132

His jaws went as hard as iron. "Bring the lamp, Carmelita."

Out on the trail he turned the body of Big Frog over and looked at him steadily for a moment, holding the lamp close to his face. He straightened up and handed the lamp to Carmelita. "Will you stay with her a few minutes?"

"I shall be glad to stay with her."

"You're not afraid?"

"No."

"I'll be back . . ."

He walked away, his long legs carrying him at a half run, his hands clenching and unclenching, his jaw marred by two ugly knots of muscle. His breast was a volcano of hate. He felt the loss of his mother the way he would feel a knife between his shoulder blades. But his eyes remained dry. She was the only one who had ever loved him, had ever showed him any kindness whatever, until Hamp Wallace had come along. His breath came in jerky gusts and never had he had such a desperate desire to kill, to rend and tear with his bare hands. So there had been two. Maybe the other had fired one of the shots . . .

He banged open the doors of the saloon and stood blinking in the glare of the three lamps. Men turned to look at him and were glad they had. They all stiffened and prepared to duck because they were accustomed to seeing men on the prod and had heard of the prowess of the new deputy. At the bar, nervously awaiting the return of his brother, Little Frog turned slowly and looked to see what had caused the sudden hush. Dunc's

eyes swept the faces of the men in the big room, paused
for a second on that of Little Frog; then he marched
directly toward the stocky man. Little Frog, having
lived by his wits a long time, knew instantly that something was wrong, something that might well involve him.
Indeed, if he could trust the sign in the hellish eyes of
the tall stranger bearing down on him, the proceedings
definitely did involve him. But he had never seen the
man before and this made him indulge in fatal hesitation. When at last there could be not the slightest
scratch of a doubt that he was in for trouble, Little
Frog went for his gun with a swiftness that showed long
practice and no little talent.

The only trouble was that Dunc's left fist was just a
shade faster and it dug like the butt of a ram deep into
the pit of Little Frog's stomach, the latter's gun coming
free and skating across the saloon floor. Surprisingly
enough Little Frog clenched and held on for dear life
and Dunc, gone mad with fury, wrestled and threw the
other like a sack of hay but still couldn't get free to use
his fists again. Finally, having recovered his wind, Little
Frog loosed Dunc suddenly and kicked him viciously
in the groin. A sheet of flaming agony billowed upward
through Dunc. With a despairing clutch he caught Little
Frog in a bear hug and now it was Dunc who held on
for his life, shaking his head to clear it from the effects
of sickening pain. He was stronger than Little Frog and
held on better, but his opponent strove manfully and
finally did succeed in breaking loose. He bounded back
and struck the bar. Dunc cornered him and drove two
terrific blows to the midsection. Little Frog turned and

grabbed his stomach, falling back to where a six-by-six support rose from the floor, studded with nails upon which coats and various other gear were hung. He rebounded from that straight into Dunc's most killing blow of the night. It flung him violently backward against the post and one of the nails sank deep into his back.

Little Frog's scream was cut short by a whistling uppercut to the chin, a blow that drove his head back against the post with a smacking thud. Dunc stood before him now, legs spread wide, and hooked him with rights and lefts. Dunc's shirt split from waist to neck from the force of his own blows. When finally his wind was spent, he dropped his hands and looked at what he had done. Little Frog's face was a mushy bag of bones and flesh; dripping blood in streams had turned his shirtfront into a gory mess. His jaw leered open, his arms hung limply. Little Frog was very dead. Only then did the hypnotized audience realize what was holding him up.

"Jesus . . . *Gawd*," breathed one man, retching violently, reeling toward the bar. "Nail . . . Hung up like a beef . . . Nail . . . Jesus, Gawd!"

Dunc flexed his hands experimentally. Nothing seemed broken, but the knuckles were battered and skinned. He raised a forearm, wiped the sweat and hair from his eyes and looked dully about. His arms and back ached and about his hips were raw spots beginning to bleed where his gun belts had punished him.

"Lordy, Dunc," breathed Les Achord, the bartender. "How come you done it?"

Dunc cleared his throat and rubbed his face with a forearm again. "Killed my maw," he said gratingly. "Him and his brother." Turning he walked weakly out.

There was no rush to take Little Frog from the nail, but after a while it was accomplished. And although they were men who could see a man shot with a big-nosed bullet without turning a hair, this was something they could not stomach and several of them had to turn and rush outside for air.

"Nail didn't kill him," said Achord, after Little Frog was lowered to the floor.

"What did?" someone asked.

"Fists. The man's neck is broke short off. Feel them bones grittin'."

"Jesus, Gawd," said the first man to be sick. "I wouldn't tetch 'im with a corral pole."

The news had traveled fast and when Dunc made his stumbling way back to the cabin there were a number of men and women gathered there, all talking excitedly.

Jim Walters put a kind hand on Dunc's arm. "I can't make no sense of all this, son. Whut'n hell'd they wanter kill yer maw fer?"

Dunc shook his head. "Mind pouring some water over my hands. That mad dog mighta poisoned me."

"But you shot 'im . . ."

"This was a brother . . . up at the saloon."

A man who had just come up peered at Dunc, then at the sheriff, his face pale. "Dead," he whispered. "That boy kilt 'im with his bare hands."

"Shet up," said the sheriff. "Come on over here, boy,

and le's wash them hands."

Mrs. Walters came up and superintended the washing, then said, "You'll sleep at our place tonight, son." She spoke so softly that tears came to Dunc's eyes. "Yes'm, but I'll have to take the kid home."

"You mean Carmelita? Well, don't you fret none. She'll get home."

"I'll take her," he said doggedly. "Sheriff, can I borry a hoss?"

"Sure, Dunc. Ed . . ." He spoke to the man who had followed Dunc from the saloon. "Trot up there to Wilfred's and tell 'im t' saddle ole Blue, and you bring 'im back here."

Ed Withers departed at a run.

They rode side by side through the purple night. Overhead, stars spangled the vault of heaven and cast soft silver upon them.

"You should not have come with me," said Carmelita, placing a warm hand on his. "It was not necessary."

He reached across her and catching old Blue's reins stopped the horse. "You walked all this way just to bring me tortillas, didn't you?"

"But I didn't mind."

"I know. You did it. Now it's night and if you walked back you'd be exposed to every two-footed dog around Big Bend. Could I do less for you?"

She was silent for a moment, turning her head trying to see the outlines of his face, blurry in the starlight. "Señor, I think you are a very kind man."

He flushed scarlet and released the reins, grateful for the darkness which covered his embarrassment. "Tell me about your trouble with Sam Peters."

She shuddered, and was silent for a moment. "I had not been here long. You see, I lived in the convent at El Paso for a long time . . . until my education was completed. After I returned here, he stopped by our *casita,* one day, and asked for water. He was friendly and polite. I could not refuse a gentleman a drink of water. The next time he stopped I knew it was not water he wanted, but me. I was alone at the time and . . ." She shivered as though the night chill had made her cold. "I managed to tear away and I outran him . . . He is too fat to run very fast. I lost him in the brush. But now he threatens to make trouble for my father, unless . . ."

Dunc, mourning the only mother he had known, was in no mood to have himself—or his friends—pushed around. Especially by Sam Peters. And in a very short while he had achieved a blind gratitude toward this girl, who had brought him a few *tortillas,* who had been willing to stay with his dead mother after the shock of seeing her brutally murdered. He realized subconsciously that she was beautiful, without letting his mind dwell upon it. But more than that, his sore heart yearned for kindness; soft, gentle, feminine kindness, of the kind she extended to him.

"I'm promising you something, girl," he said. "If he troubles you again, I'll kill him."

"*Ay,* no," she said softly. "Don't get into trouble on my account."

THE GUNFIGHTER

"I'd be plumb tickled to get in trouble on your account." He caught his breath, afraid that in his intensity of feeling he had said too much. He was certain of it, when she did not reply. However, her hand stole out of the darkness and touched him with such tenderness that his eyes filled and his throat grew thick and achy with emotion.

"Bear a little to the left," she said after a while. "See the light?"

"Yes. I remember your father. I didn't know he had a daughter."

"I've been away a lot. My father has no education and he was determined that I get some."

"He deserves a lot of credit for that attitude," Dunc said.

When they reached the little adobe ranchhouse with its stone wall, fruit trees and fragrant fields, he stopped the horse, dismounted. Catching her about the waist, he lifted her easily from the saddle. Unluckily her skirt, which she had been keeping primly tucked about her knees, caught on the saddle horn; as she slid downward it slid upward, until her beautifully sculptured legs from hip to ankle glimmered palely in the starlight.

He tried, not too successfully, to look away.

"It is all right, señor. You did not do it on purpose . . ." She laughed. He was still holding her. He could feel the faint touch of her young flesh, smell the warm perfume of her clean body.

"Please, señor, do not be so embarrassed. It was nothing . . . It is very dark."

Whips of emotion laid scalding stripes over his heart.

THE GUNFIGHTER

Weakened by his fight, tortured by the reminiscent hurt of the first Carmelita, stricken with grief because of his mother's tragic death, Duncan Stewart suddenly found his burdens more than he could bear. Crushing her to him, he wept, for in such circumstances even the most iron control cannot always withstand the touch of a gentle, beautiful woman.

In a moment or two, her own little heart loaded with sympathy and understanding, she too was weeping. Slowly her arms went about him and she accepted his hurts as her own. Artlessly, her lips brushed his eyes and cheeks, then finally his own lips sought hers with the hunger of desperation. They were welded together in an embrace that left both frightened, yet cleansed and strengthened.

"Now," she whispered, her voice seeming to catch in her throat, "come in and see my parents. I will treat your hands with a balm the sisters showed me how to make at the convent."

Old José, short, spare as a roadrunner, his lips hidden in an enormous gray moustache, took his hand. "I remember," he said in good English. "My wife used to tell me of you and your mother. They were good friends. Why was she killed?"

"A mystery," said Dunc, liking the old man instantly. "No one knows."

The girl's mother said in Spanish, "She loved the boy even more than if she had given him birth."

"And I loved her," he said shakily, in the same language. "No man could have loved a mother more." His eyes narrowed and grew hot. "Never let Carmelita go through Big Bend alone again," he said. "What were you thinking about?"

"It was a mistake," agreed her mother. "I said we would both go but she understood me to say that she should take you the *tortillas* herself. While I was out, she left alone."

"I've heard," said Dunc in a metallic voice, "about Sam Peters, José. Fear nothing from him. If he threatens Carmelita again, I'll kill him."

"*Señor*," he said, echoing his daughter, "you should not make our troubles yours. I am not afraid of Sam Peters. I told him so."

"Just the same . . ." He bit it off because he himself was just at that moment realizing what had come over him. Though he had known Carmelita but a few hours, he had fallen in love with her. He loved her with a ferocity that was frightening and the realization made him go suddenly weak. Sweat broke out in droplets, beading his forehead so that it shone in the dim lamp-light.

Even in that moment, Dunc had the insight to laugh at himself. He certainly was swift enough at falling in love! Well, he told himself, even if indeed he were overly susceptible to the charms of the fair sex, that did not make his newfound love any the less deep and sincere. His train of thought was interrupted by the girl's voice.

"He's been fighting," said Carmelita crisply. "I must dress his hands. *Mamacita,* will you bring me the jar of balm?"

She washed his hands, kneeling beside him with

141

hot water and soap, dried them with a clean white cloth, then with long slim fingers she massaged the brown fragrant balm into the skin of his knuckles and fingers. The ache went out of his heart and he relaxed, watching her absorbed in her task, her face calm and possessed of a fetching loveliness that delighted his senses.

Her hair was drawn back behind her head and tied with a red ribbon and in the lamplight it glistened like polished metal. Beneath the cloth of her colorful dress her breasts peaked high and assertive. Occasionally she would brush softly against his knee and a tremor would course through his body.

Finally she stood and wiped her hands on the cloth. "You will have to come back for your treatments. Every day for three days."

"Come at supper time," put in the mother, "and our daughter will not have to be going into town carrying *tortillas*. I promise you all you can eat."

"*Con frijoles?*" he asked with a smile.

"*Con frijoles, con carne, con mucho gusto,*" she said warmly, her kindly, seamed face glowing with hospitality.

His eyes smiled. "*Muchos gracias, Mamacita.*"

"*Por nada, chico mio. Hasta la vista.*"

He wrung old José's horny hand hard and stepped out into the darkness. He was mounted before he realized that Carmelita had followed him. "*Buenas noches, Señor Duncan.*"

"Dunc. *Por favor.*"

She placed a hand on his hard hip and he covered it with his own. "*Gracias* . . . Dunc," she said, her voice

142

lifting musically on the still air.

"I will come tomorrow . . . but I will never forget this night . . . Never!"

"I, too, will remember," she whispered, her eyes misting over.

She stood and listened to the horses' hoofs fade in the night, then she turned and slowly walked back into the house.

"Aha," said her mother, her old eyes too experienced to miss the thoughtful face of her daughter. "The young man has touched your heart, *chiquita*."

Carmelita's eyes were warm with affection as she looked at her mother. "Not touched it, *Mamacita*. He has won it. His hurt is my hurt, his grief is my grief, his fears are my fears . . ." She stopped aghast at the intensity of her own voice, then she lifted her head proudly. "And my life is his life . . . if he wants it."

"She is so young," said the mother as Carmelita went to her room.

"She is seventeen," said old José, his eyes affectionately laughing at his wife. "You were but fourteen, and no woman was ever more beautiful."

She smiled. "And no *caballero* was ever so dashing or could play the guitar so well. José, play for me."

He took down the rusty old instrument. The varnish had cracked and peeled, but it still rang true as he tuned the strings. His old eyes lighted as he drew from the strings a preliminary chord and looked at the expectant face of his wife. His work-hardened fingers were sure and sensitive as from the old instrument came one of Mexico's most celebrated songs, *La Paloma*. His voice was surprisingly mellow and clear as he caressingly sang the lovely lyric.

The fingers speeded as he ended the song and he swung into a rollicking *ranchero*. As he reached the refrain, his wife blended her own voice with his and the melody floated softly out on the night air in duet.

10

A HUNDRED yards away, on the trail south, a group of four horsemen met a fifth riding from the opposite direction, toward Big Bend. They exchanged low greetings and one of them said, "Don't sound like you skeered that there old Mex none. He's singin' happy."

The bulky horseman who had joined them cursed savagely. "I'll put the fear of hell into him, all right. One of these nights we'll pay him a visit and when his place burns pretty and bright we'll see what he sings."

A tall man older than the rest of the punchers said, "You ain't been in town for some days, Sam, or you wouldn't be talking like that. Things is done changed."

"How so?"

"Dunc Stewart's done come back."

"That orphan tramp . . . Who gives a damn?"

The older man sighed. "Boy, don't you git no news atall? That boy is pizen as a sidewinder. He took on some little town over in the territory singlehanded and burnt it flat. He kilt Hamp Wallace and if that don't tell you nuthin', nuthin' kin."

Sam Peters felt of his scarred face and it reddened with the old hatred. This news was not good. "He ain't no ghost," snarled Sam. "A bullet can puncture him just like anybody else."

"That's right," said another waddy dubiously, "but I seen sump'n tonight I never seen befo'. That fellow killed a man with his fists. Broke his neck like a stalk of corn after hangin' him up on a nail just like a quarter of beef."

"What's that got to do with old José," Sam barked angrily.

"That gal was at his cabin when this dead ranny's brother kilt Stewart's maw. They looked jes' alike and when he gunned the fust one he come lookin' fer the other'n. He brung the gal back to José's on Jim Walter's hoss. So he must be innersted."

Sam scowled blackly and said, "You boys headed back to the spread?"

The older man spoke. "Sure are. We put in that order fer posts and bob wire."

"Well, turn right around and come on back with me. I'll put you up at the hotel and the drinks is on the house. I might need you."

"Anything you say, boss."

Duncan Stewart, fatigued from the exorbitant demands he had placed upon himself, slept the sleep of youth. Jim Walters ate a surprisingly hearty breakfast in sullen silence, causing Marthy to comment, "Well, it do beat all."

"What do?" he inquired, looking up from his second cup of coffee.

"You. The doctor hardly got nowhere, but ever since young Dunc's been your deppity you been prancin' like a young stud hoss. You ain't et a breakfast like this'n in a sweat, I'll tell you."

He nodded, frowning. "Yeah, the boy do put ginger inter a body. Looks like he got so much t' burn it sorta rubs off on other people. He sure done made some tracks since he come back."

"And some enemies," she added significantly.

"And all lined up to make more." He sighed heavily. "Sure hope that boy's got sense enough t' take after some of the old-timers."

"How you mean?"

He regarded her crossly. "How you think mens like Hamp Wallace and the rest of them is left stayed live?"

"I've often wondered."

"Well, I can tell you. They done it by havin' a hid sense like a Injun. They sees things where other peoples don't. They takes two things can't nobody else ketch and knits 'em inter sump'n that tells a story. The boy's lightnin', all right, and he ain't got a jumpy nerve in his body, but it takes more'n that. He started too young and that's what I'm skeered of. He ain't wake yet?"

"No, and don't you wake him. He's still a boy walkin' around doin' a man's work. He lost his maw and he took it hard. I hope he don't wake up till slap dark."

It wasn't dark when Dunc woke up, but it was just

in time to get washed for dinner. Jim came home at twelve still in the grip of the growls and found Dunc, already seated at the table, similarly infected. His head was threaded with cobwebs and his heart beat like a slow drum.

His appetite seemed dead but reared its head like the phoenix when Marthy brought him an immense platter loaded with potatoes hashed brown with onions, thick spicy gravy and three slabs of succulent roast beef.

He ate with silent intensity until there wasn't a vestige of food left on his plate, or any more hot biscuits with butter on the table. The last four he loaded down heavily with peach jam. The coffee was hot and strong and clung to the back of his palate, making him think with unusual relish of the cigarette to come. He finished up on three fried dried-apple fritters and a second cup of coffee, then pulled out his Bull and shook tobacco flakes into the brown paper. Mrs. Marthy Walters watched the long lean fingers as they held the paper. Dunc's left hand dropped away, feeling for a match, while the right hand toyed with the cigarette, made a few preparatory moves then spun the paper into a tube. He applied his tongue to the free edge. He did it absently, as though his mind was miles away, but the fluid ease with which he had snapped the cigarette into being with one hand made Marthy gasp.

"How you roll a cigarette so good with one hand?"

Dunc looked up and studied the lady for a few seconds before the question filtered through his brown study. "Oh . . ." He shrugged. "I learned it . . ." He puffed luxuriously and returned to his thinking.

THE GUNFIGHTER

"Want to talk to you about a few things," said Walters, after he had laboriously fashioned his own smoke and had it going. "So come outa that dust storm and lissen."

"Yes, sir." The fog disappeared; the eyes became clear and intent.

"First off, you've made a passel of enemies. Maybe a couple of 'em who ain't really concerned wouldn't shoot you from ambush or in the back when you was thinkin' about sump'n else. The rest would. You're a good boy with your guns and your fists, but you won't last long if you don't know how t' stay alive. I can't draw you no map. Mebbe Hamp could but I can't. All I can tell you is to stay on your toes *all* the time. There ain't a thicket, not a boulder, not a board fence, not a dark alley, nowheres around here that might not have frum one t' four cocked guns stickin' out from it. See what I mean?"

"Yes, sir."

"Well, remember it. What you gonna do today?"

"I'm going to see Walter Koenig."

"Why?"

"Some people get their cattle rustled. This is the first time I ever heard of a cured hog getting rustled. I'm interested."

"Any special reason?"

"Yes, sir. Where did the robbers sell it? There isn't a spread in Texas that could eat all that meat. I want to check if it went into Mexico like it's been said."

"Well . . . now dagnab it, there is sump'n t' chew on. I'll be hot durned if it ever come to my mind. If that

General didn't buy it, who did?"

"I know that one of Wade's men was killed at Koenig's. Also one of Jared Walker's men was killed in that last meat raid. It's just smart operating to have a few bad eggs working for some honest rancher appear at the scene of the robberies. Know what I think? I got my doubts if those men died the way they were supposed to have."

"How's that, again?"

"It's a mighty handy thing to have a man killed on the spot what doesn't have any business being there. Maybe it wasn't done intentional, but it'd be smart."

"But on that last meat raid one of Wade's men was killed too."

Dunc nodded. "It's not a sure thing, just something to think about. On the other hand, Wade didn't have to steal that meat, remember."

"No, but he claimed the body of the dead man."

"He might not have done it. He didn't have to. He had a choice."

"Dadgummit," fumed Walters, "you got me so turned around in the head I don't know where my office is."

Dunc grinned. "I'll show you the way. You got some gun oil there, I reckon."

"Rags, oil and a whole stack of cleanin' rods."

"All my guns need cleaning. They haven't had a good going over in a long time."

"How long?"

"Two . . . three days maybe."

Walters wheezed out a laugh. "Maybe I been worryin' too much about you."

THE GUNFIGHTER

It was three in the afternoon and Dunc was still hard at it, cleaning his weapons. The beautiful .45's were loaded and lay on the desk. Their ornate barrels, inlaid with silver, gleamed richly and the longhorn steer heads on the mother-of-pearl handles looked ready to start nibbling grass.

"Durn if them ain't the purtiest guns I ever seen. That Zimmerman was some hombre. Wonder where he got the money to buy sich weapons."

"Hamp says whenever you see a saddle tramp with guns like these you can be sure he stole 'em off somebody."

"Yeah. Hamp oughta know. He's carryin' a extra pair like that hisself. Took 'em off an outlaw up nawth. Says the guns b'longed t' one of Cap'n Hays' mens who got dry-gulched up in the Panhandle . . . here, lemme see them . . ."

Two brown hands leaped and covered the guns. Dunc smiled apologetically at the blank countenance of the sheriff. "Just one at a time, Mr. Walters. The other one's got to be free . . . *all* the time."

Jim Walters swallowed noisily. He chuckled. "And I was the one tellin' you t' watch out."

"Yes, sir."

"You better be movin' along . . . The funeral ain't till tomorrow, but you'll have to hustle."

"I'll leave after dark."

"Good sense. Good sense."

Dunc surprised them by appearing at breakfast, next morning. But Walters only said, "What did you find out at Koenig's?"

151

"Not much. Those big mules were from Mexico."

"Humph . . . Mex brands. I knowed that but nobody knowed anything about the Lightnin'-on-the-Pine spread havin' no sich mules as them. It's just a reg'lar pore Mex spread. They was big as brewry mules."

"Red Raven mules . . . from New Orleans."

"How you figger?"

"They had two brands. Lightning-on-the-Pine was on the right hip. The Bird was on the left."

"Why New Orleans?"

"The nearest Red Raven brewery. And General Carlos Alvaredo was in New Orleans, exiled, until he went back into the mountains of Chihauhau and Coahuila and started gathering men."

"Hummm. Knowed about that too. About four, five years ago. The *Rurales* can't touch him because he's too strong. The Federal troops'll wait around till it's too late. He'll give some real trouble, sooner or later."

"When I was in Mexico they talked about him being supplied with money from some Texas and Louisiana outfits. Of course, they expect him to win, then get them all sorts of concessions."

"Which they might not get once he's in the seat."

"Sure, but that's the way they're hoping."

"You think them mules came from Alvaredo's camp?"

"I don't think anything yet. It's a possibility. I figure Wade's supplying him with fresh meat."

Walters sat up straight. "Well, if that's true, how come Wade wouldn't have stole the pork? He'd have the best reason yet."

THE GUNFIGHTER

Dunc rolled a cigarette deftly and stuck it between his lips. "Running hooves down a coulee into Mexico is one thing. Moving a wagon train loaded with cured meat is another. One is plain rustling. The other—well, it's got a different brand. It's another hoss. Mind you, I can be wrong about all of this."

Walters drained his coffee cup and rolled himself a cigarette. "All this means you guess there's two gangs operatin' around here."

"That's an idea I have all right."

"Sure that idee ain't thunk up so's you can include Sam Peters?"

Dunc's smile was mirthless and cold. "We wouldn't want to leave Sam out, would we?"

"There you go, cultivatin' more enemies—and wuss ones, if I know anything."

The funeral that afternoon was well attended, with most of the population on hand in their best Sunday clothes. The Reverend Lester Collins, a hawk-visaged rawbony man whose rusty black suit fitted like Lincoln's insisted that no guns be present at the ceremony but he might as well have insisted that no pants be worn. His severe lips were thin and bloodless as he saw all the male mourners wearing their hardware. He burned inside with a holy fire that soared at the sight of sin, therefore it remained at flash point most of the time. Since his edict was ignored, he promptly lost his never too steady temper, but he did manage to defer the explosion. The burial was crisp and short and after the first

153

few shovels of dirt had been cast people began to drift away, finally leaving only Dunc, Jim and Marthy Walters, Old José, the two Carmelitas, mother and daughter, and another person who had managed to remain drably in the background, completely unnoticed. Reverend Lester Collins now chose to vent his wrath on Dunc who had brazenly ignored his edict; since Dunc was the surviving relative, he appeared a logical victim to the Reverend.

He confronted Dunc, his black eyes snapping and his bony fingers working with rage. "Didn't you understand my announcement that there were to be no guns worn at this funeral?"

"Yes, sir."

"And yet you wore them in outright defiance."

"Look, Reverend," put in Jim Walters, "if there's men around who'd shoot a defenseless woman, you can be sure they wouldn't hold their lead out of respect for a funeral. The boy's my deppity and he's a marked man."

"That is what's the matter with this evil land," shouted the minister. "Too much fear of death and too much dying. God gave man reason, he gave him a will. Will yourself from these evil ways. Chain your temper to the rock of ages. Curb this ferocity. Wearing guns to your own mother's funeral . . . For shame! Hell's fire will burn bright. Curb your temper and your evil ways . . ."

"Can you curb yourn?" It was a man of modest stature, rusty and dusty from desert travel.

"That happens to be my business," snapped the

154

Reverend, now thoroughly warmed up to his subject. "However, for your enlightenment I can say that I have never lost my temper."

"Jesus hisself," snickered the little man, infuriatingly.

Reverend Collins' bony face seemed blistered with red blood. "Sir, you blaspheme. I am not Christ, but a devout follower of His."

"You been doin' yer follerin' in a safe place, if yer temper ain't never been stretched."

"I must admit," thundered Collins, his vaunted will weakening before the sarcastic assaults of this desert tramp, this nobody, "that at the moment it is being severely tested."

But suddenly all were laughing. Even the Reverend himself, realizing that this comical little man had made a pretty good point or two.

"Just the same," said Collins, before making off, "you'd better not try to tote them weapons into hell."

"We's aimin' for the other place," Hamp Wallace said mildly.

11

HAMP TURNED and grinned at the thunderstruck on-lookers. "Le's all go have a drink . . . Cepn' the wimmen, of course."

Hamp and Jim made for the saloon but Dunc, after a wordless handshake that made Hamp squeeze back mightily to prevent his fingers from being broken, followed the Mercader family to their tiny *coche* drawn by a fat gray burro.

"You didn't come last night," accused Carmelita, pouting with mock disapproval.

Dunc turned pink. "Had to ride out . . . Busy. I'll be there tomorrow night."

She touched his hand with a gentle sweep of hers.

"Tomorrow night," she said.

He watched them drive away, a tight smothering sensation interfering with his breathing. She had been beautiful yesterday. Today, in cool, freshly laundered white, she was angelic. Her face had been vital and

156

alive yesterday; today it was ethereal, other-worldish. He had loved her with all his might yesterday. Today his might had tripled.

He turned and walked toward the main drag of Big Bend. He changed directions and took the back way behind the stores and false-fronted buildings. He went into the saloon through the back entrance and almost knocked over a man standing with his back to the door.

"'Scuse it," said Dunc politely. "I didn't know you were there."

The man, hulking and thickset in range garb, having had a few drinks, was inclined to be truculent. The boy facing him, he could see, was pounds under his own considerable avoirdupois.

"Better watch yer step, you bastard," snorted the man.

Dunc's hands hung limply beside him but the eyes seemed to burn holes in the air. "Say that again, friend."

Another snort followed the first one. "Not only a bastard—a deaf bastard!"

Dunc kicked the man solidly in the stomach and as he spun around in agony the boy powered another kick into the seat of the other's pants that flung him sprawling into the main part of the saloon.

"Still makin' enemies," sighed Jim Walters, over his second drink.

"Looks like he starts out makin' 'em behave. This here oughta be good. That there galoot with the scarred face don't look happy," Hamp said.

"That's the boy Dunc cut all up the fust day you rid in."

"Growed up some, ain't 'e? Ain't changed none, though."

Dunc stood over the fallen puncher and looked down at him coldly. "Get off your feet, dog, and scramble."

Sam Peters got up swaggeringly and walked over to Dunc. "Lay off my boy, Stewart, or I'll clean up the place with you."

Dunc looked hard. It was the first time he had seen Sam Peters in four years. He didn't like what he saw. "He called me a bastard. Would you like to enlarge on that?"

Sam grinned and put his hands on his hips. "I didn't know Pat was that well acquainted with you."

Dunc pivoted and with a full-armed sweep dug a whistling right to Sam's rather full midsection. Sam's lungs emptied with a squalling grunt and as he bent over Dunc placed a spurred boot back of his neck and crashed him face first into the floor.

"Speed. That's what gits 'em ever' time," said Hamp happily. "The boy is fast as a streak o' lightnin'. Ole Rolando musta give him some learnin'. *You there . . .*" His voice lashed out like a blacksnake whip as he swung around on springy legs toward a puncher who was sneaking a gun out of leather. "Just drop it back where it was 'lessen you want t' break a fingernail or sump'n wuss."

The man paled and jerked his hand away from the gun. The man on the floor got up to a sitting position and looked hazily about. He gaped when he saw his boss on the floor beside him. He looked toward the bar and saw Dunc's back to him as he walked toward the sheriff and a dusty little stranger who wore a strange gun harness that seemed to cover a third of each thigh. He shook his head and allowed a friend to help him from the floor. He motioned toward Sam Peters. "Better git him up from there, too."

"Nunh unh," protested the friend. "I ain't touchin' him till I get sign. Might not be safe."

Dunc shook hands with Hamp for the second time and let his eyes rest on the calm amber ones of his old friend. "It's been a long time, Mr. Wallace. I haven't had a chance to thank you."

"Good boy," said Hamp enthusiastically. "You ain't no skeered young'un bein' kicked around now, I can see. How'd you leave Rolando?"

"Fine. He sent a letter to you but I left it in my warbag at the cabin."

"We'll git it in time. I been hearin' about you."

"Yeah," put in Jim Walters. "What about that rumor the boy had took you in a gun fight."

Hamp grinned. "Had a chanct t' start that there story and knowed it wouldn't do the boy no harm."

Dunc chuckled dryly. "I had a idea that was your story. Had all the markings."

"What you gonna do about your pal on the floor?"

"That depends. Did you hear him?"

"I heard 'im. You there . . ." He beckoned to the man who had tried to sneak a draw. "Come 'ere. Want you t' meet a friend of mine."

The man came over, slowly, his long face pale and sweat beading his forehead. "I didn't mean . . . I . . ."

"Shet up. Whut's yer name?"

"Alford. Dick Alford."

"Dick here," he said to Dunc, "was slippin' his iron out. Thought nobody was lookin'. Meet Dunc Stewart, the new deppity."

Dunc looked at him, his face as expressionless as an oak knot. "Would you like to pull it again?"

"No . . . I didn't . . . I mean, I . . ."

"We know what you mean," said Hamp affably. "Now, git." The fellow got and seemed glad of the chance.

"Always nice t' know who you can expect a dry gulchin' from. Now you looky here, Dunc. You got t' learn t' see outa the corners of your eyes."

"I saw him."

"Y' did?"

"Sure. I was depending on you or Mr. Walters. I could also see y'all watching him."

"Well, dang me," snorted Walters. "Guess I been worryin' fer nuthin'."

Sam Peters rolled over and sat up, his eyes glazed. As they cleared, hate-fire ignited in their depths. Sam Peters had been a spoiled brat all his life. Therefore his temper was not of the steadiest. He got slowly to his feet.

"Count your days, deputy," he snarled.

"Measure your wind," said Dunc softly. "You might blow a hole in the floor."

Sam's face flamed and his right hand made a motion toward his gun. Men faded away and left the line of fire open, though Hamp and the sheriff remained beside Dunc. Hamp smiled. "Le's git outa the way, Jim.

160

Sump'n might happen, but I doubt it."

Sam swung toward Hamp, his full lips still twisted with a hateful snarl. "Why, you old busted latigo. I'll wipe this place up with you."

Hamp grinned. "That's as may be. We'll be around to see. Seems like you got another matter a little more pressin' right now."

Sam in his rage had forgotten the advice of his oldest puncher, Buck Eldridge, and now Buck's voice called out to him, " 'Member what I tole you las' night, Sam.' "

"Go to hell," growled Sam and dropped his hand to his gun. He was fast. He knew it, but he was no gunfighter, not having the stomach for it, and now he was hesitant—a flaw in many another man who might, except for that fatal affliction, have been dangerous. His stomach congealed into a mass of solid fright and his face paled. Duncan Stewart still looked at him steadily, leaning gracefully against the bar with his left hand and gun the only ones that could be brought into play. He hadn't made a move. Sam began to sweat, then a great light burst upon him. Stewart was being openly contemptuous of him before an audience. He was underestimating Sam's ability and many a man had fallen because of that one thing, too. Sam had the jump, his hand was on his gun butt. That was a big jump.

Sam's gun snapped from the holster and he pulled the trigger with a flinch that traveled all over his gross body. Nothing happened. Then the appalling knowledge almost took the strength from his legs. For all his hard-blistering practice in private, when the chips were down he had forgotten to cock his gun.

161

Against the bar, Dunc let a dry grin decorate his lips. He was still, hadn't made the slightest move. The assembly by now had ceased to breathe entirely, Hamp not excepted save for one gusty, "Dammit . . ." Then he was silent.

Dunc straightened up and grinned toward Sam. "Want me to cock it for you, jelly belly?"

Sam looked stupidly down at the gun still extended with cataleptic rigidity. He looked up and life came back to his eyes. "I'm gonna kill you, Stewart," he bellowed, an insane rage having stung him into action. He slid the gun back into his hand and he thumbed the hammer with a smooth motion only to have the gun apparently explode in his grasp. His hand went dead and the roar of Dunc's gun came tardily to his ears. His tawdry little soul cankered with fear and hate and he was a ruined man. Those whom he had beaten with his fists would taunt him now and dare him to draw. Without another word he turned and tottered out of the saloon. His four followers, their faces showing mixed emotions, followed.

But he had a sympathizer. A shot rang out.

Hamp wiped the barrel of his right-hand gun on his pants leg and looked at the figure on the floor. "I never could abide a back shooter," he complained mildly.

Jim Walters jumped. He hadn't heard a thing. He hadn't seen a thing. It was weird but Jim didn't know how hypnotized he had been by the tense tableau he had witnessed. "What happened, Hamp?"

"This gent here . . . I been watchin' 'im. He didn't pay me no mind, not knowin' me. He was all ready to take the boy from behind. Now's where the law steps in, Jim. Got handcuffs?"

"Sure."

"All right. Let 'im wake up in jail."

"What'll I charge 'im with? He didn't shoot?"

"Now dagnab it, there's a point. Guess you might as well leave 'im there."

12

JUGG ALLISON was in the ranch office and had already broken out the whiskey when pale-haired Felton Wade entered, dressed in immaculate riding clothes, looking very fit and distinguished. He stared coldly at his foreman and took the bottle from him, poured a drink. "Well, Jugg—?"

"I didn't have a damn thing to do with it. I didn't even know them boys. What put that inter their thick heads I don't know. I hadn't even assigned them to any work yet."

"It makes a pretty story . . . a much prettier one if it ever comes out they came here first. Who knows we hired them on?"

"Don't nobody know it 'cept a couple or three here. What you reckon made 'em do sich a thing?"

Wade grimaced. "I've beaten my head black and blue trying to figure it out and I've come to one conclusion. The only one I can hang on to. Remember us talking in here, wondering if Dave's wife knew where he was going that day he got himself shot?"

"Yeah."

Wade went to the window and opened it. "Look here, Jugg." Plainly in the soft grassless loam, protected from sun and rain by a drop roof, were the impressions of badly run-over boots.

"Stood right there and listened," breathed Allison.

"Smart hombres, weren't they? Heard what I said and thought they'd hand me something on a tray. That's the end, Jugg. Not another damn drifter do we hire. Not a single one. No matter what sort of rep he brings along. We live well, we stay alive and every man jack of the hands draws pay three times what they'd get on a regular ranch. The idea of hiring anyone running from the law was good once, but we've been too lacking in choice. That bird you let your good friend have to rustle that pork was another man I had to take the responsibility for and I'm done with it. From now on you can play poker for your extra money. Now get this. No man on this spread is to go on any jaunt unless I know and approve. No lend-outs and no business with other ranch hands who want to double-cross their owners. We're on our own. Can you see the wisdom of that?"

Allison nodded. "Yeah. I can see it now."

The steel-gray eyes were slitted as Wade nodded his head. "I'm glad you see it that way, Jugg. Otherwise I was ready to write out your time. I like it here and I intend to stay."

"Me too," said Allison fervently. " 'Magine that wet-eared boy killin' Little Frog with his bare hands."

"You should have little trouble imagining it. You

absorbed a couple of good punches that didn't make you any too happy and I'd advise you to stop kidding yourself about calling him a wet-eared kid. The comparison doesn't exactly swell you in size, you know."

"Yeah? I'll take care of that end. Don't you worry."

"How, Jugg, from the bushes?"

"What do you care?" snarled Allison, his temper flaring. "Looks like you'd be glad to see 'im dead, no matter how."

"I would. I was just feeling around."

"You feel a sight too goddamned much," said Allison with an ugly grimace. "You ought to—"

"Good morning, folks."

Allison spun around at the sound of the voice, his hand going to the butt of his gun. He saw Dunc leaning indolently against the frame of the open door.

Dunc smiled frostily. "Continue your palaver. Real interesting. I latched on where you were 'imagining' about me killing 'Frog' with my hands. Let's go back a ways. How did you know his name?"

Wade sighed heavily and let his hands fall to the desk. "It's no use, Jugg . . . Mr. Stewart, how did you get in here?"

"Walked in. The Chink tried to stop me but I persuaded him that it might be better if he didn't raise a howl. Didn't see any of your riders around, so I came on up the veranda. Now, about the two I killed. They looked almost like twins. You knew them?"

"Tell him, Jugg," said Wade tiredly.

"Well, them riders come in after jobs and I hired them. I'm tellin' you straight, I didn't have no idea what they was up to. That's one thing you can't say about this outfit. We ain't wimmen killers." Felton Wade nodded in agreement.

"That's right, Mr. Stewart. I give you my word that if I'd known those coyotes had any such idea, I'd have shot them myself. The only possible reason I can offer for their actions is that they heard about your visit and thought to get back at you. Still, it was such a stupid thing—killing a perfectly harmless woman to get back at her son, neither of them even knowing you. It is hard to believe. I can only hope that you believe what I'm trying to tell you."

Dunc nodded. He had shored his mind up against further grief, especially at a time like this. He was not satisfied but nothing the Flying Y had done to date suggested any act against a defenseless woman such as that perpetrated by the Forgey brothers. It could be just as Allison and Wade said. Dunc snapped erect with such suddenness that Allison had to catch himself to prevent a grab for his weapon. Jugg Allison was trying to be very careful.

"Wade, I'm going to believe you . . . partly, at least. I wouldn't be so inclined, except I'm guessing much goes on around here that you are not all responsible for. Of course, it's nice to know you want me knocked off— from the bushes or otherwise, but that's not exactly a surprise. As deputy sheriff, anyway, I'm less interested in you than in certain others, right at the moment."

Allison was stung erect. "Look, boy, you gettin' pretty damn big for your britches. Who the hell do you think you is, bellyin' up to the biggest rancher in these

167

parts, tellin' 'im you got bigger interests, hintin' at what you'd do if you didn't?"

Dunc smiled thinly. "The difference in what you think and what is, Juggy, is this badge. I'm a properly sworn arm of the law. Some people think they're bigger than the law. Some even like to prove it. Would you like to prove it?"

Jugg stood paralyzed.

Wade's face darkened as he looked at his foreman. "I don't quite get you, Jugg. You flare up and it always winds up with you backing water. Dammit, do you like it?"

Allison's face grew dark with blood. "There'll come a day," he gritted.

Wade cursed. "The same talk. Nothing new."

"Well, I'll be going," said Dunc, the cool smile still on his lips. "But before I do, I want to say one thing, Mr. Wade. This trickle-rustling has to stop, see? You can carry on for a while, I suppose, while I work on this other thing I got on my mind, but I'll get around to lesser matters in time. So long."

"Somehow," mused Wade, staring at the spot where the young man had stood, "I kind of like your wet-eared kid. He isn't afraid of the devil himself. He covers his flanks well. He doesn't go charging into a place before he knows what he has to deal with." A smile crept over his face. "He understands that you're afraid of him—so, knowing I'm no gunman and dealing with you is routine, he blows in as the impulse moves him. You blow and bluster and turn red and he politely invites you to do whatever seems meet and fitting and you mutter something about 'There'll come a day.' I'm wondering about that day. I'm wondering who'll be buried, you or him. It'll come, sure. I'm not at all certain what the outcome will be, but I would make a guess."

"What's your guess?" grated Allison, through clenched teeth.

Wade's smile was thin. "You're a good man within certain limits, Jugg. I'd hate to lose you."

13

THAT NIGHT, Ed Peters, who had been out of town the day before, had a talk with Jim Walters.

Also, Dunc rode out to the Mercader's to have his sore knuckles treated with balm.

Ed Peters stomped into the sheriff's office just after first dark, when Walters and Hamp Wallace were getting ready to close up.

"I want to know what the hell you mean," Ed began, "lettin' that deppity of yourn whang my boy around. I'm gittin' damn good and tired of the way you run this office. First people's cattle get run off, then the stage is robbed and my money took. Now my boy is peacefully havin' a drink with some of my riders and this gun-thrower goes in there and starts raisin' hell."

It was not the sheriff who answered.

"I been in town twice," came the soft voice of deadly little Hamp, "and both times you come bellerin' about what somebody done to yer precious son. Both times he

170

started sump'n he couldn't finish when the goin' got rough."

"I ain't talkin' t' you," snarled Peters. "I'm askin' you, Jim—"

"Set, Ed, and simmer down before you bust sump'n inside. Who brung you this tale?"

"Sam, of course."

"Then I suggest you talk to anyone who was at the saloon at the time. Dunc come in the back way and run inter one of your hands. It ain't never come out what he was hunkered back in that dark spot fer. He called Dunc a name for openin' the door on 'im, and since Dunc don't take that frum me ner you ner nobody, he kicked the tail off the ranny and sprawled 'im inter the saloon. Sam took it up and practically called Dunc the same thing. Well, you oughta remember the way Sam uster bully the boys around here in town and the way Dunc was his special victim. 'Cause when anything happened to Sam you always come runnin' and bellerin' and mostly nothin' ever come of it—'cept the day my friend Hamp Wallace here was down at Dave Bridges and you come down there rippin' and snortin'. 'Pears t' me I recollect you went a sight quieter'n you come."

Ed Peters lost his ruddy cast. He turned deliberately to Hamp. "What're you doin' back here?"

"That," said Hamp with deliberate contempt, "ain't a goddam smidgen of your business. Got any more good questions?"

"Yeah. When're you leavin'?"

"Mebbe tonight and mebbe nex' Crissmuss. One damn

thing certain. There ain't nuthin' name of Peters can change my plans none."

"Don't bank on that, Wallace."

"Make you a small bet . . . Say a thousand dollars at two to one."

Peters' piggy eyes were blank. "I'd take that if I was a gamblin' man." He got up and walked out, with the heavy tread of a man past his best weight and age.

"The boy musta got it from you, Hamp."

"Got what?"

"The talent fer makin' enemies."

Hamp laughed. "Hell, Jim. I got so many enemies, I don't even think about 'em any more."

"That don't stop you from bein' careful none."

"That's 'cause I mean to outlive all of 'em. Le's close up 'fore Marthy's supper gits cold."

They took their time closing up, turned out the light and stepped out on the boardwalk. "Just a minnit," said Hamp wriggling his hips as he held his gun harness. "Don't pay none t' rush out inter the open . . . ah . . . see what I mean?"

"No. What'd you see?"

"Le's go back inside a second." They went back into the office but didn't relight the lamp.

"Hamp, I didn't see a damn thing."

"Well . . . I sure as hell did. Lemme tell you any time I goes outside I throws a good look down the street I'm 'spected t' walk on. I don't 'spect t' see a store corner with black bumps on it—'specially bumps what don't stay put. Awright. Take that there scattergun and be ready t' use it. I'm gonna do a little back-prowlin'.

172

You go on out and start walkin'. Try to strike up a little noise, like we was talkin'."

Hamp slipped out the back way and stopped for a second, re-forming what he had seen in his mind's eye. He nodded to himself, bent over and took off his boots, wriggling his toes inside woolen socks. Silently, carrying the boots, he faded into the night.

At the corner of the saddle shop, Kurt Vine waited, listening to the footsteps on the boardwalk. Kurt was hard of face and eye, a partner bouncer to the man killed riding shotgun over Ed Peters' money when the stage had been robbed. He was a dangerous man who had twice been humiliated by the crusty old Wallace and when Peters had whispered into his ear, he had clamped his square jaws shut, nodded eagerly in agreement. Wallace was everything people said, but at night from a dark alley he'd be just another sitting duck, the way Kurt looked at it. He was almost complacent about it, having no regard for the fact that better men than Kurt Vine had failed with the odds even more heavy in their favor.

He could hear muttered conversation as footsteps came closer. Suddenly he was pushed violently from behind and fell sprawling into the deep dust of a street, illuminated by the sickle of a new moon hanging high overhead. His gun was already out and cocked and all he had to do was bring it around and fire. He brought it around but when the gun went off, it was death that had squeezed the trigger and his bullet aimed at the moon fell far short of its mark.

Hamp tilted his own guns, muzzle up, his hard thumbs

hooked over the mule-ears of the hammers. A thin trickle of blue smoke was coming from each muzzle. Jim Walters looked on, his eyes dimmed by memories of the past. "Still use two of 'em, hunh, Hamp?"

"Good habit," said Hamp softly, " 'lessen you figger you might need the other'n fer sump'n else. Now where's Ed Peters' house?"

"Right on down there, around the first corner. Last house on the block."

"Unh hunh. That'n with all them winders?"

"Yeah . . . That's it. Best house in town."

"Le's go to the man and jaw with 'im a while. I got a hankerin' t' see some Christian understandin' come outa his nachal orneriness."

Ed Peters paced up and down in his huge office that was glassed in on three sides and hung with draw curtains. These were drawn but his gross shadow could be seen pacing impatiently up and down. He had heard the shots and now he awaited the news of Hamp Wallace's death. Hamp stopped thirty feet from the house and nodded. "You know that glass puts me in mind of my younger days and I got a notion . . ." Both guns flashed out and began a thundering roll, exploding with the rapidity of a Gatling. When the twelve shots had crashed out on the still air, the office glass was a shambles. Hamp reloaded speedily, cursing the impulse that had made him empty both guns. He was letting enthusiasm run away with his caution.

"Didn't know you carried full cylinders, Hamp."

"Sure do. If a gun of mine ever goes off, 'twon't be no accident. I ain't worried about shootin' myself. Now le's

174

pay Mister Peters a real nice little visit."

Two minutes later Hamp kicked a cowering Peters off the glass-littered floor. "Set up, Peters, and lissen t' the ten commandments compressed inter one. The next man what shoots at me better kill me, 'cause if he don't then I'm comin' just as straight to you as I can come and there won't be no more glass breakin'. Do that filter through that there thick skull on your shoulders?"

"I . . . Please b'lieve me . . . I didn't tell Vine . . ."

"How'd you know it was Vine?"

Peters, his face the color of dough, stammered and gulped.

"Goddam," cursed Walters sourly. "He ain't even smart."

"Naw," agreed Hamp, spitting copiously on the usually immaculate desk top, now covered with shards of glass and fresh tobacco juice. "How'n hell does cooterheads like him ever git rich? Let's go eat."

It took them a while to get to the sheriff's house because of the questions they had to answer from citizens who had rushed into the street, but they finally made it.

14

Dunc had gone through a second, and wholly unnecessary, treatment in a half daze. The closeness of
the girl, the lush warmth of her flawless skin, the gentle
affection of her every touch, all combined to shut out
the rest of the world, barricade him from his troubles.
He had already had his supper with the Mercader
family. Tender veal stewed down with garlic and *chili,
pequeños* that made it searing hot with undeniable
authority, several vegetables and fresh, hot *tortillas*. He
had eaten bountifully, pleasing *Mamacita* greatly, then
had gone out on the tiny porch where Carmelita massaged his hands with balm.

Now, it seemed to him, there was no longer any excuse to stay. "Well, I guess I'll be getting along," he
mumbled miserably. He knew the rigid attitude of
Spanish parents.

Carmelita, wise beyond her years and a true daughter
of Eve, did not need more than the tone of his voice

to assure her that he didn't want to leave. "Must you?"

"I suppose so . . . José and *Mamacita* wouldn't like it if I stayed too late."

She laughed. "Dunc, my parents are Americans. Maybe it does make them feel a little strange, allowing me so much freedom. But they are reasonable. After all, they're right there in the house. They know I can call them, if I need them."

"Sure." He felt foolish and from the ringing in his ears he knew it would only be a matter of minutes before emotion would make him behave foolishly too. A gentle sweat broke out on his forehead. "Carmelita . . ." It had to come. He couldn't stop himself.

"Sí, Dunc?"

"The other night . . . I mean . . ."

She touched his hand. "The other night we were unstrung. Too much had happened."

He choked. "Then—there won't be another night like . . . I mean, you wouldn't . . . ?"

Her hand squeezed his. "Dunc, I have thought so hard about that night. What did it mean? Did it mean that you were hurt and sad—and needed me badly?"

"It meant that, yes. It meant more than that. I need you tonight just as I did then. I need you more . . . In a different way."

"There is something you haven't said, Dunc."

"Yes. There's a lot I haven't said. I'm afraid to say it."

"Don't be afraid . . . Say anything you wish."

"You wouldn't mind?"

"How could I?"

"I love you." His voice was low and husky. "I love

177

you like . . ." He hesitated. What was there to compare with his love? What words would describe the storm in his breast, the delight she gave his eye, the leaping current that raced through him every time she touched him?

"I just love you," he said awkwardly, feeling that he ought to be able to say it better. She was silent for so long that he stole a glance at her. In the pale light of the new moon he could see that her great sapphire eyes were swimming in tears. "Did I say something wrong?" he asked fearfully.

She shook her head slowly. "No, Dunc."

His head dropped a little and he fastened his eyes on the floor. "I'm not too good with words."

Her gasp was quick and sympathetic. "Your words came from the heart and they are the only words I would ever want to hear."

He raised his eyes. "You wanted to hear them?"

"Yes . . . Since the other night I've wanted to hear them."

"I . . . I didn't expect you to say that!"

"I love you, Dunc."

And they were in each other's arms again.

José and his wife, protected by the darkness of the house, smiled at each other and walked back to their own room with careful footsteps. Soon, faintly from soft strings, came the haunting melody of *La Paloma*.

Dunc felt at peace, now that Carmelita's head rested comfortably on his shoulder. "We will be married," he said, breaking a long, comfortable silence.

"When, Dunc . . . ?"

THE GUNFIGHTER

"I have a job to do," he said carefully. "A hard job that will take up most of my time. I could easily be killed. I want to get it finished before we think of a marriage day. Once it is done, then we will speak about a date."

She sighed and settled closer to him. "I will not question or worry you about what you must do. I hate the thought of you being uncomfortable or lonely out in the wide reaches by yourself. I would want to be with you. But a man's work is a man's work and it must be done. It is not for a woman to oppose and hinder her man, but to help and encourage him."

She turned her lips up and they seemed to melt into his until his mind swirled crazily. "I'll have to go," he said regretfully.

"Yes, *corazon*. You will return soon?"

"Soon . . . soon."

He was to return sooner than he expected. If he hadn't been dazed by her shattering attraction he wouldn't have ridden his mount a hundred yards before realizing that something was wrong. He stopped and stiffened. Two red stars . . . He had seen red stars before but they could not be so low, between the horizon and himself. Like an uncoiled spring he leaped from the horse and tied it to one of José's fence posts. He sat down and took off his boots and crept circuitously back toward the house. Like a hunting wolf he circled the grounds silently until he neared the spot where he had seen the red glimmer. He listened carefully. The night was quiet. A coyote yapped in the distance and a range bull moaned fitfully. Then came the voices. He edged closer until he could hear what they said. Both were smoking cigarettes.

"The hoss's gone. We'd have been in a pickle if we'd come rampin' up here all full of noise and fuss. By now we'd be fulla lead. Me, I don't want no part of that there hombre. Pat Dawson still ain't got over that boot in the belly. The boss has been drunk ever since. I ain't never seen a man took like he was . . . Then when he fergot t' cock his gun, I thought I'd bust out laffin'."

"Well, I ain't laffin'. I like this soft job I got. Bring that coal oil on and let's git t'burnin'."

Dunc stood irresolute for a moment wondering what he should do. He could kill them with ease but he didn't kill for pleasure. There should be a better way. He smiled grimly as he followed them. They chose first a small chicken house. He watched silently as they poured the oil around the base of the shack, then one of them tossed a match. The kerosene flared, the shack caught, soon began to burn brightly. The men made a perfect silhouette, but Dunc still did not shoot.

"Awright. Let's git the barns. Boss said t' shet the doors so the livestock couldn't git out."

Dunc drew his right-hand gun and taking cool aim shot the biggest man's weapon from his right hip, tearing the tough leather belt in two and dumping the man on the hard ground.

"You, there," Dunc shouted at the other. "Throw away that iron and don't even look like you want to use it." Instantly the gun thudded on the sod.

"Now, you sons of such, grab them buckets and douse that fire. If it ain't out in three minutes I'll see if I

180

can't liven things up for you."

Stumbling and running from the blazing chicken house to the watering trough and back with buckets of water, they strove valiantly, spurred by the muzzles of the twin guns that seemed to follow their every move. They stumbled and staggered and ran with all their might. Sweat poured from their pores in torrents but they put out the fire in well under the time limit. The Mercader family stood on their back steps and watched the firefighting until the blaze was out, then José came out holding a lamp.

"Mister Alford again," said Duncan sarcastically, as the wet bedraggled men stood before them trembling from weariness and fright. "Seems like you sure like cover for your operations."

Alford wiped his grimy face with a jerky wrist. "How'n hell you know we was out there?"

"I smelled you," said Dunc. He didn't tell them that glowing cigarettes which might be out of view from the house could be in plain view of a man on horseback.

"José, got any wire?"

José brought several lengths of chicken wire and held Dunc's guns while he bound the hands of the prisoners. "Looks like the jail will have customers tonight."

"How long you think we gonna stay in that coop?" said the big man.

"Long enough," said Dunc in chill tones. "The first effort made to sneak you out, I'll shoot you down like dogs. The first scratch you make trying to dig out, I'll pistol whip you till nobody in Texas will be able to recognize you."

He made them walk back to town while he rode behind them, marching them up to the little adobe jail that adjoined the sheriff's office. He shoved them inside and locked the door.

"What about this here wire?" rasped Alford.

"Just keep bending it," said Dunc shortly. "After about five hours it'll break."

15

NEXT MORNING the three friends sat in the sheriff's office. "Now I got prisoners," said Walters, not without pride, "but what am I gonna do with 'em?"

"I wouldn't leave 'em here," said Hamp. "Them bars'd jerk outa that there mud like toothpicks. Tim Bridges'll keep 'em fer us."

"Taking them over to Claytown isn't an invitation to something?" inquired Dunc.

Hamp grinned. "I vow, if this here younker ain't shinin' brighter ever' day. What you say is fact, bub, but things has happened fast, so we gonna keep 'em jumpin'. Come 'ere." He walked to the window and pointed. "See that gully what takes off down the slope there?"

"Yes, sir."

"See them bushes all along the banks of it?"

"Yes, sir."

"See how the trail outa town passes that clump of

183

trees where this wash cuts through half a mile down yonder?"

"Yes, sir."

"Git what I mean?"

"I think so. We'll take them out back, down the gully and wait at the trees for the stage and no one will even know they're gone. Come dinner time we'll take grub in to 'em. Supper the same."

"Well," said Hamp with a laugh. "When you gits the idee you goes right along with it. I'll take 'em over myself. Jim, could you sneak some good man off after dark with my hoss and have him follow?"

"Sure, Hamp. Dunc can do it."

"Nup . . . Got a idee Dunc wants t' do some ramblin' on his own and this ain't nuthin' but a chore. Right, bub?"

"Yes, sir."

"Where you goin'?"

"Oh . . . Places."

"Now look here," snapped Hamp sharply. "Dammit, when I axes you a question, answer me."

Dunc jumped and his nostrils pinched in a little. "Yes, sir. I was going to look around over at the Broken Egg."

Hamp relaxed and smiled. "Good boy. I wasn't bein' nosy but s'pose you went over there and didn't come back? Where'd we look fer you? See my point?"

Dunc dropped his eyes, ashamed. "Yes, sir. I hadn't thought about that."

"Awright. Can't think of ever'thing but while I'm on you, don't you never let a man pull a gun and p'int it at you like you done with Sam Peters."

Dunc grinned. "I had me a hunch about Sam. I've been waiting years to shove something like that down his craw."

"Awright. But don't try it no more."

Dunc worked like a beaver all morning getting together an outfit for an extended trip. He rented a short blocky mare from Jack Wilfred, the livery stable owner, and adjusted the pack to the mare as an experiment. She took it well, so he left it on her for an hour to let it contour itself. Sweaty and grimed with horsehair and dust, he took a bath in the rear of the barber shop, donned new denims and a blue shirt, buckled on his guns and went to the hotel to eat.

As he entered he saw Walter Koenig and several other ranchers seated at a table. Walter waved and beckoned. Dunc went over to their table. Walter got up, perspiring and beaming. "Dis iss der new deppity," he said importantly. "Dunc, shake mit der hands of Jared Walker, Joe Favron, Kenny Remington und Cheff Keller." Dunc shook hands around with politeness and a touch of humility. "Friends off mine. Dis is der poy off whom I was telling you much."

Jared Walker, a grizzled old man whose years of hard riding and hard driving showed in the craggy planes and peaks of his powerful face, said, "Been hearin' a lot about you, son. I'm plumb glad the law finally got some teeth in its head around here. Ever think of runnin' fer sheriff?"

"No, sir," said Dunc stolidly. "I'm just a deputy."

Remington laughed. "With him as deputy it won't matter who's sheriff."

"It will to me," replied Dunc shortly. "I deputy under no other man."

There was a short uncomfortable silence, then Walter said, "Now, son, don't get at me wrong but dere is a question ve would like to ask you. Did Jim Walters ever tell you to not going about looking into what Felton Wade he iss doing?"

"No, sir—and that was my first official act. I went to Wade's place and persuaded him to show me where my father was buried."

The silence was thicker this time and took longer to break. "That," mused the dark Favron, "must have taken some doing."

"Damn if I ever heard of the like," snorted Jared Walker. "Then he did kill Dave . . . Why didn't you bring him in?"

Dunc shrugged. "For what? He denied everything, of course. Finding a dead man buried on a place doesn't constitute evidence against the owner of the land. All of you," pointed out Dunc, with growing confidence, "have been thinking only of Wade. It is my opinion that only the cattle end of it is him. Meat and stage robbery don't seem to fit."

"Why?" asked Jeff Keller. "It ain't but a small step from one kind of outlawry to another."

"That's true," agreed Dunc, "but I think most of these things follow a pattern. Most of you must have bumped into rustlers or bank robbers or train agents. Did they ever spread out in their operations?"

Walker shook his head slowly, his bushy white brows knitting. "Well, the bank and train robbers did, but they was always after the same thing . . . money. When you come right down to it, I sorta agree with you. Once a rustler, always a rustler. Reckon there's some exceptions but I'd go along with that idee till I was proved wrong."

The others nodded and Walter Koenig nodded more vigorously than the rest. "Dis poy he was the first to think about dem mules I haff . . . from dot last thiefing. Mex mules and to him dot means something."

"What?" asked Walker, his ram jaw jutting forward.

Dunc sighed. "It's just an idea so far . . . Something I worked out wondering where all that meat went."

"Across der porder, mine stuff," said Koenig. "Der vagons were trailed dot far."

"Yes, sir. You told me that. We know that the cattle are going over the border. I think I know where and when I come back I think I'll have some news."

"Where you going?" asked Remington.

Dunc made a big southward gesture. "All over."

"That's considerable territory," said Favron with a wry smile. "What do you expect to find?"

Dunc smiled. "I'll tell you when I get back. I just might have to call on you-all for help, too."

"You locate the drain," said Walker grimly, "and you won't hafta worry about help. Just name it and you'll get it." The others nodded assent.

Late that afternoon, his gear all in order, Dunc visited the sheriff's office. "Did Mr. Wallace make out all right with those men?"

"Not a hitch," said the sheriff, looking spryer than he

had in a long time. "By the way, Sam Peters come in wantin' t' bail the men."

"What'd you tell him?"

"I told him they were in a safe place."

"Did he want to talk to them?"

"Yeah. What he really wanted was to be sure they was here. He saw they wasn't, so he won't be tryin' t' pull the place down. Said he didn't know nuthin' about what they was doin' at José's place."

"Which, of course, is a lie," said Dunc harshly.

" 'Course. He'll git 'round t' findin' 'em, I guess. Might git bail on 'em, at that. Or he might wind up in there with them." Jim Walters looked out through the fly-specked window. "Takin' a pack?" he asked, after a time.

"I rented a mare from Wilfred. All I have to do is cinch the pack."

Walters shifted and looked at his young deputy. His eyes were warm with affection. "I got a little present for you, son."

"Present—?"

"Yeah. I'm gonna give you young Devil."

Dunc gasped. Second only to his wife came Jim Walter's horses. He had but a few, all of gray Arabian stock, however, and he was proud of them to a fault. Young Devil was the son of Old Devil, who brought the highest stud fee in south Texas. A thrill pebbled the skin of Dunc's back. "Mr. Walters, I can't take a horse like that from you. It'd be like taking one of your kids."

Jim Walters' eyes were damp but he shook his head stubbornly. "It got back to me what you told them men at the hotel t'day . . . 'bout not deppityin' fer no other sheriff. Kinda made me feel good. Young Devil needs a strong hand. He's too swift and gingery for a man my age. Tell Wilfred I said let you have 'im. Let 'im know right off who's boss and you'll have the hoss of a lifetime."

When Dunc rode out of town that night, a thin small rider who had been in and out of the saloon a dozen times made a line for his own mount. Flogging the animal into a hard run he took a circuitous route out of town.

He made contact with some friends staked out along the trail, but apparently his efforts were wasted.

Because two hours later, Sam Peters cursed his men thickly, being better than half drunk. "You mean to sit there on horseflesh and tell me a man leading a pack animal just run through you like a ghost? Five of you—and two should have been too many."

"We were spread out over half a mile," said Buck Eldridge, who was fast losing patience with his erratic boss. He drew good wages and the work wasn't too hard, but bushwhacking had not been mentioned when he'd hired out to the Broken Egg. Eldridge had had more than one brush with the law in his time and had slapped a running iron on many an unbranded maverick. He had even made free with branded stuff and knew all the secrets of the wet blanket and other methods of making brands seem what they were not.

But Buck had never dry-gulched a man. He had never

189

beaten a woman. He had a profound respect for courage. His boss had shown little of that quality and the man he, Buck, was supposed to stop had shown much. Not for nothing had Buck detailed his men so that he himself drew the stand in the bottom of the bushy draw wandering south out of town. He had heard nothing that would indicate the passage of a horse and pack animal; but then, Buck had spent his time rolling and lighting innumerable cigarettes, nor had he made any attempt to stop his horse when the animal pricked up his ears and whistled piercingly. "He,'" continued Eldridge, "mighta took out south but that don't mean he kept on this-away."

"If he didn't," said Sam, draining a pint bottle and throwing it into the brush, "then I don't care where he went. I'm meeting some important people from Mexico in a few days and I don't want him sneaking around and looking on. Hear anything at the saloon, Pete?"

"Yeah," said Pete Amber, the dried-up rider who had watched Dunc from the saloon gallery. "Wagonload o' hides is leavin' Peters' General Merchandise t'morrer fer Claytown."

Sam cursed. "Who gives a damn about hides?"

"What'll be under them hides, Pete?" asked Eldridge humorously, realizing that Amber had meant more than he told.

"Five thousand dollars in gold and greenbacks."

Sam jerked erect. "Well, why'n hell didn't you say so? Pete, you and Tom Young ought to be able to take care of that. If it's a wagonload of hides, then there won't be anybody riding shotgun."

THE GUNFIGHTER

"We'll take it," agreed Young. "Ward Smith says you was a hunnerd dollars short on his split."

"Damn pencil pusher . . . Who does he think he is, with us taking all the risk . . ."

"*Who*—takin' all the risk?" asked Eldridge softly. Sam's eyes seemed to burn in the night like an animal's. "Don't try to rile me, Buck. I'll take just so much off you. Any time you want your pay, you can get it."

Eldridge laughed. "I'll remember that—boss."

"All right. See that you do. Now all of you split up and rake these hills, washes and creek bottoms from here to the border. If you think it's safe, slide on over onto the Flying Y. Watch your step, though."

"Flyin' Y sure's got some likely lookin' red stuff over on that southwest range near the river," said Tom Young wistfully.

"Let 'em rest," said Sam. "One day before soon we'll stop all this penny ante scrounging and when we make our big run . . . You'll see."

16

When Dunc, riding out, had first reached the edge
of town he had drawn up in the shadow of Ed
Peters' warehouse, a rambling building that covered
a good quarter acre of ground. He searched the horizon
south and west for a long time. There was still a faint
glow from the sunset in the west so he gingerly threw a
leg over the swell of his saddle to wait. Young Devil be-
haved like a veteran and only shot his short satiny ears
forward to help his new master search the lay of the
land.

Dunc felt as if he was astride a bundle of muscle-
shot dynamite, so springy and strong were the big
Arabian's movements, but he knew that in a battle of
speed the horse would show a clean pair of heels to anything he would be likely to encounter. Even a superior
cowman's bronc would be left behind, for this horse
had been range-ridden and was experienced in speeding
over rugged terrain, low brush and dry washes. He had

192

never known cruelty and the first day Walters had ridden him after hand-feeding since colthood, he had trotted tamely away carrying his master like a veteran. Once allowed to really cut loose and run, though, he was hard to hold and resented being reined in. Dunc had no fears about that. He had topped and tamed some of the worst in his three years of riding for Rolando Camara-Peon.

Walters had fired both side-gun and rifle from the horse's back almost from the first, to accustom him against the day when a gun-shy horse could mean death.

Darkness settled down, but there was a pretty bright moon overhead, this fact worrying Dunc no little. He had searched all his equipment for shiny surfaces and treated them with shoe blacking, but he still did not like the light. A horse and a pack animal could be sighted too easily.

He dropped his right leg back in place and shoved a booted foot into the stirrup. Once again he examined the horizon before him—caught his breath, strained his eyes. On the moonwashed side of the draw he had seen the flare of a match. It was quickly gone but he felt certain that a cigarette butt glowed like a ruby pinpoint too far away for him to see. He smiled and turned away from the draw, heading down the trail toward the Flying Y. After half a mile he left the trail and curved toward the southeast, taking advantage of every declivity, sink and depression, hugging the shade side of stunted cedar, post oak and mesquite brush, picking his trail slowly and carefully so that his horses might not set up a clatter striking their hoofs against loose rocks. It was nearly midnight when he finally reached the Flying Y boundary. He knew he was on Broken Egg property now and nearing the place at which he hoped to make camp.

On his last ride out to visit with Felton Wade he had done considerable scouting, just as he had done every other time he had had the chance, and by now he knew the lay of the land. The spot he had in mind for a semi-permanent camp was very near the border, among a nest of badly eroded gulches and arroyos—too meagerly grassed to attract cattle, yet with enough grazing along the bottom and sides of the gulch for his own animals. This sink, known as Hell's End, almost achieved the stature of a canyon and though well-suited to Dunc's purpose was also the biggest of the many rips of erosion that spread toward the Rio Grande like the fingers of a hand.

Dunc's chief danger came from the fact that the wide gravelly bottom carried sign too well. Thus far he had done a masterly job of following trails already so tracked up that his own would be lost among the many. But he knew that here such sign would be less since the grazing was poor.

He followed Hell's End until it flattened out into the rugged arid flat just short of the river, crossed it and headed north again. Finally he reached the spot he had sought. A small deep wash so narrow it allowed just enough space for two horses abreast. The bottom was rocky with patches of gravel, cluttered with boulders that had split from the rim—bad and slow going but allowing passage with a minimum of sign. The wash came to a dead end widening into a natural circle, the rim of which was thickly crusted with a tangle of chaparrel. Unless a rider came within a few feet of the edge and peered over, he could see nothing below.

Dunc dismounted and tied the mare with a lariat to allow her browsing space, unshelled the big gray stallion and turned the saddle upward to dry out. He took out his bedroll and, crawling beneath an overhang of brush, placed it carefully, first cleaning away any rocks large enough to make bumpy sleeping. He returned to the open and sat on the saddle blanket to eat a thick sandwich Marthy Walters had made for him. She had made a huge bagful of them and these Dunc intended to make last a long time. After they were gone, he'd have to rely on bacon and beans with two big loaves of homemade bread. He decided against making coffee tonight. Tomorrow night or at midday he might attempt it but he was afraid now to make too much of a fire.

After eating, he took a swallow of water from a canteen and rolled in his blanket. But he lay awake for some time thinking of Carmelita, dreaming of the time she would warm the circle of his arms with her lovely body . . . His very own wife. He smiled and fell asleep.

Felton Wade looked closely at the squatty puncher before him. He was burned almost black from long hours in the sun and sticky dark hair was matted all over his head, crimped down on his forehead to give him a brutish look. "I'm tellin' you I seen him with my own two eyes. He was gettin' on the stage, half a mile outside of town, herdin' two of Sam Peters' boys ahead of 'im. Now if that there ol' rattler done staked out here, I'm movin'. I had a brush with the Rangers onct and I know Hamp Wallace. He don't hafta be dead certain you had anything to do with killin' a law officer. All he got to do is hope so—and you're a gone goslin'. I heerd about Zimmerman after I had been here a while—"

"But I heard that new deputy had killed Wallace."

"Heerd that story awright. Heerd another too. T'other one said he took the boy under 'is wing. Give 'im Zimmerman's hoss and guns, sent 'im t' Mexico to some high-class greaser's place and made 'im stay there till he growed up. Now they's both back, and I'm leavin'. This here range done got too damn crowded fer Alp Shofer. I wants my time."

Wade was pale. His usually fine clear skin looked muddy and old. He sighed, turned to the safe and counted out the puncher's time. "All right, Shofer. There it is. Don't guess I blame you too much, the way you feel."

"I guess you know. What if Hamp Wallace gits a look at you?"

"I hope he doesn't. I'm a lot older and I've changed since those wild days but I don't suppose I could convince him of that."

"I wouldn't try to convince him that the sun was gonna come up in the mawnin'. Well, I'm shovin'."

An hour later, Wade stood on the front veranda of the ranchhouse and watched Allison come from the bunkhouse. Wade felt old and mortally weary, wishing he had the spring of the man approaching. His lips

196

tightened and he thought . . . Maybe he's younger but, God, how stupid. At least I have a few brains left. I know when the water gets too deep to wade in.

"You look like hell," offered Allison bluntly. "What's the matter?"

"Hamp Wallace is back in Big Bend."

Allison stiffened. "Couple of fellers tole me they had heard that, but I didn't pay it no mind. Who tole you?"

"Alp Shofer. He lit out."

"Yeller," averred Allison tightly. "Yeller."

"Maybe so," muttered Wade abstractly. "Then on the other hand, taking into consideration that he's got only one life, he may be smart."

Allison's glance was blistering. "You gettin' soft?"

"I don't care what you call it, Jugg," snarled Wade savagely. "What's soft to you might turn out to be the seven pillars of wisdom all decked out in pink ribbon."

Allison didn't follow this line of talk at all and looked baffled.

Wade's laugh was hard. "Sorry, old boy. I had forgotten about the limitations of your intellectual digestion. Go take a dose of soda."

"I come to tell you sump'n," said Allison doggedly. "I been in touch."

"Is that a fact? What's new?"

"He wants two-three-fo' thousand head of cattle. Don't make no difference how good they is, just so they got meat. He'll pay ten dollars a head. He's been in touch with Sam Peters, too."

"Why so many, all of a sudden?"

"I don't know, but one of 'is men tole me he's gonna

197

cut 'em up in small bunches and gradually start filterin' 'em around southward among small ranchers and them bandits as is hid out livin' off the big ranchers. Plenty folks graze up a little grass with stole stock, and the big boys just let 'em 'cause it's sich a small-time affair. Then when this bird wants cattle while he's on the march there'll always be some not too fur away."

Wade considered. "Sounds so sensible that it's a wonder the man'd tell you any such thing."

"Got 'im drunk and he started makin' brags about what a wunnerful feller his *patron* was. Sounds like a right story to me."

Wade turned and took a hide-bottomed rocker. "Jugg, you've seen the end of a long period of good living. This country is just about to blow sky high. There'll be a lot of people go up with it, and all on account of your wet-eared kid and a salty old bastard named Hamp Wallace. With Wallace at the wheel, and that's where he is, there'll be hell to pay. I know that the men, and maybe you too, have wanted to make a big sweep here and pull stakes. I opposed it because I liked it here. However, the climate is getting a little too warm for me."

Allison looked up eagerly. "Then we'll pull it?"

Wade's eyes hardened. "Jugg, if I have to leave here, I hope to be riding my horse at a fox trot. Unless you can come up with a scheme to kill Hamp Wallace and Duncan Stewart, go away some place and let me think."

Allison got up and walked back toward the bunkhouse, his mind working furiously. It had been piling up in him for a long time, this corrosive hate of the boy who had made him take water and now he had tacit if not direct approval to do something about it. He knew his own men well, too well to include them all in his scheme, so he picked four, ordered them to arm heavily and pack food for several days.

The group mounted and rode away from the ranch-house and were several miles off before they were told of their goal. One man quit cold and without even wasting words rode back to the bunkhouse where he tarried for only half an hour. He didn't even ask for his pay.

Wade had watched them leave, chuckled sardonically. Turning, he went back to his office, took out a sheet of paper. His eyes seemed to be peering into the past. They took on a glaze of fatalism.

"Hampton Wallace, Esq.," he wrote . . .

17

Hamp Wallace stretched comfortably in the best chair afforded by the sheriff's office and grinned. "Two plumb surprised hombres," he said in his soft drawl. "Never thought they'd wind up in a fer true concrete jail. Tim Bridges was glad to see 'em. Gladder to see me. Me'n him swapped lies over a bottle which I finished on the way back. Got me a shave and a haircut, too." The puffs of side whiskers had boundaries as sharp as a mapline. His moustache had been waxed and the points sprouted insolently toward his ears. His skin was baked to a permanent red bronze which no razor could alter.

Jim Walters, recognizing the signs as of old, grinned and brought out a pint bottle. "Help yerself. The effeck must be runnin' down."

"Hit is," said Hamp and helped himself lavishly. "Where's Dunc?"

"Gone. Took a pack horse. He'll either know sump'n

when he comes back or he won't come back."

"Ten dollars . . . two to one."

"Nope. He just might do it. Fact is, I'm dependin' on 'im."

"Me too. Sump'n about that boy . . ."

"Hamp, what does it take to make a badman?"

"Talent and a gun, with a fool in between. That answer yer question?"

"Not 'xactly. Guess mebbe I didn't word it right. What I mean is this. The boy ain't no badman . . ."

"Now, looky here," said Hamp. He tilted the bottle, gurgled and put it down, wiping his mouth on the back of his hand. "No . . . Fust thing, the boy ain't bad. He's just hell on wheels when somebody thinks they is. He's on the side of the law and I grant you he done throwed his weight around some. A man's got t' do that. If he don't, ever' ranny in the country'll be wantin' t' take 'im on. If Dunc had been a killer, Sam Peters woulda been dead three times."

"What three times?"

"Fust time when he went fer his gun. Second time when he stood there like a chicken with a goozle fulla cornmeal. Third time when he pulled the gun. They ain't but three reasons t' pull a gun. To shoot it, to clean it or to hand it over to a better man. That Dunc boy's got eyes. He uses 'em. He's got a head on 'im. He uses that. He ain't no headlong jackass lookin' fer the odds to take care of 'im. He'll take some chances . . . 'course. Man who won't take one is always the one left at the waterin' trough. But he ain't got a mushmellon fer a head. I'm bettin' on 'im."

THE GUNFIGHTER

A knock came at the door and Walters opened it. A wrinkled Chinese stood in the door. He looked extremely silly in oversized range clothing. "You sheliff?"

"Yep. What's on your mind?"

"You savvy Hamp Wallace?"

"That's him right there."

The old man shuffled in and handed Hamp an envelope. "Lighting flom boss."

Hamp squinted at the celestial. "Who boss, Charlie?"

"Boss man Lade . . . Flying Y."

"Wade, hunh? Wait. Might be some answer."

He opened it, read and lifted a briar-like eyebrow at Walters. "Here's sump'n fer you to read."

Walters took the note and read the flowery Spencerian script.

Hampton Wallace, Esq.,

Honored Sir, I write this to tell you of something which might interest you. As you know, I am the owner of a large ranch and I must painfully admit that there have been times when I was not as careful about whom I hired as I might have been. Trust time to bear me evidence of that. Several of my men have ridden away from the ranch for the purpose of killing you and your protegé, Duncan Stewart. I am not a gunfighter so I could not stop them. Had I tried, you would not be reading this note. Since I have gone this far, I will go further and tell you that you will possibly remember me as Wade Murdock and understand why I am not going under that name now. I tell you this to assure you of my sincerity. Since this admission might well bring some action from you, please remember that I realized this fact when I wrote the note and be assured that I await your pleasure in an entirely peaceful manner and with no designs against your person.

In all things your obedient servant,

Wade T. Murdock.

Hamp's eyes slitted and his mind went back to a robbery, a dead man and the fog surrounding the occurrence. It had looked bad for Wade Murdock then . . . And they had come to an agreement. Many things had happened since that hot rainy night just across the Sabine river.

"Skeeters . . . Jesus, the skeeters," muttered Hamp.

"Skeeters! What skeeters?" asked Walters.

"Oh . . . er, nuthin'. I was just thinkin' back. Charlie, I'll tack a note on the back of this here paper." He wrote rapidly in a harsh upright hand and returned it to the envelope. "Give this to boss man. Savvy?"

"Me savvy. Give boss man, chop chop."

"You like drinkee, Charlie?"

"Sure as hell likem dlink."

"Take this bottle with you. Keeps off fevers, chills and boogers."

"Thankee, thankee much. Goo' day."

"What'd you tell 'im, Hamp?"

"Tole him t' keep his britches clean, that I'd see 'im when the sperrit moved me."

203

"Wonder if Sam'll bother old José again?" mused Walters. "Sure would hate to see that little gal git hurt."

Hamp chewed his bottom lip for a while and shook his head. "Sam Peters is a hydrophoby skunk. Ain't no tellin' what he'll do. Offhand I'd say, no. If he does, then right there, Jim, the fertilizer done hit the flyin' jenny."

"You gonna pay Felton Wade a visit?"

"Think I will. But first I'll sorta drift down south and ride flank on Dunc. He might need me."

Hamp saddled up, mounted and drove to a small clump of cottonwoods soaring grandly over a thick growth of lesser trees and brush. Hamp always liked to look before he leaped and not seldom was the habit productive. He dismounted, took from a saddle bag a collapsible brass spyglass that might have belonged to Jean Lafitte, and spent the next thirty minutes observing the horizon and between for suspicious indications. His inspection was tireless and painstaking. He did not miss the four riders approaching from the east. He did not miss the washing José's wife was hanging out with the help of her daughter. He nodded approvingly at the daughter after having given her a good deal more scrutiny than was strictly necessary. Neither did he miss a couple of dark masses that showed up in the clump of bush, blackjack scrub and mesquite, at the spot where he had taken his two passengers aboard the stage the day before. He noticed that the lumps, not present the day before, were far enough off the trail not to attract notice unless someone like Hamp had been looking.

Toward the northeast nearly three miles away he

brought a slow-moving wagon under his glass. It was the same one he had seen drive off from Peters' warehouse while he had been walking to the livery stable. Finally the wagon climbed the crest of the faraway hill and disappeared. As soon as it did the lumps moved out of cover and ten minutes later two riders trotted into sight on the trail toward Claytown.

Hamp twisted his moustache until the points spiked bravely. He mounted slowly and rode easily toward the northeast. He was curious.

When the riders passed out of sight at the spot where the wagon had disappeared, Hamp spurred the buckskin into a long, distance-eating lope and was soon lost in the pall of drifting dust and shimmering heat waves.

As the trail to Claytown cuts over the first of a series of low hills sliced by dry gullies and one small creek, the timber increases and near the creek it becomes fairly thick. Hamp, with the experience of years behind him, read sign before he saw it and came upon the two horses tied in a thick growth of scrub oak. He parked his own mount a hundred yards away, came back and sat out of sight of the horses, his back resting comfortably against the bole of a small tree. He bit a corner off a new plug of B. F. Gravely's Superior and sucked at it with every evidence of relish until he had dislodged several strands of lint and a couple of grains of sand. Separating this debris from the mother lode by a process all his own he spit copiously and began to sing in a low whispery voice.

THE GUNFIGHTER

*Oh, when I'm free as I can be and the Lincoln
boys don't bind me,
I'll make my way back to the gal, to the gal I left
behind me.
Oh, coffee grows on the white oak tree and Red
River flows like brandee
I'll make my way back to the gal, to the gal I left
behind me.*

He smiled comfortably and closed his eyes against
the pitiless disc of the sun that soared in midmorning
grandeur, practicing up for what it would do to the earth
in an hour or so and on till sundown. If the heat bothered Hamp he gave no evidence of it and soon snoozed
peacefully, his lips popping gently.

Fifteen minutes later a stick broke the dead stillness
with a faint explosion like a chinaberry popgun and the
amber eyes came open and instantly recorded whatever came within their scope. He might not have been
asleep at all. He stood up casually, moved a single
broad oak leaf and saw whatever he needed to see and
sat down again. Fifteen minutes later he heard the
creak of stirrup leathers as two men mounted and took
off at a run toward Big Bend.

Hamp waited for a while, then, spitting luxuriously
against a boulder, walked out into the clearing and
straight across it to a small flat rock. He stood over it
for a moment before hunkering down and lifting it. His
agile fingers delved into the loose earth and finally came
up with a heavy bag. He opened the bag and let the
gold coins slide out, then pushed them back. He threw

the bag over his shoulder, cursing the weight of gold money, and walked to the buckskin. Halving the bag by circling it with thumbs and forefingers and shaking it vigorously, he threw it across the saddle and mounted.

It was some thirty minutes past noon when he rode back into Big Bend and turned his horse down an alley. He could hear Ed Peters bellowing at men working on his office, replacing the glass that had been broken. Peters stood bareheaded in the sun and his bald spot gleamed redly and sweat glistened in beaded globules. He looked around as Hamp rode up and glowered. "What the hell do you want now?"

"Nothin', suh," said Hamp, so meekly that Peters blinked with suspicion. This was not the Hamp Wallace he knew. "Just wondered what was on that wagon you sent down the trail this mornin'."

"Then keep wonderin'," snarled Peters ill-temperedly. "I wouldn't give you the time of the day."

"Er . . . well now, that there ain't no Christian attitude, Mr. Peters. I come 'round t' pay you fer breakin' yer winders."

Peters blinked again, his mouth half open with surprise. "You . . . ugh!" The sack of gold struck him smartly in the belly, causing him to sit down with spine-jarring abruptness. Peters grabbed the sack by the throat and scrambled to his feet, cupidity and astonishment fighting each other, eventually yielding to panic. His face purpled as he held the sack and gazed at it.

"Where'd you git this here sack?" he yelled.

"Oh—up the trail a piece. Think that'll cover the glass breakage?"

"Payin' me with my own damned money. That's high-bindery. That's insult. That's . . ."

"Recovery," supplied Hamp. "I wouldn't give you a plugged *centavo* for breakin' them winders. I oughta throwed a couple of slugs inter that bag of tripe you got there where a man carries a belly."

Peters calmed down with a suddenness that looked painful. "What happened?" he croaked.

"They knowed you had the money under them hides. All they done was wait till your man forded the creek and stopped t' let the mules drink, then they jumped 'im."

Peters looked at the sack again and swallowed. "What did they do with the rest of it?"

"Buyin' drinks with it over at your own saloon, I'd guess."

"My money . . . my saloon . . . Goddammit, who done it?"

"A couple of riders. I didn't know 'em, but I will if I see 'em again."

"You seen 'em take it?"

"I was hid out at their hosses. They come back, buried the gold, put the paper in money belts and lit out. I dug up the gold. I didn't try to bring 'em in 'cause I figgered they'd stick around somewhere near here, 'lessen they thought somebody was on their trail—they wouldn't want to get too far from that gold. In fac', I think I already spotted the hosses. In front of the saloon."

Peters jerked. "Wait here a minnit."

He came back with a .45 strapped to his side. "Will you identify them mens . . .? If you do, I'll make it worth your while. I'll pay a good bounty."

"Nemmine the reward. I wants 'em for the lockup in Claytown. That's where I sent them boys of yourn what tried to burn out old José."

"Le's go," said Peters, ignoring Hamp's accusation. He strode toward the saloon, his head still bare and sweating.

A blazed-face roan with white fetlocks and a round-barreled sorrel were tied to the hitching rail. Peters stared at the horses but he didn't stop until he was inside. There were only two men at the bar. Ed Peters turned and faced Hamp. "Them's Sam's boys. You musta made a mistake. That's Pete Amber. Other one is Pecos Young."

"I don't care if they's Judge Roy Bean and Simple Simon," rasped Hamp. "They's the bucks what done it."

Peters looked undecided. "Now look, them's good boys and . . ."

Hamp cursed low and stepped in front of Peters. The men had turned around and were looking curiously at the newcomers.

Amber nodded politely and smiled at Peters who scowled and looked baffled.

Hamp pointed a finger and said, "You there, shorty. You and that other buck come over here."

"Who said?" asked Amber sneeringly.

"I said. You wanta come or be dragged?"

Amber looked at Pecos Young who, recognizing the caliber if not the identity of the little man, went pale and walked hesitantly toward Hamp and Peters. Amber, feeling that the house was about to fall in on him, did the very thing to hasten the tragedy. Half-hidden by the advancing Young, he drew, putting everything he had into it. But Hamp, falling to one knee to get out of line with Young, triggered at Amber from the right hip twice, so rapidly that the explosions seemed to blend. Amber stumbled forward as though trying to run and collapsed, digging his head into the splintery floor.

Pecos Young, frightened half out of his wits, stood trembling, his hand elevated. "What . . . what . . ?"

Hamp got up and dusted off a knee. "Young, produce that money belt you got next t' your skin and if you come out with a gun you'll make me powerful mad."

Young, his eyes denying any intention of trickery, gingerly unloaded the money belt from his middle.

"Now," directed Hamp, "perfawm fer your pal there. He don't look none too pert."

Hamp handed the money belt to Peters. "You think your son pays men that kinda money?"

"Hell, no," exploded Peters, relieved that he could command his tongue.

Young came back with the second belt and at Hamp's direction handed it to Peters. "Now—you. Who pulled that there other robbery I heard about?"

"Amber, Trask and Sam Peters."

Ed Peters dropped the belts with a thud. "That's a lie."

Pecos Young shrugged. "Ask your own warehouse clerk, Ward Smith."

Peters, face as pale as the white of an egg, tottered to the bar. "Gimme . . . whiskey. Big glass."

He drank thirstily, put the glass down and whirled

around. "I still believe it's a lie."

"Sure you do, Ed," said Hamp gently. "You never b'lieved anything against your boy before, why should you start now? What say we go see Ward Smith?"

"No," said Peters, his voice cracking. "No . . . I ain't . . ."

Hamp's eyes narrowed. "Oh yes, by God, you is. We're gonna run this thing down right now. Dunc was pretty smart about Sam, after all. Come on." He led the way toward Ed Peters' big warehouse.

Ward Smith proved a pathetic-looking dyspeptic, pimply of face and watery of eye, weak-chinned and spineless. He admitted culpability readily. "Sam made me do it," he blubbered.

"Lies . . . lies," shrieked Peters, and rushed at the snuffling bookkeeper. Hamp grabbed one of Peters' arms and hurled a hip into the fat man, hard, dumping him into a pile of second-hand harness and hames. "Any o' that done, Ed, I'll do it. Now, boy, what'd you say?"

"He made me . . . Sam did. I usta sneak him things from the store and maybe a little cash now'n then, and he threatened to tell on me if I didn't let him know when the money went out."

"Ed," snapped Hamp. "How many people knew about this last shipment?"

Ed Peters spoke from the floor. "Me and Ward . . . that's all and so help me, if . . ."

"Shet up."

Ed's face went paler and his lips shut in a hard line. But he opened them to shout, "Ward."

Hamp reached down and hauled the fat man to his

211

feet with a lunge that almost threw him again. His hot eyes bored into Ed's pale blue ones. "Now, Ed, come on back here where we can talk quiet-like."

Later Hamp was telling Jim Walters about it. "But how'd you make 'im keep Ward Smith, 'stead of firing him?" the sheriff wondered.

"I tole 'im we'd fergit them robberies, far as Sam's concerned. Never fear. Dunc was right. Now that we know, we'll git Sam on sump'n else."

"What about that Pecos Young?"

Hamp grinned, chose a hide chair and skidded down onto his backbone. "Hell, Jim, I'm gittin' meller in my ole age. He wasn't nuthin' but a paid hand. He talked plenty and didn't need no urgin'. I tole 'im t' light a shuck. 'Sides that, I didn't feel like takin' no more trips t' Claytown. It's a rat hole."

"What-all did Pecos tell you?"

"Enough to know that Dunc's got a head on his shoulders. All he had t' start with was the s'picion that Sam'd do just about anything what come to 'is mind. I guess if he'll rob his own daddy, he sure will do anything." He got to his feet and settled his middle into his gun harness with a wriggle. "Guess I'll work my way down t' the rim and go fer a little ride."

"When'll you be back?"

"Hard t' say, Jim. I might slide over to see Wade Murdock . . . That is, if me'n Dunc don't git too busy down around Rio Bravo."

"You gonna need my help?"

THE GUNFIGHTER

"Thanks, Jim. Time ain't ripe yet fer a man your age to be gallivantin' over that range."

"*My* age! Why, you wizened old runt! I'm leastways young as you, any day."

"Feelin' your oats agin, these days, hey? 'Tain't that, Jim. No insult to your old bones intended. But there's nothin' fer you to do out there—Dunc is takin' care of it, and I'll take care of Dunc. So you just take care of things in Big Bend while we're gone."

PART THREE

Lawman

18

DUNC had ridden hard both day and night. He had become a spectre that drifted with the shadows, a range ghost here one moment, then gone, light-footed, noiseless, haunting the Broken Egg like bad luck. Even young Devil seemed to realize the seriousness of the situation; he had ceased giving any vocal acknowledgement of the smell of mares, amorous or otherwise. His delicate ears would point but he swallowed his emotions like the noble animal he was and emitted no whinny.

The Broken Egg main house, a big but rough and sprawling affair of stone with bunkhouse and several outbuildings, sat sedately in a grove of cottonwoods where the Rapid wound its way southward, making a curve much like the one that gave Big Bend its name.

There was a dog hanging around the bunkhouse, a half-starved mongrel no one bothered to feed. He had to rustle for his nourishment, but his loyalty was as stout as his voice was harsh. The first night Dunc examined the place the cur had come dashing out, yelping loud enough to wake the dead and, more important, stationing himself in such manner as to give away Dunc's position. With some regret, Dunc had drawn a gun and killed it. Devil pricked up his ears at the uproar which erupted seconds later. Dunc reloaded, smiling, and watched men rush out of the bunkhouse. He spoke to Devil and they faded into the night, pulling up half a mile away in the shadow of a thin strip of timber that straggled along a dry creek bed. Dunc had left by the same route he had used going in, a route also taken by several riders earlier that day. When he had ejected the empty from his gun, he had put it in his pocket so the mounted men who thoroughly scoured the immediate area found no sign. Two of them rode close enough to Dunc for him to hear what they were saying.

"I ain't never seen Sam with jitters like he got tonight!"

"His ol' man was out t'day and give him whut fer on account of them robberies. Sam coulda done anything else in the world and ol' Ed woulda stuck by 'im. But when it comes t' money, that's the end. Money's Ed's fust love. Sam comes secunt."

"Yeah, and Sam's really been hittin' the bottle. I ain't seen 'im sober since Stewart momucked him up so bad at Big Bend. That got 'im sump'n turrible. Folks say he'n Stewart's hadda feud since they was . . ." The conversation dimmed as they rode toward the ranch house. Dunc waited until they were some seventy yards away and quietly dismounted. He leaned against a tree, took careful aim and rapped out two fast shots. Instantly the horses the men were riding went into a spasm of frenzied bucking, stung by fright and the rake of a .45 bullet through each hide, burning like salt on a fresh wound. The riders, taken by surprise, yelled, "Whoa . . . Whoa!" Probably because he inadvertently roweled his horse with his spurs one man went sailing off awkwardly into a dense growth of prickly pear, bawling louder than the stung horses. The second rider lasted a little longer, then he too succumbed to a stint of sunfishing that sent his hat in one direction, his gun in another and his body in a third.

Hoofs thudding from several other directions made Dunc rein back. Flanking the creek bed on the shadow side, he quietly melted into the night.

For two days Dunc had been avoiding Jugg Allison and his three men. He had watched them trail him, screened from their eyes by brush or peeping over the tops of washes. He wondered what their purpose was, other than to do him damage, but avoided them because his object was the Broken Egg at the moment, not the Flying Y. As night drew near Dunc would seek some well-worn and recently tracked trail and lose them. But the next day they would make a big circle and soon come on his sign again. Young Devil's new caulked shoes could be picked out easily enough as long as they were not too mixed up with other tracks. Yet Dunc managed to stay ahead of them or behind them as the humor suited him, and more often than not the trailers were the trailed.

The men whose horses had been creased were heckled

unmercifully after they had hobbled back to the bunk-house. Then Buck Eldridge, who was methodically splic-ing a brass hondo into a new grass rope, stopped the banter with a question. "Who'n hell kin shoot like that at night?"

Silence followed and the men looked at one another. Perk Bellew, the one who had come to rest in the clump of cactus, stopped pulling thorns and looked up. "By God, come t' think about it that was some shootin'. Shot ol' Jumper right atween the eyes with a side gun fer barkin' and burnt the flanks of both them hosses in 'zackly the same place. Jes' barely raked 'em."

"He didn't want t'kill the hosses," opined Buck.

"Musta not wanted t' kill us, neither," replied Perk. "Shootin' like that in the moonlight . . ."

"I don't guess," pursued Buck, "any of you bucks seen 'im?"

There was a general shaking of heads. "He seen us and that was enough," said Perk, grimacing as he touched a spot full of the tiny hair-like darts that sur-round the big thorn on prickly pear. They'd break off but were impossible to pull out. Perk knew he was in for days of discomfort that would nearly drive him crazy.

Buck sighed. "Y'know, I seen 'im yistiddy."

There was a chorus of questions and he held up his hands. "Wait. I seen 'im, but I didn't realize it. I sorta took a pitcher with my eyes but him and that light gray hoss was backed up so nachal with them bushes over in High Pocket bottom, that I didn't know what I seen till maybe an hour later."

Perk nodded. "I done things like that. See sump'n, then realize a long time afterward what it was." Others nodded too. They had had similar experiences.

Talk waned and finally the punchers turned in.

Sam Peters greeted the morning with revulsion. He hated the cheerful brightness of the sun and the noises of animals that woke him to reality. He had drunk himself into insensibility the night before; but he had still been conscious when the disturbance created by the barking dog had occurred. The memory of it did nothing now to improve his humor. He had cursed his men for craven-hearted weaklings until, reading the contempt in their eyes he had been seeing, on and off, ever since Duncan Stewart had manhandled him so badly and, worse, humiliated him, he had snapped his jaws shut and marched back into the house with his bottle, slamming the door so hard that the stout old walls trembled.

This morning Sam staggered to the kitchen where the Mex cook was preparing breakfast. "Don't want no grub," said Sam, falling into a chair with a thud. "Gimme coffee."

He gulped two hot strong cups and felt a little better. He was thirsty and drank cold water in long draughts. This made him ill and for an hour he was so sick that his normally ruddy features were a dirty gray. Gritting his teeth, he forced down a drink, then another. By the fourth drink he felt as though he might live and ordered breakfast.

While he was eating a young Mexican, slender as a

sapling and with the quiet grace of a hunting cat, walked around the house to the back porch. He shot a stream of Spanish at the cook who in turn relayed the message to Sam.

"Tell him to come in," he growled.

The young man stood in the doorway to the dining room, his eyes opaque as flecks of coal, his slim body relaxed but alert. "I am from the general."

Sam nodded eagerly. "Is he ready to talk business?"

"Sí. He is ready." The man was not insolent but neither was he obsequious. This Sam did not like.

"I can see that your general believes in discipline."

The man was silent for a moment, then he said in a gentle voice, "My general is well pleased with the discipline he has in his men."

Sam grunted sourly. "Where does he want me to meet him?"

"In the grove where your creek empties into Rio Bravo. Is the place known to you?"

"It is. It's on my property, isn't it?"

"Pues, very well. Tomorrow, as soon as darkness falls."

Sam nodded. "I'll be there."

"It would be wise not to bring too many men," said the man, still not offering Sam the usual polite title of señor.

"Why?"

The faintest smile touched the man's shapely lips. "Because my general does not desire it. That is reason enough for you, gringo."

Sam flinched, then flushed. "How would you like to

get a hole in the belly, you impudent bastard?"

The smile became more pronounced. "We have news that a certain deputy sheriff allowed you to point a pistol at him, then shot it out of your hand before you could pull the trigger. Such a man as you is not likely to put holes in my belly. Moreover, I should be seriously annoyed if you tried, and myself just might put a hole between your unlovely ears." There was a blur of movement and a big .45 stared at Sam, its sightless eye looking as big as a biscuit. The lithe man laughed softly. "It would be so easy."

Blood drained from Sam's face. "Get out," he quavered.

"Of course. I have said what I came to say. I will go now because it pleases me to go."

When he left, Sam's appetite went with him, and the fulminating hatred within Sam flared anew. They even knew about it in Mexico! That skinny bandit had been insulting, impudent. He had spoken English with the precision of an educated man and his every word had suggested the deeper shades of contempt for his host. Sam sought the bottle and sent for Buck Eldridge.

When Buck arrived, Sam motioned for him to have a seat.

"Drink?"

Buck shook his head. "Never drink this early. It ain't good fer y'."

"I didn't ask you," snarled Sam. "I called you up here to tell you that the Mex general has sent word."

Buck nodded. "I seen Jugg Allison yistiddy. Him and three of his men want in."

"Good. They can take care of . . . Wait a minute. Was Wade mentioned?"

"Nup. Seems as if him and Wade don't eye up no more. He says Hamp Wallace is done skeered Wade plumb outa his britches."

"That meddling old bastard. If he shoves his nose into this we'll make him draw back a nub."

"Now, boss, I'm gonna tell you sump'n fer the good of your soul. Hamp Wallace been around a long time and he ain't drawed back no nubs yet. He done nubbed a-plenty of people, too."

"A lucky old mossback," sneered Sam. "You think he can turn a bullet?"

Buck Eldridge sighed. "All I'm sayin' is that this is the wust time you coulda picked fer a big raid. Who you think burnt them hosses las' night?"

"Some joker. It was horseplay, that's all."

"Joker, hunh? Then whut about the dawg? How come a joker'd kill ol' Jumper?"

"You tell me."

" 'Cause that there dawg was noisy. He wanted t' git rid of the bark so's he could come back and listen in on whut we says."

Sam felt a flit of uneasiness go over him. "Well, that'll mean guard duty from now on. You may be right. Three men every night. You can break up the shifts any way you please, but make 'em stay on their toes."

"Now, that's sense," approved Buck, implying that it was about time. "When you gonna meet the Mex general?"

"Tomorrow night, in that thicket where the Rapid

empties into the Rio Bravo. I want you to be there. He's touchy, and sent word I shouldn't take too many men."

"He's careful and he ain't a fool. What's the plan?"

"Well, Perk has talked already to our men at every ranch but Favron's and he says they're all ready to pitch in and help out, one or two to each spread. The night we make the big drive they'll all be at a meeting and'll give us the location of the biggest herds. We'll only take those that we can run across the river in a hurry. That general will have men mounted for twenty-five miles along the river and they'll pick up anything we run across. All we got to do is run them across the river. I figure we ought to get something like three to four thousand head, in all. If Allison has really split with Wade I'll detail him to his own spread and let him take care of Wade's stuff."

"He won't be able to rustle much from Wade," said Buck.

"Why?"

"So much of Wade's stuff is up on the north range and scattered like dry leaves. His spread is so big and the grass is so pore that his critters have to do a lot of rangin'."

"That'll be Allison's headache. By the way, if you run into him again, tell him to come see me first chance he gets."

Allison rode in alone just as Sam, now feeling very optimistic and happy as a result of a morning of drinking, was sitting down to dinner. He clumped into the house, his face sullen and lined with chronic ill temper. His beard was nearly half an inch long and dust caked his skin and clothes.

"Just the man I want to see," enthused Sam expansively. "Drag up a chair and eat with me." Allison sat and ate with the dogged concentration of a man who has been living on camp fare for some time. He didn't say a word until he had eaten a steak, mashed potatoes and two raw onions, washed down by two cups of coffee.

"Buck tells me you're planning a big stunt," Allison said.

"Could be. Buck talks a lot."

"That what you wanted to see me about? I told him I wanted in."

"Can you take care of the run from the Flying Y?"

"Easy."

"How many?"

"Gimme the details."

Sam outlined his plans as he had done for Buck and sat back, smoking a black cheroot. "How's that strike you?"

"Sounds good," muttered Allison, picking his teeth with a broken match. " 'Specially that about runnin' 'em across the river then lightin' a shuck. Perfect, I'd say. That Mex will take over then?"

"All along the line. He'll have five hundred men mounted, ready to haze anything that crosses deep down into Chihauhau and Cuahuila."

"All right. Wade's mentioned bringin' some stuff down from the north range to that nest of washes near the canal. Pretty good grass there now, near the river. He said to bring in six, seven hundred. I'll make it fifteen hundred."

Sam gasped. "Godamighty. You think you can do it?"

"I can do it. Just one thing. How'll this pay-off be split?"

"I'll have five men on the other side, counting. The general will have a count, too. We'll have to get together on that. We'll agree on a flat number and he'll pay half before and half when the count is completed."

"What's the split?"

"We'll divide the boys up into teams. They'll estimate how many they run across and my men on the other side will be one to a team and we'll average their count up with the men's own estimate. They've agreed to take two dollars a head for the team. Then the team splits evenly."

"I'll take three dollars a head for my team," said Allison flatly.

"If you can shoo fifteen hundred head across, Jugg, you can have it. Just don't let the others know about it. Don't even tell your own men until you pay them off. Agreed?"

Allison nodded, scowling. "On the other side of us there's a little outfit, the Fish Hook. Judkins is got from nine to twelve hundred head. I'm gonna have the Flyin' Y stuff so close that we'll run them across his grazin' and pick up his stuff, too."

"Throw all you can across and it'll mean more money for you. I'll have to put another man across if you run Judkins' stuff."

"All right by me. Just one thing, Peters." Allison stood up and hunched his shoulders, his eyes gleaming redly. "Don't try no fast stuff on me. I aim this run t' stake me outa the country and I better not smell nuthin' rotten."

"I'm not in the habit of crooked dealings, Jugg."

Allison uttered a filthy word. "Robbin' your old man, stealin' smoked meat . . ." He laughed. "Don't make me puke."

Sam flushed. "You're a little white fairy yourself, I suppose."

"No, I ain't, but then I ain't pretendin' t' be one."

Sam changed the subject. "You look like you been on the trail a time."

"Four days and nights," snarled Allison, the same canker of hate that ate at Sam knifing the Flying Y man also. "I been trailin' Dunc Stewart."

Sam looked up eagerly. "Jugg, would you like to make five hundred dollars?"

"Who wouldn't?"

"Get Stewart. Another five if you get Wallace."

Allison's eyes lost some of their light. "People mess up their britches at the mention of that last one's name. I ain't never run across 'im. Five hunnerd, you say?"

"Five hundred on the barrel head . . . A thousand for both."

Allison nodded. "I'll git Stewart. I been trailin' 'im all over your place and the south section of the Flyin' Y."

"Seen him yet?" Sam leaned forward tensely.

Allison flushed darkly. "No, I ain't, but I will."

"He must be a damn owl. Come around here last night, killed my dog. When the boys went out after him he creased a couple of horses and they bucked the boys off. Playing around like a kid. Imagine creasing a horse just enough to make it buck."

Allison, like Sam, could see no humor in the incident. "Wet-eared bastard," he growled.

"I'm meeting the general tomorrow, Jugg. Like to come along?"

"Yeah. Where you meetin' 'im?"

"At the mouth of Rapid. You know the place."

"Yeah. I'll be there."

Duncan Stewart had watched the Mexican ride away from the Broken Egg from a coulee half a mile away. He sat erect on Devil, trusting his gray hat and the frizzle of pale grass on the lip of the wash to protect him from even the keenest eye.

The Mexican forked a fine palomino horse with the easy grace of one born to riding. This was no poverty-ridden *mestizo* but a man of blood and means. A man one might expect to be close to General Carlos Jiminez Alvaredo y Ozbaldo.

Dunc shifted his weight on Devil and rolled a cigarette. When it was burning evenly and his eyes were squinted against the smoke, he touched the stallion in the flanks and followed in the general direction taken by the Mexican. All the way to the river he followed, then reined in and watched the palomino pick its unhurried way across the shallow stream. On the far bank in a tremendous tumble of broken ground and stunted post oaks he could see the thin spire of smoke denoting a campfire. He choked back an impulse to cross the river and spy on the owners of the fire, for such a foray would take too long. He had resolved to watch the ranch house at the Broken Egg like a hawk from now on, except for a patrol now and then into the area between the Broken Egg and the Flying Y.

The afternoon was hot. The sun beat down on the impoverished ground with a blistering malice that seemed to pucker the earth. Sweat dried instantly and the craving for water harried both horse and rider. After a careful search of the horizon, Dunc spurred Devil toward the Rapid and there in a clump of trees he unsaddled the horse and took off his clothes.

For thirty minutes both man and beast lolled gratefully in the cool water, drinking and soaking up the sweet wetness. The sun was showing midafternoon when they left the water. Dunc saddled up, mounted, and full of the exuberance of youth, laughed softly. Short of patience and not pleased by the prospect of a long vigil of watching, he pondered the possibility of some diversion. He remembered Allison's last camp among the rocky hills and sparse timber some ten miles away, up toward the Flying Y. A grin creased his face and he touched Devil into a canter, his eyes watchful, his every sense alert. Like an animal, he sought every possible bit of cover as he rode and he paused often to scan the countryside.

His watchfulness rewarded him with the sight of Jugg Allison on the way to his camp. The first indication of the man was merely a thin sliver of reflected light lost in the shimmering haze of searing heat that rose from the hard ground. With a fluid motion, Dunc slid from the horse and moved the animal into a draw. There he waited, his impatience gone now. Then he saw Jugg break through a line of timber. The glint had been from the big silver belt-buckle the man wore.

19

WHEN the dust from Allison's horse had settled, Dunc mounted again and followed leisurely to the other's camp. As Jugg dismounted from his horse, Stump Averill, Gordy Haas and Lump Larsen sat up and watched him unfold a cloth from a tremendous pot. "Come and git some real chow for a change," he said with unwonted cheerfulness. "This here come from the new Sam Peters' kitchen. Stew and real bread."

With whoops of joy they crowded around and shoved their noses into the vessel and inhaled greedily. "Plenty of it, too," said Lump Larsen.

"Bread," growled the thick-shouldered Haas, wrenching off a piece and stuffing it in his mouth. "Seems like it's been a year since I had some real bread."

Stump Averill, a quiet, hard-eyed little man, curled a scornful lip. "Four days and you galoots act like you're starved. I'm gonna make a big pot o' coffee."

"Thaas a good idea," said Jugg. "Gordy, take them

tin plates t' the creek and scrub 'em out with sand. Lump, he'p out with that fire. Got news too. That big drive's comin'."

"When?" asked Stump, stopping in his tracks with the coffee pot.

"Date ain't set yet. Talked to Peters just now. He's gonna meet with this here Mex general tomorrow night. I'm going along." He didn't feel it necessary to tell the men of the higher divvy he had arranged for.

"Well," said Stump, heading for the creek again, "that's good news. Never could see why Wade was so all-fired careful. Damn penny-ante rustlin' never brought in nuthin' but chickenfeed."

"This ain't no chickenfeed deal," said Jugg, rolling a cigarette. "This is gonna be big."

Stump came back with a pot of water and, arranging two stones, shoved fire between them and placed the pot over it. He shoveled in ground coffee and moved himself back from the fire.

"Don't know about you boys," said Jugg, dragging hard on his cigarette, "but when this drive's over I'm slopin'. Too many laws around and the boss is gettin' old and soft."

"I'm fer that, too," agreed Stump while the other two nodded.

"Let's take it out t'gether," said Larsen. "Might run inter sump'n good. Damn if I don't hate t' hafta run from a kid and a ol' Ranger pappy, though."

"We'll take care of them before we leave," snapped Allison sourly. "I got fifty bucks fer the first one who plugs either of 'em."

"Money in my pocket," said Larsen, exposing blackened teeth in a grin. He rolled a cigarette and went to the fire for a light. Stump moved closer and stirred the now boiling coffee with a stick, while Haas brought more wood. "Just as well heat that there stew up good . . ."

He didn't get to finish.

Two six-guns bellowed, fire and scalding water erupted in a geyser blown up by the two big bullets. Two more bullets scattered the fire, the embers flying wide. The clearing was large and didn't afford good cover but Jugg's men made the most of what was there. Jugg himself took the best cover, a thick-boled cottonwood. Haas had the poorest, a boulder that barely covered his head. Worse, his back pocket had caught an ember, was beginning to smoulder.

Haas cursed and wriggled, drawing fire from a dense thicket up the hill from the creek. A rifle bullet took off a boot heel and another one drilled the crown of his hat. He writhed and turned the air smoky with the sincerity of his epithets. Finally, bawling like a cut bull as the combustion gained headway and began to sear his behind, he got up and raced madly for the creek. In he plunged then rolled out on the other side and behind a cottonwood stump.

Jugg fired one gun empty and stopped to reload. Stump and Larsen both fired wildly but without seeing anything to shoot at. A probing rifle bullet filled Larsen's eyes with sand and a second later other shells pierced his holster and gouged a painful furrow in his foot.

The rifle spoke again and a horse squealed and began

to buck furiously. Another shot and a second horse tore loose, squealing frantically, pursuing the antics of the other. Soon all the horses had torn loose and after a few hysterical circles straightened out and raced toward the north.

Dunc grinned and reloaded his rifle. The sun was low now and he had had his fun, so he mounted Devil and returned to his watch of the Broken Egg ranch house.

Dunc was not aware of it but there had been a second stalker, a small undistinguished-looking little man on a buckskin gelding. He blended perfectly with a background consisting of a yellow hump that gave him a forty foot elevation on the side of the creek away from Dunc and a perfect seat for the festivities. His mouth was split so widely by a grin that his upper dentures came loose and made him close off the grin and chomp down hurriedly. Then he touched the buckskin and, with the reins wrapped around the horn of his Flick, headed the horse for the ford singing in a hefty baritone:

> Ooooh Mary doncha weep, doncha mourn,
> Ooooh Mary doncha weep, doncha mourn.
> Pharoah's army got drownded,
> Ooooh Mary, doncha mourn.

"Well, hush my mouf wide open," ejaculated the little man stagily as his horse forded the shallow stream and climbed to the other side. Jugg Allison and his frightened men were clustered about Larsen who was wash-

ing off his foot. They had heard the clattering hoofs of
their assailant's horse as he had made off, so felt secure
in coming out and taking stock. Larsen cursed steadily
as he laved his foot with cold water. Jugg Allison stood
by watching, his eyes flaming redly, his lips compressed
tightly. "What'n hell do you want?" he snarled at the
little man.

"What you got?" retorted the other equably.

"Some ranny tried t' dry-gulch us a few minutes ago."

The horseman grinned and looked about. The coffee
pot had two punctures; Haas, the heel of one boot gone,
moved about with a one-sided hobble; the fire had been
scattered widely.

"Either damn poor shootin' or damn good shootin',"
said the little man. "Where's yer horses?"

"Gone," said Jugg bitterly. "That feller, after he had
us on the run, started shootin' at them horses. Creased
'em and made 'em spook."

"Musta been damn good shootin'."

"Who're you to say so?" snarled Jugg, his head swimming with the force of his fury. This grinning mounted
man was turning out to be an irritation.

"Hamp Wallace, I been knowed as in some sections.
Well, hope you fellers kin ketch your hosses."

He rode away from the group and was soon swallowed
in the brush . . . And they all stood, mouths open, staring
after him. Then they turned and stared at each other.

Jugg's face gradually resumed its accustomed dusky
red.

"I didn't," he said, "see nobody fallin' down tryin' t'
win fifty dollars."

Larsen, who had camouflaged his emotions by resuming his foot-bathing, looked up. His dark eyes were blank with quiet rage at this unfairness. He glared deliberately at Allison.

"I didn't see you fallin' over yo'self tryin' t' save fifty dollars, neither."

Allison stiffened. "You tryin' to say I'm skeered of that old mossback?"

Tension suddenly ruled the air.

Stump Averill hadn't liked Allison's innuendo any better than Larsen had. "He meant just what you meant when you made the fust remark," he said in a low, hard voice. "That satisfy you . . . *Mister* Allison?"

Jugg whirled on Stump but the bandy-legged little man was in a half crouch, his fingers spread like hawk's claws, his eyes hard and steady. "Just grab when you git the notion," he hissed softly.

Jugg, his inner being boiling but his rather overblown caution still holding the fort, turned and lunged away from the men, taking the direction of the fleeing horses. The three looked at each other then Haas and Larsen concentrated on Stump. "Well," said Larsen, "look who rammed the big man's words right down his throat and made 'im like it."

"Ol' Stump was right there, warn't 'e?" Haas was openly admiring of the little man's courage.

"Always did think he blowed harder'n he could suck," snorted Stump contemptuously. "Now you know what jes' come to my mind? I just hadda idea that we better take real extra good keer o' *Mister* Allison, 'specially after he gits his hands on that drive money. I think he'd

237

love for to leave us with empty pokes if it meant he could fill his'n."

"Thassa thought," admitted Haas. "Wonder if he'll find them broncs."

"If he don't, he got hisself a long walk," opined Larsen.

Allison dogged the horses until the trail curved toward the Broken Egg ranch house. Probably led by his own mount who had been there before and had been well fed, Jugg reckoned.

He stopped, his feet burning and sweat pouring from every pore in streams. He cursed hard and bitterly until he had exhausted himself of breath. His head ached with his rage. He turned around, his heart blackened with thoughts of murder directed toward Hamp Wallace and Dunc Stewart, and troubled by the backing down he had been doing of late. He, Jugg Allison, the cousin of the famous Clay Allison, gunman extraordinary. His soul curdled, and he suddenly realized that he was feeling nauseated. His hate was gradually shaking him to pieces, because in no small measure it was hate directed not at others, but at his own weaknesses; but Jugg was not the sort to delve into the workings of his own mind. Had he been the least bit introspective he would have realized that most predicaments of the kind he had just run from were the results of his own blundering ill-temper.

He reached camp at last, tired, hot, and horseless. His feet hurt like the devil and his body ached with fatigue. "Gordy," he snapped, "run over t' the Broken Egg. Git rigs and broncs fer us so's we can round up them hosses."

"You look like you done a good job of walkin'," said Haas, with thinly veiled contempt. "If you want a hoss, go git 'im. I ain't never been good at runnin'."

Allison went cold with fury but the hostile eyes of his men left him but one course to follow. With a soundless groan he set out on foot toward the Broken Egg. He had hardly passed from sight when the horses, having completed a circle, came back, trailing their bridle reins sidewise to keep from stepping on them.

The men's eyes were especially gladdened at the sight because they had thrown down the gauntlet, but one of them still had conscience. "Think we oughta chase 'im with his hoss?" asked Larsen.

"Let 'im walk," was Stump's heartless opinion. "Might take some o' the orneriness outa 'im."

Haas nodded. "Yeah. Maybe he'll reelize what the ground's fer."

Jugg Allison got himself a mount in time to go riding to the rendezvous the next night, but he was hardly in a state of mind to care much about what would be accomplished.

Sam Peters was taking Buck Eldridge with him, Allison making the third man. While Allison was away from the house roping a horse in the corral, Eldridge said, "What's eatin' him, y' reckon?"

Sam shrugged. "I don't know. Jugg used to be a bet-

ter tempered feller than he is now. Must be something
on his mind . . . His horse ran off last night. Made him
walk in."

"I hear tell from a round-about way he's got the same
thing eatin' him as what's eatin' you."

"Nothing's eating me," flared Sam, his face reddening.
"Remember that!"

Buck laughed.

"Not even Dunc Stewart?"

"Not even him," retorted Sam grumpily. "And get off
it, will you?"

"They tell me he's sweet on that Mercader gal, too,"
continued Eldridge, who enjoyed turning the knife.

"Don't talk about it." It was so softly spoken that
Buck turned to look at his boss. Sam's face was livid and
his eyes burned with a fire that for once was not alco-
holic. "Make you a bet, Buck," he continued in that soft
voice. "He'll never get her."

"What's to stop him?"

"Me."

"You . . .?" Buck grinned. "No offense, boss, but
how're you gonna do it?"

"I'll kill him . . . or I'll kill her. Maybe both. I'll take
care of them right after this last drive."

"The last one, hunh?"

"That's what I said. It might be too hot for us after
we make this push. The old man's getting hard to deal
with since that last robbery. I swore I had nothing to do
with it, naturally."

"Naturally," echoed Buck slyly, making Sam glance
at him hard.

Allison rode up, so Sam and Buck got their horses and mounted.

The moon was riding high and bright as they cautiously approached the little grove. They looked about carefully and listened but they heard no sound.

"Let's get down and wait in the clearing," said Sam. "Seems like we're early."

They dismounted, tied their horses to saplings and walked into a small natural clearing that was washed white in the clear light, tufts of hardy grass spiking through the sand.

They rolled smokes and when they had them going realized that they were under scrutiny.

Two men stood in the shadows thirty feet away and watched them out of shaded eyes.

"Well . . ." said Sam uncertainly, his face reddened by whiskey as well as uneasiness. "Come on out so we can talk."

The watchers did not come immediately. When they did, seven soldiers with crossed bandoliers and rifles drew up behind them and spread out in a semicircle.

Sam glanced quickly behind him and saw several more soldiers, their faces darkly impassive and their eyes expressionless as pebbles.

Sam licked his lips and faced the two who had approached. "I thought there were to be no men?"

The man who had visited him earlier in the day smiled thinly. "Then something is amiss with your thinking. I said for *you* not to bring too many men."

"Why me and not y'all?"

"It is simple, really," said the speaker with patient

241

resignation. "*El General* is an important man. General Carlos Jiminez Alvaredo y Ozbaldo, here is the one who wishes to deal with us."

The general, a tall imposing man, tilted his arrogant head slightly in acknowledgement. "It is well that we meet," he said in a smooth cultured voice, his English perfect. "Now possibly we can sit and discuss certain matters of interest to us both."

Sam thrust out his right hand, his face beaming with good fellowship. "Put 'er there, General . . ." He stopped and choked. The general had turned his back and was searching for a comfortable place to sit.

When he was seated, he spoke again, his voice level and somewhat steely. "*Señor* Peters, I know much of you and none of it is such that I am aching to be your friend. We have business to discuss. Let us therefore proceed with that."

Sam sat down, his breast churning with fury. The man had insulted him, had refused his hand and as usually the case with Sam, when he thought of one wrong others crowded in and added weight. Allison and Buck remained standing, the former's own brain afire with the fury that never left him, that grew from day to day until it was now the ruling passion in his mind. He had wanted money. Now he wanted revenge. He had come to include Felton Wade in his hatred. And now without any personal reason he accepted the insult to Sam as his own and hated the general.

Alvaredo tilted his head and for an instant the moon touched the strong face with its lean aquiline cast, the severe thin lips and the patrician beak of a nose. His chin was somewhat pointed but it did not distract from the power of his aristocratic features. "You have cattle to sell, I believe."

Sam nodded sullenly. "Thousands."

"How many thousands?"

"Between thirty-five hundred and five thousand. It is hard to say, because they are to come from a number of ranches and things might happen to cut the total."

Alvaredo shrugged his big shoulders. "That is unimportant, except that I am glad to know the total might be so large. Other revolutions have failed because soldiers cannot fight on promises. They must eat. So far I have fed my men well and their numbers grow daily. I will need more food as the size of my army grows."

"Where will you keep such a large herd?" asked Sam.

"I will not keep it as a herd. It will be scattered along the route of my march toward Mexico City. My price is ten dollars a head American money."

"That's not enough," Sam said bluntly.

Alvaredo got to his feet. "Then we have nothing further to discuss. *Adios.*" He was tall, menacing and overwhelming. Sam changed his tune immediately.

"Wait . . . If that's the best you can do, I'll consider it."

"Very well. Begin your consideration. I have no time to waste."

"If you don't buy from us, where would you get such a drove of stuff?"

"That need be no concern of yours. I can get them more cheaply, though not as handily. Moreover, I would have risks to run for which I have no liking. However,

243

it makes no great difference to me. Make up your mind."

Sam got up, nodding. "All right. I'm being robbed, but . . ."

A smile split the lean, strong face, showing even white teeth. "Who is being robbed?"

Sam managed to hold on to his temper, helped no little by the ring of brown men carrying rifles. "Let's talk about the tally and the crew I'll have on your side of the river."

For an hour they talked over details and finally came to agreement.

"Now," asked Alvaredo, rolling a husk cigarette with long slim fingers, "when will the drive be made?"

"Three nights from now," answered Sam cautiously, with a glance at Buck and Allison. They nodded in agreement. "That suit you?"

"Perfect. In three nights . . ." He turned abruptly and strode away with a long graceful stride.

20

Two hours later Alvaredo sat in an adobe hut, sparely furnished for his personal use. He sat at a table bearing a bottle of tequila, a saucer containing diced limes, and a salt cellar. He crushed a quarter of a lime in his strong teeth, took a stiff drink and tasted some salt from the back of his brown hand. His hair in the dim lamplight glowed like a golden helmet. It displayed a slight wave, the only concession that Castile made to native Mexico.

"Reymundo, we have made a good bargain—if it is kept."

"It will be kept," said the slim emissary. "Peters is a dog, he is greedy, he has no morals whatever. The Mercader family—their daughter, I'm told, is beautiful—has had cause to learn of his beastliness. It is said . . ."

The bottle crashed against the side of the hut and shivered into a thousand shards. The big man was on his feet, his pale brown eyes flaming with a mad light.

"Why was I not told of this?" he said in a voice like a saw striking a spike in soft wood.

"*Mi jefe* . . . I did not know you were interested in peons who are citizens of *Los Estados Unidos*." Reymundo was pallid and not a little frightened. Alvaredo, his nostrils flaring like a stallion's, his face blotchy pale beneath its bronze, stared at him for a long moment, then he slowly collapsed into his rude chair.

"Forgive me, Reymundo," he said softly. "I forgot myself for a moment and of course you did not know. I might as well tell you. José Mercader is a distant cousin of mine, my only relative. I was married in New Orleans, Reymundo. This also you did not know. She was lovely . . ." He stopped as tears came to his eyes. But his voice remained strong. "She was the most beautiful woman on earth," he resumed. "We loved, Yvette and I. Such love does not exist today. Men and women have little capacity for love in these times. They marry, fight and scream at each other . . . We never exchanged a cross word. Thus it was for five years—then come little Carmelita." His voice shook now. "When Yvette died I went out of my mind, but not so much so that I did not realize my responsibility. I sent little Carmelita to José Mercader, and they reared her as their own. She does not know. I have told them never to tell her."

"Might I tell her?"

"Please do not. She reveres and loves the Mercaders as her very own parents, and they are fine people, Reymundo, believe me."

"*Sí*," mused the slim soldier. "Did you know, sir, that I too have a Carmelita? My younger sister. When I

246

joined you, I left her in the care of Don Rolando, at the hacienda of—"

Alvaredo leaped as though stung. Reymundo spun around, his hand flashing to his gun. But the young man's draw, swift and effortless though it was, left him so far behind that to raise his muzzle further would be foolhardy. The stranger had drawn his weapon even more swiftly.

"Relax, *amigo mio*," said Alvaredo gently. "I am never wrong about men. This one came to talk, not to murder."

Dunc stood tall in the doorway and looked carefully at the big man, his eyes narrowed and calculating. His face relaxed and he shoved the gun back in its holster. A thin smile touched his lips.

"My name is Duncan Stewart," he said.

The general got to his feet and thrust out a hand. "I'm General Alvaredo. This meeting is my pleasure."

Dunc took the hand and shook it hard. He recalled his days with Don Rolando Camara-Peon and, speaking in Spanish, replied, "It would not benefit me, your junior, to argue. But might we not share the pleasure?"

The general smiled his appreciation. "Sit down and join us in a drink. May I present my aide, *Señor* Roberto Reymundo-Cartardas. He will bring another bottle."

Dunc sat himself at the table. Done with amenities and feeling the tingle of his first drink, he spoke bluntly.

"You've agreed to buy rustled cattle, *verdad?*"

"He is the young deputy of whom I spoke," interposed Reymundo.

"I had realized that," the general said impatiently. "Of course, *Señor* Stewart, they will be stolen cattle. Where else would I get food for my impoverished men so cheaply? My funds are not unlimited."

Dunc nodded slowly. "I can see your point. Can you see mine?"

"You are interested in having the law prevail in your domains just as I hope to see it prevail in Mexico. If you say you have heard similar statements from other men in my shoes, I shall not be offended. I must point out, however, and in this you must accept my word, I shall do what I have said I would do. Mexico, in the corrupt upper strata has scant reason to love me. Yet my soldiers must eat. Where shall I turn? Do you understand?"

"Yes, sir. I do. I wanted to speak to you, not because I thought I could make you change your mind—but rather to help me make up my own. I could go back across the river tonight and stop the whole thing."

"You could, yes . . ." Alvaredo looked deeply into the young man's blue eyes. "You say you could. You will, then?"

"I was hidden in the brush when you talked to Peters. I heard every word that was passed. I can stop it . . ." Dunc lowered his eyes and poured a glassful of tequila. Slowly he got to his feet. "*Caballeros,* may I ask you to drink to the Mexico to be?"

Silently they stood, lifted their glasses and drank.

They returned to their chairs and the general again examined the straightforward eyes of his guest. "How did you get into my camp?"

Dunc grinned. "The same way I got into the grove

248

where you met Sam Peters."

Alvaredo's face grew black and his long fingers curved like talons. "Peters! Tell me of him . . . and Carmelita."

"He molested her. She was civil enough to give him water once. The next time he visited, she had to run to save her honor. I will kill him for that."

Reymundo spoke. "Then it was you who saved José from being burned out?"

Dunc nodded. "Peters had sent two of his men to destroy his place. They are now in jail."

"Señor Stewart," said the general gently. "What is your interest in the girl? Your indignation does you credit, but it seems extraordinarily strong."

"I love Carmelita, sir. As much as you loved your Yvette."

"Ha, then you heard! And she? Does she love you also?"

"Yes. She has told me so."

Dunc turned to Reymundo.

"Once I was a guest at the hacienda of Don Rolando. I met your sister there. How is she?"

"Fine. She is to be married soon. . . . But what a coincidence! You say you knew Don Rolando—?"

"Señor, I must ask you again," the general broke in impatiently. "You are sure you love her?"

"Your Carmelita? Most certainly I do," Dunc swore.

The older man held out his hand. "I am never wrong about a man. You will be good to her. You will make her a good husband."

Dunc took the hand and squeezed it hard. "I will do the best I can and our children will be your grandchildren. May I not tell her who you are?"

Alvaredo's eyes were on distant horizons and his fingers clenched into fists. "If I succeed in giving my country back to the people who have made it what it is —then, you may tell her." Tears came to his eyes. "Then you will bring my daughter and grandchildren to see me."

21

"PUT up them there guns," came the complaining voice. "It's me, Hamp!"

"Sorry," said Dunc, thumping his guns back into their holsters. "How could I know it was you?"

"What'd the general have to say?"

"How do you know I saw him?"

"I watched you cross the river and come back. Any coffee left in that pot?"

"Sure. And some coals to heat it on."

They drank coffee in silence and Dunc rolled a cigarette. "Hamp, I'm going to tell you something you might not like."

"I don't like beatin' 'round bushes. Speak up."

"I know when Sam Peters is going to pull that raid and I'm going to let him pull it."

"Why?"

Dunc explained the details of the raid to come. "All the ranchers will lose some cattle. But none of them will be cleaned out except Judkins over on the other side of the Flying Y. I'll get his cows back."

"Y'will? How?"

"I told Alvaredo I could stop this whole thing, but I wouldn't. As strange as it might sound, I'm on his side. He's out to do his people some good. I'm going to marry one, you know."

"She's American," Hamp reminded him.

"Anyway, I hope he gets away with what he's going to try. He'll let me have that Fish Hook stuff back. The others will lose some cattle, but it'll be the end of rustling in these parts. We'll catch the rustlers, so they should be satisfied."

"Not necessarily," commented Hamp dryly. "Just partly satisfied, le's say. You gonna tell 'em afterward?"

"You think I should?"

Hamp shrugged eloquently. "I got a funny way of lookin' at things, son. You made a bargain. As fer's you're concerned you had good reasons. Since you made it, you'll hafta keep it. It ain't fer me t' say you done wrong. I didn't come back in this country t' ride herd on you. I got a few rows t' plow of my own. You go ahead and run this here business just like you think it oughta be run, but I wouldn't tell them ranch owners a thing. I guess Allison'll run off some of Wade's stuff fer his part."

"Yes. He's to take care of the Flying Y and Judkins on the other side."

Hamp nodded abstractedly. "As you say, they'll all lose some, but that'll be the end. I'll let you catch them rustlers red-handed. How you gonna work it?"

"I'll send a note to each rancher after it's too late to stop the drive. I'll give the whole setup with names. Unless I miss my guess, it'll mean finish for Allison, Sam Peters and his bunch."

"I'll buy in on that deal . . . pussonal. Want me to take care of that end fer you?"

"If you would, Hamp, I'd sure appreciate it. I'll be kind of busy."

"Awright. Now le's have all the news you got."

They talked until dawn streaked the east with a long gray finger.

Jugg Allison and his men rose a couple of hours after sun-up and did without coffee because their pot had two gaping holes in it. Allison still bitterly resented the treatment accorded him by his own men the day before.

"The drive," he said to them, when they were ready to mount, "will be on three days from now. Seems to me I heard you boys say you might like other climates. If so, you'll make enough of a stake to be on your way. But if there's any more tricks like yesterday, you can git right now. If you don't want to play like I holler, then I don't want you around. That plain?"

"You firin' us, Jugg?" asked Stump Averill softly.

"No, I ain't. But I'm layin' it on the line. If you stay here and make this run you'll take my orders. What'll it be?"

There was momentary silence, then Larsen said, "We'll stay."

The others nodded and Allison, anxious to get off the subject, said, "Le's git back t' the Flyin' Y and start them cows offa the north range. We'll need to take some of the boys t' help."

"We lettin' them in on it?" asked Stump.

"No. We won't need them, later, 'cause I'm runnin' the stock right down there close to that overflow swamp. Water runs outa the lake when the Rapid is up and settles down there. The grass's good and they'll all bunch for us. All we got to do then is t' run 'em across the river and it ain't no distance from the swamp. No need t' split the take more'n fo' ways."

"What about Wade?" asked Gordy Haas.

"I'm countin' 'im out. He had a chance onct but he's too careful."

"S'pose he gits wind of sump'n?" Stump asked.

"He won't. If he does, I'll take care of Mister Felton Wade."

At that moment Mister Felton Wade was being taken care of in quite another manner. He sat with a guest in his elegant office and each had a glass of whiskey in his hand.

"Murdock," Hamp Wallace was saying, "you used De Courtland's money well."

Wade Murdock nodded, his pale hair shining in the early light. "You told me to do well with it, didn't you?"

"So I did," mused Hamp. His mind went back to that night on the trail out of the Sabine country when he had surprised Wade Murdock standing over the fallen body of a certain Jasper Hunt. Hunt had been mortally wounded but with the dogged stamina of an alligator had refused to die, had led Hamp's men astray with false trails, had broken the posse into small contingents and single riders trying to beat the wasteland for him. Hamp was riding alone when he surprised Murdock bending over the fallen man, who lay to one side of a faint trail firmly embraced by a murderous thicket of catclaw.

"You said you had just come on the body," remarked Hamp reminiscently. "I knowed that there money hadn't evaporated."

"Why did you let me get away with it?"

"Because I knowed De Courtland too well. He set over there in Lake Charles and backed the worst gang of hide-snatchers what ever hit Texas. They murdered cattle by the uncounted thousands just fer the measly dollar the hide'd bring . . . no matter whose cattle. When his strong-room was busted I was all fer the buster but I was a lawman and I hadda take out after 'im. I hit 'im at long range with a rifle bullet and he rid two days and give me a hell of a run before he fell off. You happened by, saw what he had and hid it. Truth is, I was glad somebody'd got it. I'd been thinkin' how'n hell I could swallow handin' that money back t' ole De Courtland. 'Course, you wasn't no angel, but I didn't never ketch you with a dishonest dollar . . . Not that you ain't picked up plenty of 'em in your time."

Murdock smiled. "You always was a queer one, Hamp."

Hamp nodded. "I guess so. People is curious . . . But I will say you follered my orders pretty good."

The pale blue eyes danced with amusement. "I'll never forget that night, Hamp. The mosquitoes were fierce, weren't they?"

"Wussest damn 'skeeters I ever seen in my life. That's one part o' Texas that's too much like Louisiana."

Murdock laughed. "That was quite a conversation we had, but I can remember it almost word for word. You said, 'All right, Murdock, I ain't gonna stand around here with these here gallinippers eatin' me alive and hunt for no money. You do like I say and I won't never look for it.'

" 'What do you want me to do?' I asked.

" 'Take it,' you said, 'and go some place and go as straight as you can. Hire every law-dodger you can find and ramrod 'em with some tough man and I'll be along some day t' round 'em up. That's how you'll pay me off.' "

Hamp nodded. "Well, from what you say you got a right nice collection fer me. Thanks for them three you sent me at Yucca City ... or did you really think they'd git me?"

Murdock chuckled. "I knew that if they did get you, you'd have lost your grip and couldn't come and collect the others. They were ready to cause me trouble anyhow. I knew what'd happen."

"This Allison, now," murmured Hamp. "Is he the same Allison what killed them tramp farmers over Marshall way 'bout ten years ago?"

"The same. He had heard that they had a poke from some skinning deals. They had exactly ten dollars. He killed two men for ten dollars."

"I'll enjoy takin' care of him," said Hamp, nodding his head with satisfaction. "Now, Murdock, I hear you ain't no gunman."

"I've carefully let my gunmanship stay hidden. I came here for some peace. I have a good place, too much land maybe but plenty of stock. I didn't want to be the target of every proddy gunthrower riding through."

"Unh hunh. How come this two-bit rustlin' you been pullin'?"

Murdock shrugged. "I never really hurt anyone and my poke wouldn't stand the wages I would have had to pay to keep these lice in line." Murdock's lips curved in a wide grin. "I did it for you, Hamp. To keep the collection together."

Hamp chuckled and emptied his glass. "Well, it's done and all my pretty boys is right here ready fer the pickin'. When I'm ready. By the way, Murdock, you gonna lose maybe fifteen hundred cattle."

"The hell I am. When? How do you know?"

"I knows ever'thing," said Hamp complacently. "This is the big drive I bet your boys been waitin' t' pull a long time."

"They've worried me to death about that drive," said Murdock. He got up and walking to a huge safe, opened it, took out two of the most ornate guns Hamp had ever seen. The handles were of carved ivory and the barrels were rich in gold and silver engraving. He strapped them on and flipped his hands carelessly. They came up with the shining weapons. He spun them expertly and thudded them back in their rich holsters that were dark with age and use.

"No rheumatiz, yet?" observed Hamp.

"Not yet. Hamp, I'm glad you came along. I won't try to tell you I've played it four square and down the line, but I've never entered into any wide-scale lawlessness. I shot young Stewart's father because he was trying to shake me down. He was a worthless sort, anyway."

"Yep, he was a ornery cuss," agreed Hamp. "The day I first seen 'im he was beatin' Dunc. Kicked his wife when she tried to help the kid. I'da plugged 'im right there but he was a yeller belly."

"Yes . . . As I was saying, I'm glad you came. We'll weed this place out and I can settle down to a comfortable old age and live right."

Hamp got up. "Well, don't bother them boys when they try t' run your stuff. I'll count that off on what I figger you owe society. When it's all over, I'll explain."

Murdock frowned. "Well—if you say so. I hate to see a lot of my stuff run off."

Hamp's eyes narrowed. "You just keep on doin' like I tell you, Wade, and you'll see that peaceful ole age you talkin' about. Try t' buck them men and you'll push up grass some place. I 'magine they is all set t' slope when the run is made. If you tried to stop 'em they'd mow you down."

Murdock nodded. "I guess you're right. Can you tell me more about it?"

Hamp twisted his longhorn moustaches until they spiked valiantly. "Drop over t' Big Bend t'morrer night loaded for bear. We'll be able t' use you. You can stay

258

overnight in the hotel. That's all I can tell you now."

"I'll be there, Hamp."

Hamp grinned. "I didn't know what I was doin' that night in the Sabine country, but I gits notions like that. Mostly they turn out all right."

Hamp had been gone two hours before Allison and his men appeared. Allison dismounted, gave the cook orders to fix a big meal of steak, eggs, hot biscuits and plenty of strong coffee.

"Hurry it, too," he added sharply. "We been livin' on pine straw fer a week."

He was dirty, his beard a bristly stubble whitened by dust and salt. His feet felt as if he had dipped them in boiling tar, his limbs were still sore from the long walk he had taken, and his temper as usual was at the boiling point. He strode into the big house and on into the office. He nodded at Wade and dropped into a chair, but not before he had purloined the bottle and a glass.

"Well," said Wade with infuriating cheer, "I suppose you buried Stewart, your wet-eared boy—and Hamp Wallace?"

"You're so damn funny I'm about to bust out laffin'," snarled Allison. He downed half a glass of whiskey and snorted, glowering at his employer.

"Indeed? I had never thought of myself as a comedian."

"You ain't," Allison assured him shortly, pouring more whiskey. "You mentioned runnin' that herd off the north grazin' and puttin' 'em down near the river, didn't you?"

259

"Ah . . . Yes . . . so I did. You think it's about time to bring them down?"

"Yeah. That grazin's gittin' short up there."

"Very well. Bring them down."

"Unh hunh . . . Say what you wearin' them circus guns fer?"

Wade shifted and his right hand made an unbelievably swift motion and Allison found himself looking in the eye of a .45 before the question was well out of his mouth. He gasped and turned as pale as dirty milk. "Jesus," he breathed.

"Quite. Things are due for a change and I thought I'd best bring out my pets. Am I fairly fast, Jugg?" he asked innocently.

Allison, fear and his stale chronic ill-temper mingling, looked murder at Wade. "You'll do," he said grittily and got up. "Gotta eat."

He stalked out, almost foaming with rage. At that moment he hated every living creature on earth. Most of all he hated Jugg Allison, but he didn't realize that.

22

ONE of Kenny Remington's newest hands asked for permission to go to town and was refused. An hour later he was seen riding his own horse away from the ranch. He wore a gun and the stock of a Winchester could be seen protruding from a rifle boot.

Remington called his foreman, Ed Hatcher. "I thought you told him he couldn't go to town."

Hatcher glared at the back of the departing rider. "I did. Well, good riddance. He wasn't no good nohow."

Remington frowned. "I been havin' a funny feelin' lately," he said. "Things is too quiet for some reason."

The unimaginative Hatcher grunted. "The quieter, the better, if you ask me."

At about the same time it was noticed that one of Jared Walker's men was unaccountably missing. Ordinarily it would have been presumed that the man probably was following the trail of some lost stock, but Walker was also jumpy and suspicious. Like Remington, he found it hard to explain the reason for his feelings.

Joe Favron had taken a shot at two riders he saw hanging around a trail of beef that were being moved to better grazing, and he too felt nervous and restless.

Jeff Keller was away from his ranch on a business trip, but Monk Simmons, his acute old foreman, had been riding with the Favron men the day Joe took a shot at the strange pair. He wished heartily that his boss was home. He wished it more than ever when two of his men reported sign indicating two riders had circled a herd of Circle O stock.

Jim Walters, seeing several strange riders—hard lean men with tight lips—passing through Big Bend on their way south, wished for something else. He wished Hamp Wallace would come back.

And that afternoon he did.

"Better git your ridin' gear in shape," were Hamp's first words.

"You got news?"

"Plenty. Now Jim, this is the way we'll do it." They talked until evening, then they walked over to the sheriff's house where Hamp took a much needed bath Later he went back to town and visited the barber shop, then returned to Walter's place.

Hamp and the sheriff sat on the front porch and planned further.

"I don't like the idea of lettin' 'em git all them cows," complained Walters.

"Well ... I don't fancy it none neither, but Dunc went and traded the cattle for information. He'll kill rustlin' in the valley here for all time. It ain't too big a price t' pay. Wade Murdock stands t' lose the most and he knows it."

"He didn't buck none?"

"Oh, he raired around a little, but I got Mister Murdock where the hair is short. He'll do what I tell 'im. Think you can find enough men t' run them errands?"

"Yeah. I can git 'em. I'll hafta pick 'em, though. Them ranchers might not like it that I tole the men t' deliver the notes right on the nose of a watch and not as soon's I found out about it."

"I got a better idee. Tell 'em you 'spect to git the news but don't let none of them go till they just got long enough t' reach the ranch where they're goin'. Think you could time 'em like that?"

"I guess so. I been to ever' one of them spreads and I know about how fast a man can make it."

Sam Peters paced up and down in the Broken Egg ranch house. As with Allison, hatred and a continuous state of futile fury had abraded Sam's nerves to ragged edges, were flogging his body and mind mercilessly. He drank whiskey but its calming touch seemed to have been lost. It was the last night before the big raid and all the details had been carefully gone over with the men who were to take part. They had departed on their missions and now Sam was alone with his hatred of Duncan Stewart and Hamp Wallace, his desire for Carmelita Mercader, and a new plague that had grown steadily with the approach of the raid. What would his father do if he discovered that Sam had been the leading spirit in the venture?

Ed had been brutally direct when he had visited Sam the day after the hide wagon was robbed. Sam was his son and had been pampered all his life but the business of stealing from his father had been the last straw. Ed remembered the stage that had been robbed, too, and though he steadfastly chose to believe that his son had had nothing to do with it, evidence was mounting to such a formidable degree that the raid would be enough to make Ed take a new and closer look; so Sam believed.

Yet at this moment Sam wanted to flee to the protection of the man who had always stood up for him. Whenever frightened or beset by trouble, Sam had invariably gone to Ed and now with his next-best friend, whiskey, settling dead on his stomach, he had an almost irresistable desire to run off at top speed yelling for his father.

The way Sam looked at it, he was faced with the absolute necessity of killing Dunc Stewart and there seemed no easy way to do this. Dunc had to go or Sam would never know peace. Carmelita must also be conquered. She had wounded him grievously and deep down he was certain that nothing he could ever do would make her come to him of her own free will. He groaned in an agony of desire as her calm lovely face appeared in his mind's eye. Both she and Dunc must be made to suffer for the indignities they had heaped upon him. A kind of desperate courage quickened his pulse.

He snatched a gun from his belt and took aim at the

gaping hole made by the front doorway outlined against the night. "I'll kill you, Duncan Stewart," he snarled aloud.

"I don't believe it." It was a gentle voice but Sam jumped like he had been touched with fire. He wheeled around and there stood Dunc in the door leading to the dining room. Dunc's hands were at his sides, his eyes were gleaming like an animal's, reflecting the bright light of the lamp. Sam's breath hissed audibly as he inhaled, his limbs shook at the sight of his enemy.

"Yes," he whispered, "I'll kill you. I have a gun drawn and cocked. You think I can't pull the trigger, don't you?"

Dunc's smile was as chilly as the breath of doom. "I don't believe you can even lift the gun, Sam . . . And if you do, I'll kill you the moment the muzzle starts upward."

A hard rigor shook the gross body and sweat started from every pore. The hand that held the gun shook so badly that the barrel beat softly against Sam's leg. His breathing rasped in the still room. "I'll kill you," he whispered again, his voice breaking.

"I heard you the first time."

"Yes," whimpered Sam. "I said it . . . I'll do it."

Dunc suddenly seemed to explode into blurred action and his Colts appeared in his hands, lined up without a tremor on Sam's shuddering belly. "Where do you want it, Sam?"

Sam's face went pasty white. He seemed about to collapse at the knees. "Don't—" he croaked raggedly. "Don't shoot me, Stewart."

The knees caved in and Sam fell to the floor, his limbs jerking crazily. They stopped with a final spasmodic lurch that turned him over and his sightless eyes stared upward at nothing.

Tough Sam Peters had fainted. Dunc's lips curled with contempt and, holstering his guns, he turned and walked softly out of the house.

Nip Carter and Tony Hardy were the new hands hired only a few hours before. They wanted to talk to the boss and Eldridge told them where to find him. They were thin vulturish killers who boasted no loyalties except to themselves. They heard voices coming from the house and knew no one was supposed to be there except Sam.

"Might be sump'n up," said Nip, in a low voice. "Le's go 'round back and come in through the kitchen." Just as they started up the steps to the back porch, a tall figure loomed in the moonlight directly above them. For a split second they stared at the shadowy figure, then went for their guns with the smooth effortless grace of finished gunmen. Dunc drew and leaped at the same time. His first bullet caught Nip just below the breast bone and knocked him backward into Tony, spoiling the latter's first shot. Tony got no chance to pull the trigger again. From a position flat on the ground, Dunc triggered lead from each gun. The bullets tossed Tony backward, dead before he struck the ground.

From the bunkhouse came an uproar of sound. Dunc, springing to his feet, tossed four slugs at the square building. The big bullets thudded heavily into the pine planking, tore hunks of wood from the door facing and sent up a cloud of dust. The men nearly broke their legs falling back into the bunkhouse. Dunc, his face in a tight smile, wondering who his victims were, trotted quietly out of the yard to where Devil stood, his reins trailing on the ground. Dunc vaulted aboard and with another shot at the bunkhouse turned the big Arabian and thundered away into the night.

An hour later Sam Peters sat huddled in a rocker, his hands on his knees, his eyes staring vacantly at the floor. "He got in here, Buck," he said tonelessly. "I don't know how."

"I does," said Buck carelessly. "He come in through the kitchen. Julio is back there now groaning over a egg on his skull. What'd he do?"

"Nothing," said Sam listlessly.

"Bound to have did something," opined Buck irritably. "When I come in you was stretched out there on the floor with not a mark on you."

"He must have pistol-whipped me."

"If he did, he musta used a gun upholstered in sheep hide. Ain't a bump ner a scratch on you nowheres."

Sam lifted suffering eyes. "Get out, Buck . . . Goddammit." Even the blasphemy had no life.

Buck didn't bother to hide the sneer on his lips. "Well, we got two less t' divide the take with t'morrer night. Them boys didn't even make a payday."

Sam shuddered but gave no other sign that he had heard. Finally he tottered to his feet and, opening a fresh bottle of whiskey, drank nearly a pint before he took the bottle from his mouth. He placed it shakily on the table and fell to his knees. He stayed there for maybe five minutes. He tried to get up, falling prone in the effort. His mind went blank and finally his snores could be heard with stertorous regularity.

23

DUNC sat on a high knoll and listened. A hundred yards away was a whitewashed boulder marking the eastern boundary of the Flying Y. Dunc had watched since late afternoon and just as the sun turned red he saw seven riders come at a gallop from the direction of the Flying Y ranch house. They began to haze the cattle that had bunched around the swampy grazing area. The beasts were driven directly to the river and across. The operation took a very short time, most of which was devoted simply to getting the cattle moving. They were reluctant to leave the good graze and each rider had used double ropes and quirts to get the cows into motion.

Dunc got up and stretched. Men were racing toward various ranches now, carrying messages to assemble in force against the raid that was already under way. The raiders, after their fast quiet drive, would return to the Broken Egg to await the official tally and get their money—or so Dunc supposed, on first thought.

Dunc frowned. The Broken Egg was the obvious place for them to go, therefore he found himself suspecting it for that reason. What if they went elsewhere? The posse would miss and maybe lose them. The more he thought of the matter the more he fidgeted. He mounted Devil and touched the big horse into a long easy lope. It was time for the meeting with Hamp Wallace.

He rode for some time then stopped in a boulder patch and let the horse catch his wind. Devil was a tireless runner but Dunc was too experienced a horseman to demand unnecessary speed when there might be a need for hard riding before the night was over. So absorbed was he in his problems, that his youthful concentration overcame his natural caution. He rode out into the moonlight in full view of Jugg Allison and four riders. They had been following a soft-floored trail and Dunc hadn't heard them.

For a split second the opposing men stared at each other, then the explosion came. With a hatchet-like pitch of his right hand Dunc drew and snapped a shot at Allison, reining Devil back on his haunches. The bullet spanged off Allison's saddle horn and thumped him solidly in the center of a silver belt-buckle. The other men, in action swiftly, made Dunc the center of a hail of whistling lead. A bullet gouged the cantle of his saddle, another pinched a piece of hide from his chin, a third struck his left side, and one slammed into his left shoulder, almost knocking him from Devil's back. Dunc's return fire dumped Stump Averill, dead, from his saddle, broke Larsen's right shoulder. Devil, stung along the left flank, took the bit between his teeth, fought off the pressure of the reins and with a lunge like a striking lion crashed into the chaparral, found a trail and went rocketing downhill with wild prodigious leaps. Dunc reeled drunkenly but managed to stay in the saddle by dint of desperate leather-pulling which under different circumstances he would certainly have scorned.

Thus, hand hanging on to his saddle horn, he gave Devil his head and the horse, sensing that distance from those snarling rifles was important, literally exploded into a run as if shot from a catapult. The beast cleared dry washes and low bushes like a soaring bird. He crashed bodily through undergrowth, his magnificent frame functioning with steel-muscled coordination that left pursuit far behind. The raging Allison, his belly aching and his wind still not recovered from the blow that had bent him double, soon gave up the night-shrouded chase.

Allison reined in and stared with boiling futility at the settling dust. "Even his goddam hoss can fly," he snarled helplessly. "But I'll git 'im. If it's the last thing I ever do."

Straight for his home corral went Devil, lacking the guidance of a hand on the reins. A canny animal, now that he had successfully outdistanced pursuit and mindful of the uncertain balance of his master, he slowed to a gentle trot which he held until he felt his burden grow even more precariously seated. He slowed to a fast walk but kept his direction. Dunc, his mind foggy

271

and his body racked by pain, breathed deeply, gritted his teeth and held on with a grim, implacable determination.

Some time later Devil stopped in front of the livery stable and gave voice to a piercing whinny.

Dunc, seeing that he was back in town, sought to relax and overdid it, sliding from the saddle to the soft straw-spread ground. Devil nuzzled his prone body and pawed hard at the straw with frantic impatience. Something was wrong and he knew he had done all he could to put it right. He wanted help.

Wilfred, whiskery face blank with question, walked out of his lighted doorway in response to the noise and saw Devil. "Now, what'n hell . . .? Dunc! You hurt? By God, the boy's shot. Hey, Rufe. You and Bob come 'ere and gimme a hand with this boy."

Twenty minutes later they had stripped him, carried him out, and laid him in the bed he had used previously at the sheriff's house. Big Bend's sole doctor, a young man who had acquired a good deal of experience with respect to gunshot wounds, was examining the casualty.

"He's lucky. That there in the side is painful but it just furrowed up the skin. The one in his shoulder missed bone and artery . . . Went clear through him, so I won't have to probe. He'll be sore and he won't use that arm for a while, but otherwise he's in the pink." He nodded to Mrs. Walters. "Feed him all he'll eat, and force fluids. He'll need plenty to help keep the fever down and restore the blood he's lost. But by fluids, I don't mean whiskey—"

272

"Don't you worry," said the good Marthy. "I'll watch him like the eye in my head."

The doctor smiled tiredly. "Let me know if there are any changes . . . Especially if he gets too feverish. The main thing is rest."

He left and the three men looked at Mrs. Walters. "Anything else we kin do?" asked Wilfred.

"No. Y'all go on about your business. Thanks a mighty lot fer bringin' the boy home."

"Not atall, ma'm," replied Wilfred. "We was real glad t' help. Ain't heard nuthin' else 'bout the raid, is you?"

"Not a word. Don't 'spect to fer a while yet."

When they had gone she turned and looked at Dunc, surprised to see him eyeing her steadily. "What they say about the raid?"

"They was askin' fer news. I didn't have no news, naturally. How you feelin'?"

"Weak," he said shortly. "Reckon I could have something to eat?"

" 'Course, you can. You lay right there till I rustle up sump'n. How 'bout some cool water?"

"Please."

She brought the water first and he drank thirstily, wincing as he moved his shoulder. When she had gone, he reached out his right hand and pulled the chair holding his clothes and guns closer to the bed. His eyes burned feverishly, glazed with pain and irritatation the rest of his face did not betray. It was frozen into a tight unrevealing mask, his lips thinned and pressed against his teeth. He had played a stupid trick on him-

273

self and was missing the raid because of it. His stomach curdled with acid disappointment. What bothered him most was fear for Carmelita's safety. He knew something of Sam Peters' mind. Should things go badly for Sam and his rustlers, there was no telling what they might do out of revenge. Or, if they were successful with their drive, elation might make them equally dangerous.

Dunc found himself eating ravenously of Marthy's cooking, however, and felt considerably better after he had finished his meal. He lay back, sighed heavily, and smoked a cigarette.

"Now you try to get some sleep," she admonished him. "It's gettin' late fer young boys." She blew out the lamp and pulled his door almost shut so the light from the kitchen wouldn't bother him.

He closed his eyes, inwardly tortured by the knowledge that he was definitely out of the fight he was certain would come. But fatigue, weakness, took their toll and he drifted into deep slumber.

Hamp Wallace stood stoically while Jim Walters wrapped the tail of a shirt about a creased forearm. "Looks like ever'body got inter it but Remington," he observed.

Walters grunted and tied the last knot. "Good deal all around. Ned Butler says we got seven of 'em. He kept tally. I figger Barnes got slowed down somehow and didn't git t' Remington's in time."

Wade Murdock drifted over from the big group that

274

stood in the light of the burning Broken Egg ranch house. "No sign of Sam Peters," he said.

Hamp buttoned the cuff of his sleeve and nodded. "I didn't figger to find him. Any sign of Jugg Allison?"

Wade shook his head.

"None. That foreman of mine has his trail tricks!"

"He took off to the north?"

"Him and his crew, so our boys think. I got fastened down by that shot horse . . ." Murdock's face twisted harshly as he spoke. He had loved the big cream-maned sorrel. "I didn't get into the last round. Not a cow saved, either," he said with a sidelong glance at Hamp.

Hamp bit off a chew and sniffed. "If I was a rancher, I'd trade a hundred cows fer a dead rustler any day of the week."

Joe Favron nodded. Jared Walker expressed sulphurous agreement, winding up with: "If we can just git the rest of 'em, I'll be glad to write off my losses."

Jeff Keller grinned. "Me too. What happened to the young deppity, by the way?"

Hamp frowned and bit a mouthful of bristles from his moustache, a sure sign of perturbation. "Damn if I know. He was supposed to 'meet us at that there dead cottonwood up toward Big Bend a ways. I ain't seen 'im since we 'greed to meet there."

"Well," averred Walker positively, "he done his part. I reckon sump'n happened t' 'im."

"Sump'n sure did," said Hamp. "Wile hosses couldn'ta kep' that boy outa this mix. Awright now, before we goes rushin' off like a covey o' partridges le's make some plans. Mr. Walker, headed nawth where would you try fer—t' git outa the valley, I mean?"

Jared gnawed his lip and pondered. "Well, they can go through the Flying Y but that'd git 'em inter territory where there's telegraph lines, head 'em fer San Antone or Austin. Northeast would take 'em out t' Claytown. They got a real sheriff over there and I bet Sam Peters won't go in that direction."

"What about the east and west rims?" asked Hamp, squinting at the sun.

"East shelf's got a climb-up goin' t' the Flying Y. Trail t' Yucca City is the onliest outlet to the west."

Hamp still was not satisfied.

"They couldn't go straight nawth?"

Jared's lips thinned. "Not lessen they can fly. 'Ceptin' the places I mentioned there ain't nuthin' but sheer wall, hundred or more foot tall."

Joe Favron did not agree. "I think there's one other way."

"Spill it rapid," snapped Hamp.

"Directly north, I've heard, there's a notch in the rim. Old José told me once that there is a sort of tunnel almost choked with brush, a cut that water or wind made. They could take their hosses single file through that."

Hamp snapped erect. "Mr. Walker, this'll be a sorta smoky idee because we ain't got no time. Send a man with a fresh hoss to old José's place. Git José to show the way as fast as they c'n go and either hold that place or stop it up. If they kin kick up any dynamite they could maybe close it. I'm dependin' on Allison and them stoppin' in Big Bend long enough t' crack some safes and clean that place out. I pick him t' try fer that nawth gap if he knows about it, then curve wes' 'cross the border and contack the Mex general. But I'm bettin' he won't be able t' pass up Ed Peters' safe. Git goin'."

24

JUGG ALLISON, a desperate band of men and a beaten, cowering Sam Peters had torn through a thin cordon of attackers and raced northward. True to Hamp's prediction, Allison had no intention of passing up what pickings could be had in Big Bend. Jugg stopped his riders there, talking fast.

"You . . ." He pointed to one man. "Head up the Claytown road and look out fer Remington's outfit. He wasn't in the fight and they must be late. First hair you see, lemme know. If they don't show, you stay there and we'll know that way is clear. You . . ." He pointed to another. "You's the one who tole me about that climb-out up there in the nawth notch. You know where it is?"

"Sho', I been up it a coupla times."

"Hit fer it right now. If you don't come back we'll know that route's open."

To the third man he said, "You pick two more and

y'all spread out south and listen fer the posse. I don't think they're too close behind us 'cause they got some killed and wounded. They'll take keer of them first. First sign er sound you see er hear, beat it back here fast. Rest of y'all round up fresh hosses and change saddles. That'll give us a good lead, later."

Then he told them what was on his mind. They would ransack Big Bend. They would commandeer the saloon and into it they'd pack every woman and child in town as hostages in event that escape routes were cut off and they couldn't get out. The loot promised from Ed Peters' warehouse safe as well as the saloon safe was enough to make the men willing to wait despite the obvious risk.

The man who had ridden toward Claytown was the one from whom they could expect the first report if he sighted opposition. Sure enough, he came galloping back after a while, announcing he had run into Kenny Remmington's crew at the crest of the long hill where the pass cut through the rim and had fired wildly and rapidly, sending them to temporary cover.

Allison nodded grimly as the men came from the Mercantile store with bags of loot, including food. Ammunition would be along later.

"Awright . . . We only got a little more time. All them women and kids rounded up yet?"

A few, it seemed, had not yet been located and he ordered the search speeded up. "We still got a road nawth, but we better be on it soon. Now, y'all git t' work on that there saloon safe."

Buck Eldridge had something to say. "Look, Jugg,

we'll stretch a rope if you fool with them women and kids. We won't have a chanct."

Allison's smile was derisive. "Ain't you boys ever heard of a hostage? They have got to take us to hang us, and the more I thinks of this hostage idea the better I like it. Think a man out there, say, would fight us if he knowed we was holdin' a hot iron t' his wife's feet?"

There was a murmur of assent, and hope lighted eyes that had been shifty and frightened. Buck Eldridge nodded with the others but made to himself a profound decision. Buck had a horror of the hangman's noose and at the moment it seemed terribly close.

Allison put all hands to work piling furniture against the storm doors of the saloon, chopping holes in the walls for rifle ports and one big square hole in the floor, giving on a crawl space which was to be their means of entry and exit. All doors were nailed shut and the windows covered with boards. Allison still could see a way clear to flee but he was taking no chances. He had gambled big. He would not be stampeded even if the road out were cut off. Should he be trapped here, his hostages were packed into a back room ready to be the price of his freedom.

Haas and Groat appeared through the hole in the floor with a frightened man helping drag additional loads of ammunition. "Hadda shoot that damn fool of a Ward Smith," announced Haas. ". . . Wonder where old Peters is?"

"Nemmine all that," snarled Allison, "break them cases open. Ever'body . . . come 'round and fill up. Notice anything goin' on, Haas?"

"Nup. Ever'body skeered t' death. Lights goin' out all over the place."

"Good," growled Allison. "Now let 'em come . . . Where's that Sam Peters?"

One man spoke up. "When you mentioned women, he ducked out." The man grinned, showing broken ugly teeth. "Musta had a special one in mind."

Allison scowled but forgot the matter. Sam Peters would be no help in a real fight. Jugg had learned that much.

Sam, his mind closed to everything except his hatred for Duncan Stewart and his pride which had been effectually crushed by a slip of a girl, rode a fresh horse hard for the Mercader ranch. He knew he was running a risk but, as with Allison, ire had conquered caution and desire was dulling his wits. At the moment all he could think of was that he had it in his power to possess Carmelita. Even if not for long, she would be his to do with as he wished. For him this would mean a double victory. Triumph over the girl, and a kind of revenge on Dunc Stewart. Fiercely he roweled his horse with cruel Mexican cartwheels.

Suddenly the little adobe house stood before him and he reined in and slid from the saddle.

Dim light shone from the windows. Sam gained the low porch in a single bound and hammered on the portal. He could hear a stirring in the house and slithering footsteps approaching the door. He drew a gun and waited tensely, wishing he had a drink. Even the thought

281

of fighting old José set his teeth on edge.

The door opened and Sam lunged, bringing the gun down in a sweeping arc. The barrel struck Mama Carmelita a stunning blow on the head. With a stifled cry she crumpled to the floor. The young Carmelita ran into the room, dressed in a flimsy cotton nightgown. Sam grinned and holstered his weapon. He leaped forward and gathered her into a bear hug. José was nowhere in evidence.

Hamp Wallace halted his men and motioned them into a circle around him. "I'm hopin'," he said, "that Remington got word and is jus' late, not missin'. If he's late that'll stop up the Claytown pass. Now common sense would make Allison put sentries pretty far in our direction to make sure we don't come up behind 'em, so we won't. We'll split here and leave a few men to stop any break in this direction. We'll approach Big Bend from both sides and do it as quiet as we's able so they won't run off."

"S'pose they didn't stop in Big Bend?" asked a rider.

"If they didn't," said Hamp caustically, "then we got a ride on our hands."

Dunc woke with a start. A scream reverberated in the dim reaches of his sense and that with the pain of moving made sweat break out on his face. He heard a scuffle in the front room and a smothered cry that made him skid dizzily out of bed and fall across the chair

282

on which his clothes were hung. He gritted his teeth against the pain and faintness and wiped the sweat from his face with a palsied hand. Brilliant lights burst upon his vision and for a long time he remained in sprawled position, fighting the pain and waves of nausea that churned through him. There were sounds of further scuffling outside his window, then voices. "Crack the old bitch over the head with yore gun butt before she wakes up ever'body."

Someone laughed. "Who's to alarm? We got the whole town, ain't we? She has to walk 'cause we got other wimmen t' bring in and she'll slow us down iffen we has to tote her."

They passed out of hearing and Dunc tried to digest what he had heard. He straightened up and managed to sit weakly on the chair. Gradually he worked into his clothes, favoring the injured left shoulder. He fought for concentration and an answer to the words he had overheard, but neither seemed to come. He weaved into the kitchen, found a pint of whiskey and drank some of it. He gasped and dippered up a gourd full of water, took a few swallows. He thrust the pint into his back pocket, testing the fit of his guns. He found that though the left shoulder hurt like the devil he could still use the arm after a fashion. His lips pulled back in a mirthless grin. He went out the back door and stopped dead in his tracks. Fear froze him as the meaning of the words he had heard finally drifted through to his fogged brain. At the same time he remembered Carmelita. He turned and ran for the livery stable. He slowed carefully as he neared the sprawling barn, approaching it with the

silence of an Indian. As he got near the combination
office and sleeping quarters Wilfred used, he could hear
men talking guardedly. He drew a gun with his right
hand and slipped up to the partially closed door. Wilfred and the two men who had helped carry Dunc to
the sheriff's house stood lined up against the wall, their
eyes dull with fear in the dim lantern light.

A lanky gunner with his weapons lined up on the
men was talking in a thin hard voice. "Awright, dump
them guns. You's comin' up to the saloon like the rest
of the town. We'll see how much the posse'll like to
shoot at us knowin' their women and kids is in there
with us."

"What you want us for?"

"To carry ammunition and stuff."

Dunc slipped in and with a pantherish leap slugged
the man hard on the back of the head. "Wilfred, saddle
young Devil . . . *Move!*"

Wilfred moved and the other men relaxed a little.
"Y'all get ready to ride out with Wilfred," ordered
Dunc. "You two contact the posse. It ought to be get-
ting back any time now."

"You look terrible. Where you goin'?" asked one.

"Hunting," said the white-faced Dunc, his lips almost blue. He hoisted the pint again and felt the harsh
burn of bad whiskey shock his vitals. He was feeling
much better now and when Wilfred came to the adja-
cent stable door holding Devil's reins, he believed himself ready to ride and fight.

"Better slope, Wilfred," said Dunc, going into the
stable. "How about a hand up?" Wilfred helped him

mount then ducked as the man Dunc had slugged came charging from the room, both guns leveled. Dunc saw him, cursed the stupidity of the two in the room and threw his gun from the right side even as the twin muzzles facing him snapped up. Dunc ducked swiftly under Devil's neck and shot the man squarely at the base of the throat. "Better get out fast," he yelled and was gone, with Devil's hoofs thundering a tempo of unleashed power. "Easy, boy," Dunc said, as they passed the last shack on the outskirts of town. He swayed in the saddle and Devil, feeling, as he had before, the insecurity of his master, slowed to an easy canter. Dunc clung to the saddle and fought with all his might for possession of himself, for strength. After a time he shook his head and clenched his jaws tight against the pain and urged the horse into a swifter run. As his head gradually cleared, he sent Devil faster and faster until it seemed that the sleek stallion was skimming the bunch grass and low brush like a bird. He saw the house as soon as he cleared the last rise because it was lit. Devil went over the ridge in a snapping, soaring leap that almost unseated Dunc when the horse struck the ground. He catapulted down the slope. With a bound he cleared a pole fence, again almost spilling his rider, then the beast was plunging to a halt before the house.

Sick with pain, his head reeling and body aching from the pounding run, Dunc slid from the saddle. He staggered up the stone walk just as Carmelita's mother opened the door.

"She all right?" gasped Dunc.

"*Por Dios, señor,*" she screamed crowding close to

285

him. "Hunt him down and kill him like a dog. He has taken her."

She was caked with blood about the face, frantic with anger and fear for her daughter. "Just a little while ago, señor. I have but just recovered my wits . . . why, you yourself . . . you're bleeding!"

His whole left side was beginning to show blood through his shirt, but he scarcely bothered to notice. "Do you know what direction he took?"

"Back toward the town," she said eagerly. "I could hear his hoofbeats as they went out of hearing. She fought him greatly and he had a hard time getting her into his saddle."

With a muttered curse, Dunc wheeled and ran to his horse. Mama Mercader trotted after him and helped him into the saddle. "I will follow you, señor. I will find my dove, my darling."

"Stay here," ordered Dunc harshly. "Hell's broken loose in Big Bend. Ride out to the south trail and wait for the posse if you must, but don't come to town." He wheeled Devil away and disappeared into the star-lighted darkness.

Back in town Dunc stabled Devil after discovering that no one was hanging about the stalls or corral. Clinging to the darker shadows, he made his way up the alley behind the Main Street stores, on the side opposite the saloon. He seethed with frustration and raging turmoil because he had not the faintest notion where Sam might have taken Carmelita. Would it be to the saloon where the rest of the hostages were? Would it be to some deserted shack? Would it be to his father's place?

Ed Peters' house was Dunc's first stop. He walked boldly up to the front door and tried it. Locked, as he suspected it would be. Drawing one of his guns he whipped the muzzle through the glass. Putting his hand through the break, he drew the bolt. He stepped quickly inside and waited. Sounds began in the back and soon Ed came through a bedroom door in a nightshirt that hung almost to his ankles. In one hand he held a gleaming lantern and in the other a glinting gun. He peered about, failing to see Dunc who had backed away into a shadowy spot near a rack upon which hung several coats and a hat. When Ed was nearly to the door, Dunc stepped out. "Drop that gun," he rasped, without bothering to draw his own.

The fat man gasped, but his weapon thumped to the floor. "What do you want?" he quavered.

"I want Sam." Dunc's eyes seemed to burn holes in Peters', who took a fearful step backward. "He ain't here. He's at the ranch."

"That's a lie," said Dunc quietly. "Sam headed a rustling drive tonight. It was broken up by the posse led by Sheriff Walters and Hamp Wallace. Sam escaped and kidnapped Carmelita Mercader. The rest of the outlaws are holed up in your saloon with the women and kids of the town as hostages."

Peters turned pale. "Jesus, gawdamighty," he gasped. "*My* saloon?"

"That's what I said," spat Dunc contemptuously. Patently Peters was more concerned about his property than he was about the hostages.

Peters swallowed noisily. "Well, maybe he ain't at the

ranch, then. But I ain't seen Sam. I ain't!"

Dunc believed him and stepped backward through the door, melted into the darkness around the house. But seconds later a thought came to him and he retraced his steps on an impulse, confronted Peters who was still frozen in the doorway. "Are there any other houses in town that Sam knows well? Any he might take a notion to hole up in?"

Peters seemed to shrink and wrinkle into a shapeless lump of resignation. His throat worked and a croak came out. "No."

"That's another lie," said Dunc stepping close and grinding a gun muzzle deep into Peters' stomach. "But this one you won't get away with. Which house?"

Sweat started on Ed's face and trickled down the creases of his fat neck. Dunc drew back the hammer of his gun and the metallic click sounded like an explosion in the quiet air. "Three seconds, Peters. I don't need you in my plans. Three seconds. One . . . two . . ."

Ed's face was doughy and bluish He licked his lips and said in a stuttering breath, "His Aunty Ella's place, maybe."

Dunc nodded. "That's better. Well, they probably have Aunty Ella in the saloon, and her being an old maid there wouldn't be anybody else around her diggin's." He turned and disappeared into the dark again and Ed Peters, who had looked at death too closely for comfort, sat with a thump in the middle of the hall floor.

The effects of the whiskey Dunc had consumed had long since worn off. But he was too angered and worried to feel pain, and his desperate concern whipped flagging muscles into action.

Dunc ran down the dusty street until he reached the unpretentious cabin in which Ed had housed his sister for years. It seemed deserted, but Dunc stopped at the door and listened attentively. Then the voices came to him, dulled and muffled, but voices. One a man's, the other a woman's.

"I will not scream," Carmelita was saying, and although Dunc could not see them, her blue eyes were hard as diamonds. "Because I know it will be no use. But I will fight you while I have breath. And I will hate you until the last day of my life, you frog, you pig . . ."

Sam's face was livid under the searing lash of her tongue, his pride bleeding afresh and his mind nearly cracking from the knowledge that he might take her but could never truly possess her. His eyes rolled and shone with a mad brilliance. "I'm going to have you," he mumbled, saliva flecking his lips and chin. "And after I'm finished, I won't leave anything for him . . . I'm going to break you so that not even he will know you. I'll play with you as I like, then I'll spoil what's left. I'll bruise you and smash your bones. I'll cut you into slices, and I'll take my time about it."

She breathed a little faster and clutched the nightdress where a great rent showed down the front, a memento of her first efforts at resistance. She knew she had no chance against this gross, meaty brute but she intended to sell herself as dearly as possible. Sam stepped forward and catching the gown, ripped half of it away with a bestiality that made her scream despite herself. She tried to cover her flesh with what was left. He took a few seconds to feast his eyes on the pristine lines of her lovely body with its pure flawless skin reddened where he had bruised her. Again a big hand reached out and ripped, and she was left holding a tiny rag. This she dropped in a proud gesture of defiance.

Sam drew in a sobbing breath of brutish gusto. She was his, a succulent plum ready for the plucking . . . He took a step forward but sprang back as her nails raked his face, leaving bloody trails. He laughed maniacally. "I'll pay you for that!" He wiped his face, and seeing blood on his hands he began to tremble and his eyes bulged. "Just look what you did to me," he said in a childishly complaining voice, the old fear of blood stabbing him. Thus it had been ever since Dunc Stewart had raked young Sam's face with a bottle. A blinding wave of rage poured over him like a flood of scalding water. With a wild scream he leaped for Carmelita, crushing her to him.

He bore her irresistibly to the floor . . .

"Get up, Sam!"

Like the crack of a rifle bullet the words stung through the red mist that clouded the shredding mind of the animal on the floor. The words meant little to him, but the voice he recognized.

A peculiar dribbling whine came from Sam's throat. His eyes rolled fearfully at the sight of the twin bores of the big guns pointed at him.

Dunc's face was icy white but the eyes seemed alive with living fire. The way he saw it, there was not a single reason for him not to kill Sam Peters. He had laid profaning hands on the girl Dunc loved.

The never-banked fires of hatred forced Sam to his feet. He rose slowly, moving like a sleep-walker. Even in his demented state, Sam seemed to know what was coming, and belatedly he found the courage or the desperation to act. His draw was fast but Dunc's lips writhed in a contemptuous snarl as he triggered the gun in his right hand—a gun aimed low.

The explosion shook the close hot air of the room and Sam grabbed his fat abdomen with one hand, sinking slowly to his knees. Dunc lifted the muzzle of the left gun, snapped it down with his thumb hooked over the hammer to cock the weapon with a minimum of effort. Again came a shattering blast and this time the bludgeoning of the heavy bullet set off a muscular reaction and Sam's gun went off.

Dunc spun half around but maintained his feet as the bullet took him in the left leg.

A wintery smile touched his lips. Again he sent a bullet into Sam . . . This time the big man folded over and stretched out on the floor.

Dunc reloaded his guns carefully, concentrating on the performance as though to stretch it out as long as possible. Finally he shoved the guns back into his holsters and looked mistily at the stiff figure of Carmelita who had risen from the floor and was standing silently nearby. He passed a hand over his face. His eyes were clouding but he could still see in a hazy fashion. His vision told him plainly enough that while she had been handsome with her clothes on, nude she was unbelievably, gorgeously, beautiful!

She maintained her frozen stance, her eyes on the fallen body of Sam Peters. Unconsciously her hands went to her head and pushed back the heavy masses of stygian hair foaming about her perfect shoulders in disordered shimmering richness. Dunc swallowed, feeling like a man strangling. Numbly he picked up a fragment of her gown and handed it to her. She took it and with swift motions fashioned a covering for the sharp erect bulk of her breasts. He picked up another piece Sam had torn from her. This she managed to wrap about her slender waist so that it hung to her knees.

Dunc's lips moved. "Come."

Together they drifted silently from the house and became one with the night shadows. By the look of the stars and skies, Dunc judged with surprise that dawn could not be too far off. He halted, his good arm sheltering Carmelita, as a number of mounted men came racing toward them. Quickly he pushed her into an alley. He faded southward with her and made a circle toward the sheriff's house. His bleeding leg dragged as they walked on and he fought the darkness threatening to engulf his mind.

In the rear of the Walters' home, he indicated an open window. "You'll be fairly safe here," he said in a croak. "Climb in that window. Don't move around . . . stay quiet. Just put on something, then stay out of sight."

She clutched his shoulders, making him almost cry out from the pain. Carmelita, overcome by all that had happened to her, suddenly crumpled to his feet, kissing his bloody hands.

"Get up," he croaked distractedly. "Get up, for God's sake. Get into the house."

"You can't go," she begged in a shrill whisper. "You can't. You're shot all to pieces."

"Please," he said, his face hardening, then he turned and abruptly walked away.

Allison surveyed his men and took stock of his position. Theoretically the north pass was still open. He had had no reports of the posse from the south. And Remington, if he were still around, as yet seemed in no mood to tangle with an opponent of unknown strength and was holding back.

Only the situation to the south immediately worried him. There had been ample time for the wounded to have been taken care of and pursuit mounted. Now his men, he could see, were becoming nervous, were beginning to mutter among themselves. A dull boom sounded from somewhere far off, shaking the building slightly. For a long minute all within the saloon remained still, glancing at each other with apprehensive eyes.

"What was that?" asked one man, at last. No one answered.

Nervousness grew. The tension snapped with brittle suddenness when John Hawk, the man sent to watch the north pass, crawled in through the hole in the saloon floor. His face was white and his eyes seemed bugged like a crayfish's. "I run into a bunch fixin' to dynamite the pass," he said chokingly. "I run to the east tryin' t' pick up the Claytown pass and run spang inter a bunch o' men . . . So I had to come back . . ."

Allison drew his gun and shot the man dead before the horrified eyes of his men.

"That," he grated, his chest aflame with a murderous hate, "is what happens when a man runs out on his pards. Tryin' t' get gone by way of Claytown. Wasn't thinkin' about us. For all o' him we coulda stayed here and rotted." He holstered the gun and surveyed the others carefully. He was about to say something more, when a burst of firing was heard to the south. The rattling sound of shots trailed off, leaving a blank silence.

"I guess you all know what that means," Jugg said.

The assembled owl-hooters, saddle tramps, running iron specialists, gunhands amateur and professional, hardcases from the hills and sandy flats, desperados all, drew deep breaths and fingered their hardware.

The shots to the south could mean only one thing. The posse was moving in and had made contact with Jugg's sentries. It was now too late even to make a try at the Yucca City trail. Jugg Allison's band of badmen were trapped. Their only hope was to fight their way out or bargain on the strength of their hostages.

Allison hitched up his trousers. "Well, here we is and there they is. It's gonna be a lot hotter before it gits any cooler and you can take my word for that."

25

Dunc plodded on with an implacability as foolhardy as it was magnificent. He could think only that there were men in town who needed killing, men he knew were at the saloon. He had no plan and at the moment, had no support. Actually, Remington's men and the rest of the posse had already made junction only a half mile south of town, but were wasting time in pointless conversation, trying to figure out what next to do.

So Dunc and his guns moved toward the saloon alone.

Meanwhile, Andy Eli, Jim Sheppherd and a hunchback named Butcher Boone had been scouting around for signs of the posse. Feeling safe with only women and a few inconsequential men in town, and despite some unexplained gunshots which had mysteriously left Sam Peters to die in the starkest agony, they didn't even bother to keep their voices down. Dunc allowed them to walk within a few feet of him, placing their position accurately by the sound of their voices.

These were enemies, dark blobs in the faint starlight. He gave one warning shout so they could draw, and opened fire. Eli took a bullet first, squarely between the eyes. Boone slashed his weapon up and blazed at the flash of Dunc's gun, then went down screaming, belly-shot. Sheppherd fired three times with staccato rapidity, then took to his heels when the seemingly bullet-proof wraith didn't go down.

Dunc cocked his head slowly, somnambulistically, listened carefully for the retreating footsteps; he fired, breaking Sheppherd's foot where it joined the ankle. The wounded man bawled hoarsely, yelling for help at the top of his lungs, but Allison and the men inside the saloon could see nothing through the firing-slits knocked in window and wall, save a murky blanket of black. Several of them fired wildly, one almost shooting Shep-pherd, who then roared to them to hold their fire before they killed him. By a bit of fast scuttling, Sheppherd managed to crab his way beneath the saloon and climb up through the hole in the floor. Jugg Allison was waiting for him. Sheppherd, caked with dust, rested on his knees. Blood was welling out of the torn boot.

"Was that the posse?" Allison demanded.

"Nunh unh . . . Some feller. Tall and skinny. He got Andy an' Butcher. We walked smack inter 'im."

Allison nodded, his face darkening beneath its coating of beard and dirt. "Stewart," he snarled.

Sheppherd whimpered and tried to pull off his boot. Failing, he took out a Bowie knife and cut the leather away, then fainted. Allison looked at him callously. "Haas, tie 'is foot up so's he won't bleed t' death. Thing's

296

damn near shot off. Wrap it up and pour some whiskey over it . . . You—git back in that there room." He drew a gun and pointed it at the sheriff's wife. "Git back, I say."

"I'm going to talk to you," Marthy said, holding her ground. "You let us out of here this minute or every one of you will hang in the morning."

"So you say. Now git back 'fore I loses my temper." To punctuate the threat he threw a bullet that missed the woman a scant inch, tearing out a sliver of wood as it drilled the door. A woman screamed and fell with a thud inside the room, and the muffled crying of children grew sharper.

Marthy Walters paled but kept her eyes level. "If you killed her, we'll burn the church down tomorrow with you settin' on the steeple." She went back into the room and closed the door.

Outside, Dunc could scarcely see. He prayed for dawn. The buildings on Main Street were giant black mushrooms and he was an ant. The saloon, with faint yellow lights shining through the loopholes, seemed bloated in the darkness, an enormous toadstool crouched athwart the town.

"Come out of there, Allison," he yelled at the top of the voice, then frowned confusedly.

Who was Allison and what did he, Dunc, want with him? The colossal toadstool turned into Allison and ignoring the lurid stab of pain the motion threw into his shoulder, he drew both guns and fired into the bloated flesh until his guns were empty. He noticed that all was quiet inside now, except for a faint keening that sounded like children crying. That couldn't be, because Allison was a toadstool, not a child. With a maniacal laugh, Dunc turned and lurched off into the night, which along its distant edge was beginning to pale into fragile dawn.

A few minutes later, Carmelita, huddled in the darkness of the Walters' home, heard a thud on the doorstep. Being a brave girl, she managed to swallow her fears and investigate.

Cautiously opening the back door, she gasped. Dunc had returned . . .

Wilfred and the two men who had been in the livery stable with him had found the posse about a half-hour before dawn, had informed them of what had happened in Big Bend.

After the curses and exclamations of futile rage had died down, Hamp Wallace beckoned to Wade Murdock, Jim Walters, Jared Walker, Kenny Remington, Joe Favron and Jeff Keller. "Want yer council here, now. They got the women and I don't think it's a safe thing t' figure rattlers like Allison wouldn't make use of 'em."

"I can vouch for that," said Wade. "There's nothing he wouldn't do."

"Well, I'm a sorta newcomer here. All of you tell me what you knows about that saloon."

"Things like what, Hamp?" asked Walters.

"What it's made outa, how stout, how high offa the ground, how easy t' barricade . . . Ever' damn thing t' the dirt writ on the walls."

At this point José joined them, told them briefly of dynamiting the pass and of the single man they had fired at, who had retreated in the direction of Yucca City. "It was nothing," answered José to the congratulations that came his way. "The walls were soft and a slide was easy to start. They are trapped now."

Hamp stuck to the subject.

"Now, I'm axin' again. Who knows that there saloon from top to bottom?"

José, who was listening, seemed to know more of the construction of the saloon than anyone else and gave a good description of it from top to bottom. "I helped build it twenty years ago, señores," he finished in explanation.

"That's good," said Hamp. "Now y'all just camp here and stay outa sight till I makes a scout and sees what I can find out."

Daylight almost caught Hamp in town and one of the bandits did throw a shot in his general direction. But Hamp returned with information.

As he was slipping on his boots, he motioned to José. "Ole feller, make me a diagram of that bottom floor."

José swept the dust into a smooth plane and drew an accurate diagram with a stick. "Now this is the bar . . ."

"What's this room off to the side here?"

"A storeroom. Or it used to be. The regular storeroom is directly behind the bar now."

"What's in there now? The old storeroom, I mean."

299

"I do not know. Possibly . . ."

"One big card table," said Jared Walker. "I been in there. Why?"

"That's where the wimmen and kids is. I set right under it and heerd 'em talkin'. Now, I couldn't find no winder, José."

"There are no windows. There was one but it has since been boarded up."

"From the inside or outside?"

"From the inside."

Hamp frowned. "Hit's a bullhide cinch we got t' git them wimmen and kids outa there before we starts anything."

"If I might be permitted a suggestion, señor."

"Talk, man. This ain't no time fer manners."

"*Pues,* it would seem that if we scattered through town and took position across the street from the saloon, at a given signal we could commence firing at it—from the front. That would make a great deal of noise and draw attention from the back. A man could sneak up Rapid Creek, crawl over the bank and knock open that window. It would be no trouble. It's a swing window, on hinges."

"Does it open to the inside or the outside?"

"To the outside, señor. If it is the old window, it will be easy. By now it should be as brittle and dry as a weed."

"Yeah . . . If they don't realize that and do sump'n about it. Well, looks like José's got my vote. Anybody got any better ideas?"

No one, it appeared, did. But several objections were

300

raised by men whose wives and children were inside. Hamp listened patiently and said, "I'm still axin', any of you galoots got a better idea?"

That reduced the complaints to vague mutterings and the motion was carried. The men were ready to mount and throw a semicircle around the front of the saloon, planning to tether their horses handy in case anyone tried to break out of the trap. But at this point a disturbance was created by Buck Eldridge, who walked into full view with his hands elevated.

"Mawnin', gents. I come with a message."

"Spit it out," rapped Hamp ominously.

"I been tole to warn you that ever' shot fired against the saloon means a dead woman or kid. The bunch wants for all the posse t' go down the trail toward the Flying Y, stay in sight and let 'em git a good head start. Else they'll kill your folks one at a time, till you does what they says."

Hamp's eyes narrowed and a rumble rose from the men. "That a fac'? Well, let just one of them wimmen or kids git a scratch and ever' man in that dump'll stretch hemp."

Eldridge went pale. "I ain't in that bunch . . . I ain't makin' no waw on children and wimmen. Another thing, I seen the young deppity ridin' out that fust night. But I never let on though Sam Peters wanted him shot bad. I lit cigarettes till my mouth was sore, so's he could spot me and steer clear. I'll fight with you mens if you'll let me. They done already shot one woman."

The bunched riders gave a start, and a hubbub arose that Hamp waved down.

"Shet up and lissen. Who's shot?"

"Don't know 'er name," admitted Eldridge.

He was roundly cursed and one hot-head went so far as to draw a gun but Hamp's sizzling glare cowed the fellow. "We got one more and they got one less. Le's be glad and git t' movin'." He frowned, "But this here news is done changed plans. We cain't start no shootin' from in front, or from the back, neither. José, is there a opening on the roof?"

"Sí. A pigeon house with stairs going down from the cote between the two upstairs gambling rooms."

"Them's the ones opening out on that gallery above the bar, ain't they?"

"Sí."

"Any way to git up there?"

José looked dubious. "For a young man, possibly. For señor Duncan, but he is badly wounded."

"So Wilfred tole me and ain't no tellin' where he is now or whut shape he's in." Hamp swallowed jerkily. "Well, seein' as I'm the youngest . . ."

Walters stopped him. "Wait hard, Hamp. You ain't neither no spriggins. They's lotsa younger mens'n you here . . ."

"Yep. True as you spoke but this here is a job for me. Now one of you boys with two sideguns and a rifle gimme yer hawglegs. I might not git a chance t' reload."

He took the proffered guns and thrust them into his belt. "Now y'all kin go on and take yer stands as we said at first . . . Only, dammit, don't bust a cap till you hear me open up. Then start blazin'. If I can git them

302

wimmen and kids out like I aim to do, you can set fire to the place. That'll bring 'em out."

Later, after a considerable stretch of crawling so as not to expose himself, Hamp eased over the lip of the Rapid's low bank and, still in the bushes, began to squirm through piles of debris; whiskey bottles, cast-off saddle trees, tin cans and other junk. With infinite care he wormed his way under the room he had previously located. There he spent a few minutes, listening. Inside the saloon he could hear considerable activity; chairs and tables were being moved, and heavy boot treads shook the stout building. Hamp eased up to the most likely looking crack, struck the boards a single sharp blow, thrust a dirty square of paper through the crack and began crawling out from under the building. He could hear a soft scurry of feminine feet as the women rushed to learn the contents of the note.

Feeling as revealed as a raccoon on a flagpole, Hamp shinnied up a giant cottonwood standing over the saloon. It had been many a year since he had climbed trees and by the time he reached the huge branch that swept out over the roof of the building he was winded and wet with sweat. Laboriously Hamp 'cooned the limb until he was over the eaves of the saloon. Then, with great caution, he lowered himself to the tinder-dry shingles.

His stockinged feet drew crackling noises from the shingles as he made his way to the pigeon house, whose occupants vented their displeasure by flying away with their wings popping like firecrackers. Hamp frowned.

To anyone below who knew pigeons, their flight would mean the same thing as the barking of a dog. Intruders. Hamp had to take his chances, however. He kept on, finally reaching the top of the narrow stairway that Achord, the bartender, used to carry feed to his pets.

He cautiously descended the creaking steps. When he finally reached the balcony that ran around two sides of the building, above the bar and above the gambling tables on the south side, he stopped and peered over the railing. The men were all clustered at the front and sides looking out of their loopholes at figures taking up positions about town—figures moving with deliberate lack of caution in order to attract attention. One man threw up his rifle, fired and missed, earning a round cursing from Allison. "That's the way graveyards git started," roared the bearded leader, grinding his gun into the middle of the outlaw. "We're after a dicker, not a fight. All of you remember that," and with careless malice he clubbed the man viciously between the eyes with the butt of his gun. "This goes for keeps . . . The next feller what shoots without a order gets a slug."

Hamp gauged the distance and seeing that it was only ten feet to the floor, took one jump and cleared the low rail. His drop would have been relatively noiseless had it not been for a table he hadn't seen, directly below him. It went to pieces with a thundering crash and he sprawled on the floor. He didn't come to his feet to meet the startled opposition but remained where he had fallen, his borrowed guns lancing flame and thunder. Hell broke loose inside and outside. A hail of bullets stormed through loopholes, filling the saloon with the nasty drones of misshapen ricochets, the crash and clatter of broken glass. Dust began to eddy in clouds, vying with the blue blanket of powder smoke. A beam dislodged above the bar and fell with a shattering crash among the ruins of the bar mirror and stacked bottles. Men yelled frenziedly and fired wildly at the ballooning cloud rising above Hamp's position, a pall of gun smoke shot through with orange flashes.

A man screamed wildly and ran headlong into a wall. Another fell limply on his face. Some were trodden on by others frantically seeking cover. Hamp dropped three empty guns and scuttled behind his smoke screen to the door of the improvised prison. A gun crashed in the room as he opened the door and he smacked it shut after him just as the back window crashed bodily outward. As it did, a wave of women and children poured to freedom through the opening, falling, running, screaming, a tide of terror bent only on escape.

Hamp slid a bar in place and followed them, but squared off to send two shots through the door panel as blows began to fall on it. He turned to leap through the smashed window and saw two forms below on the ground. One was a tremendous woman who must have weighed two hundred and fifty pounds, the other a tall rail-thin creature with stringy colorless hair. The big woman was shot through the heart and the thin one's neck appeared to be broken, her head twisted to an unnatural angle. But her hand was clutching a gun.

Hamp's face twitched tightly then he stepped over them and sought his men.

He found Jim Walters and Wade Murdock behind a

watering trough near the sheriff's office. He hailed them. "Come back here a minnit. Call Walker and Remington . . . the rest of 'em."

There was a conclave held in the protected area behind the sheriff's office. Hamp pointed out four men. "Git across that creek and don't let 'em git out the back way. Beat it, now, in a hurry."

When they had gone he looked at the others. "Been on that damn roof. If we burn 'em out, might as well set the whole town. That place'll burn like gunpowder and send sparks all over the place. We'll have to shoot 'em out or wait 'em out. The kids and wimmen is all free—'ceptin' two. That one Allison wounded got out, but them two didn't."

"What two, Hamp?" asked Walker.

"Don't know. One gret big woman and a little skinny string of a female . . . Both dead."

Wilfred spoke up. "That big 'un is Miz Shaffet. Her ole man is a swamper fer Ed Peters at the saloon. The skinny 'un is Ella Peters, Ed's sister."

Hamp's eyes narrowed and only then recalled the big gun Miss Ella had clutched in her dead hand and he wondered. "Anybody got any news from Dunc?"

"Back at the sheriff's house with Carmelita," put in José. "He got to her just in time. He's shot up bad. Young Peters is dead."

Hamp nodded. "I guess she got 'im in bed."

"*Señor*, she has but is barely keeping him there. Only weakness is her ally. He insists on drinking enough whiskey to enable him to come out again."

"I oughta go over there and bat 'is head in fer 'im,"

306

growled Hamp. "Well, le's get back to business. Two women dead. If a man comes outa there alive he'll just be borryin' time. We got ropes and trees, o'course—but I favor a fair trial."

"Not me," said Murdock. "I wish there was some way for me to line up Allison in my sights."

An hour passed during which the men in the saloon tried to storm out the back way, losing a man in the attempt. Their horses, hidden in the cottonwoods and brush, had already been found and dispersed.

Then, unexpectedly, came Allison's hoarse shout. "How about if we put up three men. Three of you go out in the street and we'll meet you. If we wins, let us go free. If not, you get all of us. It will save a lot of you galoots becoming corpses."

All fell silent, thinking over Jugg's desperate words.

Hamp frowned. "That's some deal, all right," he grumbled to his aides. "Thing is, I ain't of a mind t' lose even one good man fer that trash and I certainly ain't of no damn mind t' let none of 'em get away."

Murdock stepped up and loosened his beautiful guns in their holsters. "We wouldn't need three, Hamp," he coaxed. "Two is plenty."

Hamp gave him a glance that approximated affection. "Good boy, Wade."

"I say let's do it," Jim Walters said, his jaw tight and his eyes hard, "But three he axed fer and three it'll be."

Hamp looked at him. "Jim, I'd be the last man on earth t' doubt your guts. I'm just 'fraid you done got stiff some."

Buck Eldridge stepped up. "I got some smut t' wipe

307

off myself. Lemme be number three."

Hamp squinted at him. "Awright, you got yourself a place." He raised his voice. "*Jugg Allison . . . Open up and start comin'.*"

The massive twin storm-doors flew open and three men walked out, spreading one to each side of the door with Allison himself in the center. A leather-tough gunhawk named Hammat with a dark murderous visage took the right, and an exceptionally fair-skinned man, bald as a beetle, covered the left. Hamp sucked in his breath at sight of the hairless gunslinger. "Well, now who do I see but Curly Craddock! Eldridge, sidle over here and lemme take this end. I know Mr. Craddock and ain't no use'n you gettin' killed just cause you's smutted up some. He's lightnin'."

Murdock, standing stiffly to Hamp's left, said, "Trade me too, Eldridge. That'll put me and that big-talking Jugg in the center."

26

CARMELITA had been out of the room five minutes while the sheriff's wife took darts in one of her own dresses so it wouldn't bag so badly on the girl's slim figure. The girl was clad for the moment in a chemise and a single undergarment, the ampleness of the clothes doing little to obscure the delightful contours of her delicate, but quite sufficient charms. On an impulse, Carmelita had stepped back to the bedroom to look at her patient—and had found him gone.

For Dunc, again conscious, had instantly reached for the whiskey bottle. It was gone. His body racked with pain and his mind boiling with but one feverish object, he crawled out of bed and stumbled back to the kitchen. He found another bottle, and taking a long pull from it, proceeded to search closets and alcoves for anything that would shoot. In a curtained corner he came on a weapon the sheriff had recently bought but of which he was mortally afraid, distrusting repeating shotguns with the deathless skepticism of a man born in the tradition of the London Twist and the bat-eared double. It was an almost new Winchester lever-action, ten gauge. Dunc eagerly stuffed buckshot loads into its magazine, more into his pockets, levered a round into the cannon-like chamber and staggered down the back steps. Keeping to the alley he managed to reach the rear of Peters' General Merchandise. With infinite care and untold agony from his wounds, he crawled beneath the store and wormed his way to the other side, which abutted the saloon with only an alley between. The store was built high enough to give a man on all fours plenty of room under its floor; Dunc, keeping a big timber foundation post between himself and the saloon, sat down where he could command the entire crawl-space beneath that building. He was just in time. He heard Hamp's stentorian response to Jugg Allison's challenge. He heard the big storm-doors of the saloon fly open. He listened closely to Hamp's disposition of Buck and the fancy-gunned Wade.

"Slap leather, Curly," said Hamp silkily. "I been wantin' t' see you fer a long time."

Curly Craddock turned harshly on Allison. "You didn't tell me Hamp Wallace was messed up in this. You underhanded—"

"You didn't ask," rasped Allison. His hate burned within him like a tormenting disease and still he didn't know from whence it stemmed. He just hated . . .

Slowly he walked with his flankers toward the three

men facing them, who also approached until there were less than thirty feet separating the two groups. Then an unforeseen factor disturbed the scene. Carmelita came running down the street, in a semi-dressed condition that got quite some attention in spite of the tension.

"Where's Dunc?" she shouted. "Dunc is gone!"

As all were watching her, a rifle slaughtered the silence from beneath the saloon.

Bushwhackers! Planted by Jugg Allison to add to his firepower! The rifle slug was joined by another from the hidden dry-gulchers, and Buck Eldridge took both loads full in the stomach. He jackknifed face first into the dust.

Like startled snakes Hamp's Colts appeared in his hands and volcanoed fire and explosion and Curly Craddock died with his guns half drawn. Simultaneously Murdock fanned his hips with the grace of someone going through the sequence of a dance but there was no grace in the slamming big-nosed bullets that took Jugg Allison high in the chest. Allison stumbled forward and brought one gun up but Murdock ignored him, fell full-length in the dust and slammed out two bullets at the lanky Hammat whose opposition had been killed by the hidden rifle before anyone had drawn a gun. His shots, those of Murdock's and two quick ones from Hamp's guns were drowned in a shattering fury of detonations that suddenly seemed to lift Peters' store from its very foundations. *BALOOOM!* . . . Four times the roar repeated and beneath the saloon a cloud of dust and splinters boiled. When the noise died away men stood with eardrums ringing, stupified into momentary inac-

311

tion by tension and the shocking thunder of gunfire.

Carmelita raced like a doe for the edge of the store and disappeared beneath it, old José following. They emerged, dragging the limp figure of Duncan Stewart. Dunc shook his head, managed to get to his feet, propping himself with an arm about José's shoulders.

"Well," said Hamp, gustily sheathing his weapons. "I guess a man could say that Dunc done his part in this here fracas. Four-five galoots with rifles under there hidin' out. We's lucky mens, all but smutty Buck— cleaned up some but died doin' it."

"Godamighty," breathed Jim Walters.

"Unh hunh," grunted Jared Walker, his eyes moist, his face dripping bitter sweat.

"I go fer that, too," said Kenny Remington.

Joe Favron crossed himself and muttered in his mother tongue. "*Sacre nom du bon Dieu.*"

"*Gott in Himmel,*" contributed Walter Koenig, who had just arrived.

Jeff Keller jerked a bandanna from his hip pocket and blew his nose loudly.

Hamp Wallace was indulging in a favorite pastime. He was voluptuously stroking his bump of justice, allowing himself to gloat upon the long arm of retribution that once again had reached out and cast evildoers into hell's fire. There was one off-color patch on the otherwise clean slate, however, so with characteristic forthrightness he set about to correct it and ease his curiosity.

"Miz Walters . . . lots doin' and fever still runnin'

high but I'd like t' know one thing. Won't take a min-nit."

"Heatin' water fer the doctor," she said crisply. "But since you're in my home, I guess I got a minnit t' spare fer the saloon hero."

"What happened in that back room, Marthy? I heerd a shot—and that skinny one I found dead, a gun in her fist—"

"Ain't got a idea even. Always did say Ella had a bat in 'er belfry. Had that gun all the time . . . Wisht I'da knowed it. Well, when you slid that there note in there you 'lected Sary Shaffet. Sary was the biggest one in there, and didn't she ever buss that winder to flinders! Well, when we all read it, Ella she went white as a pair of drawers and backed up t' the winder. Didn't nobody notice 'er too much—too excited. When your first shot come, Sary wheeled round and got set t' crash through but Ella drawed the gun and started screamin' somethin' about 'The dear boy won't have a chanct if we gets out.' Well, we didn't know what the devil she meant and Sary with 'er five kids didn't give a damn—'scusin' the lan-guage—so she hauled off and run slap over Ella and rammed that there winder like a runaway bull. Well, Ella shot Sary comin' on but Sary took her *and* the winder out . . . Didn't none of us stop to see what . . ."

"That's all right," said Hamp. "They's both dead and no help fer that. Thank yer, Marthy."

Hamp walked out of the house, wriggled himself more comfortably into his gun harness and set a course for Ed Peters' house. He knocked hard on Ed's door.

"Come in," said the haggard Peters, after a moment.

313

"You'd do it anyhow! So I might as well invite you right off."

" 'Wisdom cometh late but welcome at any date'," quoth Hamp wisely as he walked in. Peters looked deathly pale, old. He was a deflated bag of fat with hope, pride and stiffening gone and a tattered conscience squirming palely in the dim reaches of his soul.

"Set down," said Hamp. "I'm gonna ask some questions and I want straight answers, no hackin' and hawin' around the bush. What was the matter with yer sister?"

"Matter? Why—What are you talking about?"

Hamp drew a gun and laid it across his lap, and the effect of this gesture was instantaneous and profound.

"She was kinda queer," Peters said quickly in a strangled voice. "Liked men, you know . . . Though she never was much to look at and I don't suppose a man ever looked at 'er."

"Not even one?"

Enough blood squeezed up into Peters' pasty face to make it mottle. "Once . . ." His breath seemed to catch in his throat. "Never thought much about it, though . . . Allison, Jugg Allison got drunker'n a lord one night and started makin' the rounds. Jack Hawkins knocked him in the head with a stick of stove wood and took his guns fer comin' around to his house lookin' fer a woman. Guess he musta staggered inter Ella's house that night 'cause I seen him come out the next mornin'."

Peters wiped bitter sweat from his brow. "I didn't never mention it to her. She wasn't never very happy but fer six months afterward she went around all prettied up and actin' like a mare in heat . . ."

314

Hamp got up. "Ever'body's got a weak spot . . . Or in her case, I'd call it a strong one. Nachur diddled her out of her dues and she bit back the only way she could. Things like that happen."

"That's a surprise—comin' from you."

Hamp shook his head. "Nup, Ed. You just don't know me very well. Right now I feel sorta sorry for you 'cause you had t' wait so damn long before you could tell the woods from the trees. Your only son dead in your sister's house, and her dead back of your saloon. All brought on by a man your son connived with and your sister loved. God bites hard sometimes when a man lets a skim git over 'is eyes. At least, you ain't dead. You got some time te look around and see what's been showin' all the time."

"I'll change," whispered the defeated man. "God believe me, I will."

"Well," said Hamp lightly, "at least you callin' on the right One now. It don't matter a damn what I think about nuthin'."

He turned on his heel and walked out of the house.

Dunc mended, in some weeks, under the expert ministrations of Marthy, to whom gunshot wounds were an old story, and with the loving attendance of Carmelita.

Hamp hung around, whittled, masticated plugs of B. F. Graveley's Natural Leaf Superior and, from time to time, took surreptitious looks at certain parts of the Bible.

"Didn't know you was a churchgoer," commented Jim

Walters, a little nettled because these days he couldn't get an argument out of Hamp. Not even decent conversation. Hamp seemed to have something weighing on his mind.

"Well, a drifter like me often ain't much on churches. Happens I'm a well-qualified knot-tier, however, and I don't never like t' git rusty."

"You mean you can marry people up?" exploded Walters, outraged. "Why that's the damndest lie you ever tole in your born life and days."

Hamp grinned. "Well, now that ain't a bit kind of you, Jim. Matter of fact, I done married several couples in my time and after all, what is it to a marriage 'cept sayin' the right words in the right spot at the right times, keepin' yer I do's and sich lined up proper . . . And of course seein' t' it that the groom kisses the bride and don't stand around scrapin' his boot on the floor while ever'body holds their breath."

Jim Walters sank back, his eyes glazed with astonishment. "Well . . . I reckon so, come t' think of it. I don't s'pose nobody ducks around axin' if the preacher got a diploma or whatever it is they got."

"Sense, pure sense, Jim. You're wakin' up some."

"Who you practicin' fer?"

"Bub and Carmelita. I got a idea that there priest down to Mission City will take the job offa my hands, but you never can tell. You're out of a deppity, either way."

The sheriff frowned.

"How's 'at again?"

"Wade Murdock wants the boy t' ramrod his spread."

316

Walters' eyes slitted. "Looks like I see your fine hand in that deal, somewheres."

Hamp grinned. "Maybe I did mention it casual-like to Wade."

Walters nodded profoundly. "Let's mark that down. Hamp Wallace done done sump'n casual, aside from shootin' somebody."

THE END

GUNS OF HELL VALLEY

An
Epic
of the
Untamed
West

by
JOHN
PRESCOTT

A GRAPHIC GIANT

35¢